BETTER OFF WED

PORTIA MACINTOSH

Boldwood

First published in Great Britain in 2023 by Boldwood Books Ltd.

Copyright © Portia MacIntosh, 2023

Cover Design by Debbie Clement Design

Cover Photography: Shutterstock

A CIP catalogue record for this book is available from the British Library.

Paperback ISBN 978-1-80426-660-1

Large Print ISBN 978-1-80426-659-5

Hardback ISBN 978-1-80426-661-8

Ebook ISBN 978-1-80426-658-8

Kindle ISBN 978-1-80426-657-1

Audio CD ISBN 978-1-80426-666-3

MP3 CD ISBN 978-1-80426-665-6

Digital audio download ISBN 978-1-80426-664-9

Boldwood Books Ltd
23 Bowerdean Street
London SW6 3TN
www.boldwoodbooks.com

1

You only get one chance to make a first impression. Absolutely nailing it, the first time you meet someone, is all that matters. The details, the long story, *the truth* – all of that can be figured out later.

'Olivia Knight?' a tall, skinny man with longish blonde hair and dark blue eyes asks me.

'Yes?' I reply, with enough (but not too much) enthusiasm. 'Scott Mason?'

I instantly feel stupid for saying his last name, but he did say my full name. Wow, I'm overthinking things already.

'The one and only,' he replies unenthusiastically. 'Take a seat.'

I sit down at the table opposite him. The butterflies in my stomach are going berserk.

'So, how are—'

'Listen, I'm a busy man, I'm sure you're a busy woman, so I'm thinking why don't we skip the pleasantries and cut to the chase?' Scott suggests.

Scott has seriously pronounced smile lines, which is ironic, given how immediately unfriendly he seems. His light auburn hair is receding, but only from the sides, so he has this sort of vampirical peak of hair in the middle of his forehead, only made worse by the way he quite literally is looking down his nose at me. Oh, this is going *so* well.

'Oh, right, yeah, okay,' I babble. 'Sure, let's skip the formalities.'

'Why are you still single?' he asks me.

Oh, boy, that really is cutting to the chase.

'You're, what? Thirty-five? Thirty-six?' he presses.

'I'm thirty-one,' I reply.

Yikes. I hope he's read my profile wrong, as opposed to getting a much older read from my face in real life. I don't feel like anyone looks thirty-six. Either you can still pass for your twenties, you're wrongfully assumed to be in your forties, or you simply look 'in your thirties'. No one can pinpoint thirty-six. At least, I'm hoping not, anyway. I'll be fiercely maintaining that I'm in my 'early' thirties until I hit thirty-five. After that, I imagine I'll style out 'mid-thirties' for as long as I possibly can. It's not so much that I'm bothered about my age – it's just a number, and one you can't do much about anyway – but when you're in the position I'm in, you have to think about these things.

'Thirty-one?' he replies.

God, don't say it like *that*, whatever *that* is.

'Thirty-one,' I say again.

'Okay, why do you think you're still single at thirty-one?' he asks. He awaits an answer with a furrowed brow and a curious stare.

Wow, he makes it sound even worse when he puts it like that.

'Well, I do think it's worth noting that thirty-one isn't really the sort of age where you're *still* single,' I point out. 'I guess single is just single these days. Some people are "still" single, I suppose, but lots of people are single again. And it's a tough world to figure out when you're thrown back in the deep end – especially with dating apps.'

'Surely the good thing about dating apps is that it shows you that there's plenty more fish in the sea, though?' Scott replies. I feel like he's making a point, rather than asking a question.

'I mean, yeah, there's plenty more fish in the sea, but do you know what else there is in there? Loads of rubbish, and a whole host of terrifying creatures that would murder you in a heartbeat.'

Scott smiles.

'Do you think women especially are embracing single life?' he asks curiously.

I glance across the table at Scott as I sip the glass of water in front of me. God, I feel like some sort of experiment, some scientific sample he's curiously trying to figure out, except I'm nothing fancy like a cell or a blood sample (as you can tell, I'm not a scientist, I don't even remember how I secured that impressive GCSE C grade), I'm more like a bit of dung being pawed through, to try to work out what some animal ate to kill it.

'I don't think women feel like they need a man to be happy,' I point out. 'I think plenty of women live very happy, full, contented lives without a man or a woman – I think lots of us are doing it without cats these days too.'

I narrow my eyes ever so slightly as I try to work out whether or not my jokes are landing.

'You think women are single by choice then?' he persists.

'Yes,' I reply. 'Either by their own choice or the choice of all the people who meet them.'

'At least you have Galentine's Day now,' he reminds me, as though it's some sort of big win for women's rights.

'Yes, we'd been waiting for that one, since we bagged the right to vote,' I reply, deadpan.

'Do you find Valentine's Day hard?' He continues his line of questioning.

'I keep myself busy,' I reply. 'If I'm not touring the restaurants near my apartment, walking up to random couples and pointing at perfect strangers, screeching, "Oh my god, I knew you were cheating on me," then I stay at home and enjoy the free time. I clean, I binge shows on Netflix. I sit, staring at the wall, wondering if it's possible to forget how to have sex because it's been so long...'

Okay, I definitely got an amused snigger out of him for that one.

'Sleeping alone doesn't bother you?' Scott asks. 'That other half of the bed doesn't feel empty during the cold winter months?'

'Oh, the other half of my bed is never empty,' I reply. 'If not because I'm sleeping diagonally across the bed then because I usually pile up clothes on the other half as I routinely try on everything I wear before going back to the first outfit I chose. I suppose, if I were ever that lonely, I could form some sort of man-shaped pile out of it all. Of course, in the rare event I did bring someone home with me, I'd have to make sure I moved it all first – that would look pretty tragic.'

'One-night stand?' Scott asks, shuffling in his seat, briefly far more interested than he has been thus far.

'Nope, I have two,' I joke proudly. 'One on each side of the bed. One is full of condoms, the other is full of flat AA batteries, so make of that what you will.'

Scott tilts his head curiously. There's a look in his eyes, something that suggests he believes that he knows exactly why I'm single. I guess I'm lucky that this is a job interview, and not a date, or it would be a definite non-starter.

'Well, I can tell that you can make jokes,' Scott says – which is not the same thing as telling me I'm funny, but never mind. 'We have several comedians up for the role. What do you believe makes you the best person for the job? Why are you a relatable host for a dating show?'

Welcome to Singledom is a new reality TV show where sexy single twentysomethings all live together in a made-for-TV compound for a number of weeks. It's like a cross between *Love Island*, *I'm a Celebrity... Get Me Out of Here!* and *Married at First Sight* (if you can imagine such a thing) where people who aren't just looking for love but specifically are unable to find it live together and complete crazy challenges – all with a view to figuring out why they're single and helping them improve. I suppose the winners will be the newly formed couple who, I don't know, seem the most in love? Win the public vote? Something like that. I read in the brief that they have to get married live on air, if they want to win the prize money – imagine that.

At this stage, show bosses are looking for a male–female duo to host it – they specifically want comedians for the tone of the show which, roughly translated, I think means they want to try to come across as something light-hearted, rather than something harshly judging people for not finding love yet and subsequently trying to fix them in a way that makes good TV. Yes, of course I'm pretty cynical about the whole thing, but when you work from job to job, project to project, doing something like comedy, you have to take what you can get. It's one of those jobs that, when you haven't quite been able to show that you've 'made it' yet, people find quite funny (not in the way you want them to, though). My bank balance is no laughing matter

– I need this shitty job, in the hope that it leads to other less shitty jobs, which eventually result in me getting a good one.

'I think I'm someone who understands what it's like to be single,' I reply. 'I know all about the good, the bad and the ugly – and most of my routines are on love and dating, so I feel like I could bring exactly what you need to the presenting.'

'And you would be okay with potentially long filming days – say, in the middle of a forest, even in horrible weather conditions?'

'Oh, yes, definitely,' I reply. I knew that farms and forests were going to be the potential filming locations. 'An old boyfriend once told me he was taking me on a weekend break to Nottingham Forest – you can imagine my disappointment when it turned out to be an away game. Crystal Palace was another place that sounded like it was going to be a lot cooler than it was. The only time I was ever truly excited was when he sent me a message saying, "Reading tonight?" and I assumed he meant books, rather than a trip up the M4 to watch the footie.'

I'm so pleased I got to do that bit because, last night, when I was looking up football teams, I wondered if I might be wasting my time.

Scott doesn't seem overly amused, so perhaps I was.

'Well, Olivia, I think we've covered everything we need to today,' Scott informs me, his face giving nothing away. 'We'll be in touch.'

'Great,' I say, once again trying to maintain that cool balance between enthusiasm and aloofness. 'Well, have a good weekend.'

'Yep,' he replies, picking his phone up, and punching a button. 'Sarah... yeah... yeah... no!'

As I leave the room, I wonder what questions Sarah just asked him.

Did she seem like a single loser? Yeah.

Did she try to make jokes? Yeah.

Was she actually funny and should we give her the job? No!

As I leave the air-conditioned office and head out onto the sunny streets of Soho, the sweltering June weather is like walking into a wall. It's that thick, hot air – the kind that almost seems as though you can reach out and grab it. Ick. I'm dressed for my interview in a smart but stylish blue body-con dress over a series of complicated underwear items all designed to give me the best advantages for bagging myself a telly job. Basically, everything either sucks something in or pulls something up, and all in a way that seemingly defies physics, and also demoralises me to my core. The thing is, I just need to secure the job, then I can let the real me turn up for the gig and the details that got me the job won't matter. My performance will speak for itself. This is all for that stellar first impression. Here's hoping I nailed it.

I grab my phone from my bag.

'Hello,' Teddy answers.

'Hey, I'm out, is there somewhere you can stop and pick me up?' I ask.

'This is London, so no,' he replies, sort-of joking, but I take his point. 'Where are you now?'

'I'm just strolling down the road,' I reply. 'I'm near Shake Shack.'

'Hang on then, if we time this right, you can jump in,' he says.

I feel the subtle buzz of my phone – a notification. I quickly glance at it and see that it's an email from Scott *already*.

I listen to Teddy's instructions and make sure I'm in the right spot for a drive-by pickup. He'll be here any second. I can wait until I'm in the car before I open the email. Opening it right this second isn't going to change what it says, is it? I wonder, if it's good or bad news, that it's come through so quickly – the chair I was sitting in won't even be cold yet. Oh, I've got a real Schrödinger of a situation on my hands now, but whatever it says in the email is already in there.

I spot Teddy's black Porsche pull up next to me, so I quickly jump in.

'Go on then, Liv, how did it go?' he asks.

'I've got an email already,' I reply.

I glance at Teddy as he drives. There's a look on his face that doesn't make me feel good. Well, he runs a business, and even though he works in a different industry, I imagine he knows what it means when you get an email immediately after an interview.

'Did you pretend to be single in the end?' he asks.

'I did,' I reply, suddenly feeling the slightest bit guilty to have denied the existence of my wonderful boyfriend, but we did discuss it together beforehand, and he really wasn't bothered by it. He always says that, when it comes to work, there isn't anything he wouldn't do to succeed.

'Do you think it helped?' he asks.

I take a deep breath and open my email.

'Oh, my god,' I blurt.

'What? What?' Teddy asks, briefly glancing at me then back at the road.

'Well, I didn't get the job, but pretending to be single didn't make a bit of difference in the end,' I reply.

'He thought you weren't funny enough?' Teddy replies in disbelief.

'*Worse*,' I reply. 'He thought I was too *old*.'

'You *just* turned thirty-one,' he says.

'*I know*,' I reply. 'I'm sure he's just covering his back, but he's basically saying that the only way they would give the role to someone my age was if they were in an established relationship, elevating them to a sort of mentorship status – and I can't exactly go back in and tell him I lied about being single.'

I sigh.

'See, in real business, your age is never an issue,' Teddy reminds me. 'In fact, the older you are, the more respected you are, it's as simple as that.'

That might not just be in business, that's probably in a patriarchal society generally, but I take his point.

'Yeah, I guess show business isn't like a normal business,' I reply. 'Ah, well, I tried. Back to writing funny stuff for younger, cooler people to say, I suppose.'

'I know you hate the ghostwriting, but it pays the bills,' he reminds me.

I mean, it doesn't literally pay the bills, Teddy pays the bills, but I take his point on that one too. It's income, at least.

'Yep, those reality TV stars' romcom novels aren't going to write themselves,' I say with a sigh.

'I remember when you used to talk about writing your own,' he says. 'Never knowing if you could get it published. At least with household names, half the battle is won.'

'Maybe I could write my own,' I reply, not sounding all that sure about the idea. 'I can write jokes, I can write things to order.'

'But writing an entire book from only your own material... You've got the com down though,' he tells me. 'If you've not got enough rom in your life, maybe that's on me.'

'Shut up,' I tell him with a laugh, reaching over to squeeze his thigh for a second. 'You know I love you, Ted.'

'And you know you don't need that job from those hacks,' he reassures me with a smile. 'You know you don't need to work at all.'

I just smile back. It's nice that Teddy wants to take care of me, but I couldn't live like that. I need to have a job, I need to work. It's not that I don't think I could find things to do with my day, because of course I could. I never really understand it when people say if they were rich they would still have to go to their job every day or they would go crazy – I could think of a ton of things to do like travelling, charity work, enjoying more lazy days, spending more time with my family – it's not that I desperately crave paid labour, it's just that I can't stand the idea of not contributing financially.

I know that people live in all kinds of situations, with different partners being the one who makes the money, while the other person doesn't have a job for perfectly valid reasons. What anyone wants or needs to do is their own business, I just know that, for me, if I were to give up working to live off Teddy's money, just because my chosen career was proving difficult to make a success of, I would not only feel like I was giving up on my dreams, but I'd be giving up some kind of control. And we've only been together nine months, with Teddy working long hours – we don't even live together, although I suppose this would involve moving in with him, but I haven't exactly had an official invitation, it's almost as though he's expecting me to, one day, just stop going to my own home occasionally, like I do now, and wind up living with him that way.

'Thanks for picking me up,' I say, to change the subject.

Usually, even if we're going to the same event, Teddy has to meet me there – and that's when he can make it at all. He's always so busy, but family events always go much better when you have someone there by your side, don't they?

'Well, I didn't want to risk you being late today, not when we have a party to make.'

I smile. I'm so lucky to have him.

Being single again, even if it was only for a matter of minutes, even just for the sake of trying to land a job, has reminded me just how lucky I am.

'We're actually going to be early,' I point out, almost excitedly, because I am never *ever* early.

'Actually, I need to talk to you, before we arrive at the party,' Teddy replies, his face giving nothing away. 'But let's wait until we stop, I need to focus on getting through the traffic first. You know what it's like getting to Oxford in rush hour.'

'Oh, okay,' I reply, not really knowing what else to say.

That can't be good. 'I need to talk to you' is basically a 'We need to talk' and no one ever followed that statement with good news, did they? Everyone knows it means bad news. I remember, when I was a kid, my mum would have all these phrases that she used – she had something for pretty much every event and occurrence, making everything a teachable moment. All of these little phrases have stuck with me and right now, in light of everything that has happened today, there is one phrase in particular I can't get out of my head: a lie told often becomes the truth. I've just – essentially – proudly (and unsuccessfully) renounced Teddy, just to try to get a job. Be careful what you wish for, right?

Teddy fusses with the controls on his steering wheel until music plays. He already has my parents' Oxford address keyed into his in-car satnav. It's currently estimating two hours, although that is subject to change on a Friday afternoon/evening.

I'll just have to wait and see what he says, and try not to panic in the meantime. But I've already lost the job I was up for today. Please don't let me lose my boyfriend too.

2

Now that I think about it, perhaps my alarm bells should've started ringing when Teddy offered to pick me up from work and drive me to Oxford, to the party.

Teddy works for Osa Solutions – truthfully, I have no real idea what they do, only that it's something to do with finance. Something along the lines of if you're rich, and your 'problem' is that you want to stay rich, they solve that for you. Somehow. I'm pretty much the only person in my social circle who isn't rich in her own right, so it doesn't feel much like it's of any concern to me.

It's a family business, started by Teddy's granddad. When his granddad died, the business was taken over by Anne, Teddy's grandmother. Given that she is in her eighties now, she's looking to put someone in charge, so Teddy has been working overtime (quite literally) to prove that he's the right person for the job.

You would think being Anne's only grandchild would make him a shoo-in for the job, but Osa is Anne's baby – sometimes I think she cares about it more than she does her own child, Alicia, Teddy's mum. Teddy is always talking about what it's going to take to bag himself the job, given how seriously his grandmother takes the reputation of the company. I've only met her once, in the nine months Teddy and I have been together, and I can't help but pick up on a vibe that perhaps she doesn't think a lowly comedian is an ideal girlfriend for someone who is potentially going to be the head of a company that tells billionaires where to invest their money.

Suddenly it hits me. Trust my anxious brain to hear the words 'We need to talk' and automatically assume it's going to be bad news. Teddy doesn't seem anxious at all, he's driving me to a family party – of course he isn't going to break up with me. Ooh, wow, perhaps Anne has finally decided to give him the promotion he's been working himself stupid for. Perhaps that's what he's going to tell me.

I perk up a little, smiling to myself, because perhaps if my face smiles, my brain will get the memo that there's nothing to worry about. I swear, when I'm on my death bed, I'll dwell on all the time I wasted worrying about things before there was anything to worry about.

Oxford was a great place to grow up but, as soon as I was old enough, I knew I needed to move to London to give myself the best chance of making it as a comedian – whatever 'making it' means. Coincidentally, my brother Dougie also moved to London to pursue his career as a stockbroker. That's where he met his fiancée, Eden. The two of them live not too far from Teddy, actually, in Kensington. I, on the other hand, have a place in Camden, which feels a million miles (in so many ways) from them all.

Teddy and I tend to spend the most time at his swanky pad, because he prefers it, but as stunning as his apartment is, I am much happier at my place – a one-bedroom flat that is far from boujee. I know, it sounds crazy, and completely unbelievable, but it's true. I like to feel like I'm in the heart of a community, surrounded by real people, with places to go where I can relax, where I can feel like I belong. I'm not so much into the hustle and bustle of the city, though, I'd much rather be living my best Hallmark life in a cute village or by the sea, but while I need to be in London, I think Camden is where I'll be happiest – it's not exactly the cute, quaint life I dream of, but it's a great community full of down-to-earth people.

Where Teddy lives, I don't know, everything is so perfect, so clean and neat – but have you ever tried to relax on a white fabric sofa? It's almost like you're scared to move. Teddy's sofa, apartment – world, even – feels exactly like that. It's definitely taking some getting used to.

Growing up in Oxford, I wouldn't exactly say we were rich. Dad was a builder who eventually scraped up enough money and support to build a house to sell. Then he did another, and another, each house being bigger and fancier than the last. Eventually he made enough money that he and my mum could build one last house – for them to retire in – although Dad didn't actually build this one himself, he paid people to do it, but the super-swanky pad is very much his brainchild. It's so cool I can't quite believe my sixty-something dad had such a hand in it. It must be worth a fortune now it's finished.

Honestly, I really do feel like a regular Cinderella, surrounded by people with so much money. Mum and Dad's house is stunning, the perfect place for parties, and Dougie and Eden live in a dream of an apartment too – although his plan is to retire soon after they get wed and buy a big house in the country. All of this is to say that being creative is a wonderful thing, but it's not the best job for paying the bills.

I always thought I would be so much happier, that if I got myself a job that I loved, that it would never feel like I worked a day in my life. Ha. It turns out that all the money is in, well, money. It's in investments and portfolios and buying and selling and everything that I decided sounded too boring for me to do every day for the rest of my life. While I was sitting carefully crafting witty Wagatha Christie tweets, Dougie was doing a deal that ensured he could retire before he hit forty. He probably made more millions than I got retweets.

We've been driving for over two hours now. Teddy glances at his watch.

'Where are the caves you always tell me about?' he asks curiously.

I'm briefly taken aback by his question.

'*My* caves?' I reply, although obviously they're not my caves. They are the caves I used to play in growing up. 'They're in Botham Estate.'

'Okay,' Teddy says. 'I'm curious. Let's stop off briefly. We can walk and talk before we arrive at your parents' place.'

Botham Estate is a country park – the home of the famous Botham House, which is a museum and tea room these days. The grounds of the estate, which used to belong to a wealthy businessman in the 1800s, have been a tourist hotspot for decades – probably more than a century. Growing up right next to it, naturally it was the place we loved to hang out in as kids, with so much woodland to explore, and of course the caves.

Teddy keys it into his satnav.

'I hope I haven't oversold them,' I joke playfully – well, half joke. Have you ever rewatched a movie you loved when you were a kid, or visited a place you haven't been to in years, and suddenly it's not at all like you remembered it being? Everything seems dated, smaller, nothing compared to things you've seen or places you've been since. It's the nostalgia that makes a place special sometimes. Without context, caves are just caves.

'I've visited the caves at Cheddar Gorge,' Teddy tells me.

'Lower your expectations,' I snort. 'These are man-made caves. It's basically a fancy garden. They do look and feel real but they're probably smaller than you're expecting.'

'We'll see, won't we?' he replies.

We park up at the south entrance of the stunning Botham Estate. There's nothing like a little time in London to reset you in a way that makes you appreciate things like just how gigantic the trees are here, how long they must have been growing for, the conditions they must have survived over the years. Although the main road is only a matter of metres away, as we walk into the woods you could forget where you are. You only have to go off the track a little to feel like you're in absolute wilderness, with only the faint roar of cars to anchor you in reality.

'It's gorgeous, right?' I say.

Teddy kicks a rogue twig from the laces of one of his smart black leather Brunello Cucinelli shoes. He pulls a face at it, as though the twig targeted him, like it went out of its way to attack him.

'Yeah, it's better when you look up,' he reasons. 'Although you have to look down, to watch where you're stepping.'

I was fortunate to have my trainers in the car with me. Teddy, however, is suited and booted for the party already. It's so unlike him to want to interact with nature generally, never mind when he's wearing a Brioni suit.

He looks good as we make our way through the woodland, the summer sun shining through the gaps in the trees. His suit makes him look like something from a romantic movie, like he's the big business hunk who is only in town to bulldoze the family business I run single-handedly a matter of days before Christmas. If he was, we would probably end up passionately kissing up against one of these big trees at some point during our walk.

'Ta-da,' I announce as we happen upon the hidden caves.

'Oh, they're cute,' Teddy says, not exactly making it sound like a good thing, more like a euphemism for small.

'Anyway, let's get to the party,' I insist, hurrying things along, because of course one of my childhood memories was never going to mean much to Teddy, and because I want him to spit out exactly what he wants to talk to me about.

'I want to see this wishing well,' he insists.

'Buddy, listen, if you think the caves are underwhelming, then the so-called wishing well is really going to disappoint you,' I reply. 'It's not actually a well.'

I've told Teddy all about how my friends and I used to come here, to explore the caves, and to make wishes in the well. Of course, it's nothing like a real well, it's just a large well-shaped stone that sits inside one of the caves – it doesn't even have any water in it – but we would still chuck pennies into it and make wishes with high hopes.

'We've come this far,' he insists. 'Go on.'

'Okay,' I say with a laugh. 'But look, I'm not saying you're trying to avoid my family by killing time, but...'

'You know I love your family,' he reminds me.

'I know, I know, I'm joking,' I insist. 'Come on, this way.'

We make our way through the caves that, okay, looking at them as a thirty-something woman, aren't that impressive, but they really did seem magical when I was a kid. Being man-made, they were never going to be as spectacular as the real thing, but they always seemed huge to me. Half the thrill of exploring them when I was younger was being scared of what might be waiting for me inside. A long, hot summer's day felt like living out my own personal (slightly less scary) version of *The Goonies*.

As we venture in deeper, the daylight begins to fade slightly. I direct Teddy through the dark tunnels until we get where we're aiming for. Once we're in there, a carved window-shaped hole allows the sunlight to flood the area we're standing in, illuminating the well with a sort of natural spotlight.

'Here it is,' I point out, in case it isn't obvious.

I peer inside. There are still pennies inside, so people are still making wishes here, but there's a crushed drinks can and a few empty crisp packets too. Thinking about it, it makes sense that I was making my wishes in a bin. No wonder most of them haven't come true.

'Are you going to make a wish for your promotion while you're here?' I joke.

'Hmm, you know Grandmother,' he reasons. 'If she found out I was wishing for it, she would probably give it to someone else just to teach me a lesson.'

I smile. That sounds true but I can't say things like that, can I? You can only talk about your own family that way.

'I'm hopeful, though,' he continues. 'Taking over the company is a big part of my life plan, the centre of it really, and hopefully things are finally falling into place. The decisions I make now will shape the rest of my life.'

'Well, if anyone knows what they're doing, it's you,' I reassure him, squeezing his arm.

The smell in here is exactly as I remember it. It isn't a nice smell, although it isn't an unpleasant one either. I kind of like it, because it reminds me of when I was a kid. Whether I was running in and out screaming because someone at school had heard their mum talking about a ghost that lived in there, or standing around corners, kissing my first boyfriend while we drank cheap Kapop alcopops his older brother bought us, it felt like I had my whole life ahead of me back then.

I remember the celebrities I had crushes on – in my late teens, it was usually a different one every week – and I would always look at their girl-friends who were these fun, happy, thirty-something babes who seemed like they were living the dream. I would always tell myself that I didn't need to worry about my twenties passing me by, because my thirties were going to be where it was at. I guess you could say I'm off-track, seeing as though I'm not getting papped enjoying romantic dinners with a Hollywood A-lister, and I only write for household names, rather than being one myself, but teenage dreams are exactly that.

I glance over at Teddy. He looks uncomfortable. Of course he does, he's in a cave.

'Sorry, I know it's a bit gross in here,' I say. It's not that bad, but I know Teddy hates stuff like this. 'You should have seen the place after me and my friends drank too much bright purple alcohol.'

Teddy ignores that fun little fact (I don't know why I thought he'd appreciate it) and fumbles around in his inside jacket pocket for a moment. In one swift, ultra-cool movement, he tosses a penny into the well before opening a small red ring box that I didn't even realise he was holding. The diamond sparkles so brightly, even in the dim light of the cave. Now that's what you call a rock.

'Olivia Knight, will you marry me?' Teddy asks, cool as you like, although I suppose he's had longer to process the concept than I have.

I feel my lips part ever so gently. I am stunned into silence. This is the last thing I was expecting him to say – my best guess (with no real reason other than considering who I am as a person) was that he was going to break up with me, I never considered that he might be popping the question.

'It's customary to reply,' he prompts me with a smile.

'Oh, my god, sorry, yes,' I quickly say. 'Yes, of course.'

Is there any answer other than yes when you've found someone who makes you happy?

'Finally,' he says, sighing with relief. 'Look, I know we've only been together for nine months, but when you've got a good thing, why not let the world know? Plus, it turns out, it might help your career too, so that's a happy coincidence.'

I laugh at his joke. I always appreciate a joke, no matter what is going on.

Teddy takes the ring from the box and places it on my finger. It's snug but it fits. My god, it's beautiful. It certainly looks too expensive for a girl like me to be wearing because anything I don't lose, I tend to break.

'Wow, it's gorgeous,' I tell him. 'And I can't believe you brought me here to do it!'

'Well, I had this whole night planned, I was going to take you to Le Gavroche for dinner, hire a string quartet who would be waiting for us in Hyde Park, where I would pop the question to you under the moonlight but then I thought, well, we're here anyway, and I know you love all that senti-mental crap, so...'

'Ah, I do love all that sentimental crap,' I say with a smile and a sigh. It really feels like he knows me. I would've been so embarrassed if he had done the other option. Still, I would've said yes.

I scream with delight.

'Oh, wow, I can't believe we're engaged,' I blurt. 'Honestly, that's the last thing I expected today.'

Or ever, if I'm being honest.

Truthfully, Teddy and I haven't really talked about marriage all that much, and if I'd had to guess, I wouldn't have been confident that he was even the marrying kind. I suppose when you know, you know.

'I just dropped what most people pay as a house deposit on a ring, am I at least going to get a kiss for it?' he jokes.

'Blah, sorry,' I say, suddenly all goofy. I do a strange little jig on the spot before stepping forward so Teddy can take me in his arms.

I'm expecting your typical kiss but, of course, this is Teddy, so he lifts me up and pushes me back against one of the walls – thankfully one of the smoother parts – and kisses me passionately. Using his weight to hold me in place, one of his hands finds its way to my chest.

'Oh, my god,' I blurt gleefully when he gives me a second to get some air. 'Teddy, not in a cave.'

'Why not?' he replies between kisses. 'Anyway, these aren't real caves.'

We're interrupted (thankfully before Teddy has the chance to try to sweet-talk me into taking this celebration any further) by a loud, theatrical cough. You know the kind, one that is designed to make a point, rather than to clear a person's throat.

'No fornicating in the caves – there is a sign, you know,' an elderly-sounding man's voice interrupts us.

Wow, really? There's a no fornicating sign? I don't remember that from my childhood, although I probably would've ignored any signs when I was a teen. Then again, hopefully I didn't know what the word 'fornicating' meant when I was a kid.

'Sorry, sorry,' I insist, mortified, as I compose myself. 'We just got engaged.'

I'm not sure why I say it, because it hardly excuses it, does it? And I know that there's no way I would have, you know, *fornicated* right here, right now. It was never going to get beyond light petting.

'Olivia Knight?' the man says as he steps out from one of the dark tunnels.

Oh, my god. Is he still here?

'Owen?' I reply. 'Wow, hello, it's been a long time.'

I straighten my dress, making sure my boobs are covered, because another two seconds and Teddy might have breached my bra. Teddy backs away from me slightly. I can tell he's stifling a smile.

Owen was one of the groundskeepers here when we were kids – and he still is, it turns out. At first, he was like a nemesis to us, a party pooper who was always trying to ruin our fun, who figured out where we lived and would always report us back to our parents – who, of course, he already knew. He once negotiated an unofficial three-day-long community service order with my and my best friend Heidi's parents, where we had to spend half-term picking up leaves (in the woods – why?) because something along the lines of Heidi broke a branch off a tree by swinging on it, and allegedly swore at him when he told her off for it. I can't remember what she said to him, but Heidi has always been Heidi, she's never liked or respected authority. Eventually, me, Heidi and the rest of the neighbourhood kids developed a playful understanding with 'Old Man Owen' (who, in hindsight, must've only been in his fifties).

'I can't believe you still work here,' I point out.

He's instantly recognisable but he looks smaller, with more rounded shoulders, and the lenses of his glasses are much thicker than they used to be.

'I still manage the grounds – I'd be lost without my job, although I don't do much work these days, I mostly just patrol, looking out for gunge smokers and fornicators – I can't believe you're still causing trouble here,' he adds, but there's a smile on his face. 'You said you got engaged? Your parents must be thrilled.'

'Oh, they don't know yet,' I tell him. 'So this is just between us.'

'Your secret is safe with me,' Owen replies. 'Although I imagine Vic knows, even if Erica doesn't.'

I look at Teddy.

'No, no one knows,' he says. I can see his jaw twitch slightly, as though he's annoyed that a perfect stranger is grilling him. 'Why would I tell him?'

'Oh, it's bad form, not to ask a man for his daughter's hand before you propose,' Owen tells him.

Teddy furrows his brow.

'That's a bit old-fashioned, isn't it?' Teddy turns to me. 'Isn't it?'

'Yes, no, of course,' I babble. 'I'm sure Owen is joking.'

Owen gives us a look which very much suggests he isn't joking.

'Anyway, we've got a party to get to, but it was lovely to see you again, Owen,' I insist as I take Teddy by the hand and lead him towards the exit.

'Yes, and you, Olivia,' he calls after us. 'Give my best to Vic and Erica.'

'We used to run rings around him when we were kids,' I tell Teddy once we're well on our way back to the car.

'It's a good job you were running, or else he might have locked you up in that stately home and read Bible verses to you,' Teddy replies. 'What a nutter.'

'Ah, he's harmless,' I reply. 'To be fair, we were just almost fornicators,' I point out.

'You can get me later,' Teddy says with a wink as he climbs back into the car.

I strap myself in before sinking back into the comfortable car seat and admiring the ring on my hand.

'I still can't believe it,' I blurt.

'Believe it,' Teddy insists, reaching over to squeeze my leg before setting off to my parents' house.

Gosh, it really is a beautiful ring, and Teddy is a gorgeous man, and I love the way he proposed – it just goes to show how well he knows me. I'm surprised, pleasantly surprised, but it's still a shock.

Now that we're in the car, and things are quiet, I pause to consider everything that just happened. It's soon, isn't it? Really soon. Some people are going to say it's too soon. But there's no point in waiting, is there? Plus, it's not like we have to get married tomorrow, and engagement doesn't come with any kind of countdown attached. We don't even live together yet so, first of all, we need to figure out what that looks like. But this could be my chance to reinvent myself, to figure out what my life looks like moving forwards. To have a relationship I can be proud of, that might even give me a boost I need at work. Suddenly I feel like I have so many opportunities at my fingertips. To build a relationship, to shake up my career, to build a family home with Teddy. We don't need to get married right away, we can figure it all out as we go, but both secure in the knowledge we're committed.

'I'm thinking, if you're up for it, it would be great to get married pretty much right away,' Teddy says, right on cue.

'Huh?' I blurt.

'Yeah, well, why wait?' he says. 'I love you, you love me. Look at Dougie and Eden. They've been engaged for ages and their engagement party is only tonight. Then it's months of planning, months of parties, stags and showers, and rehearsals – blah blah blah. If you love someone, you just want to do it.'

I smile in pleasant disbelief.

'Wow,' I say. 'I mean, I guess you're right. But don't you want something special?'

'Well, I know there's only one place you'll even consider getting married,' he says thoughtfully. 'But we have the resources to make whatever we want happen, when we want it to happen. Why string it out? Let's make it official.'

'Yeah,' I say, nodding as I come around to the idea. 'Yeah, that makes sense.'

'Great,' he replies.

'Oh, you're going the wrong way,' I quickly point out.

'Yeah, I figured, we're still quite early – that actually happened much quicker than I thought it would, and Oscar or whatever his name was moved us along. I thought we could grab a quick bite somewhere.'

'There's food at the party,' I remind him. 'You know what my mum is like – there will be five times as much as is needed.'

'Yeah, but you know I hate buffets, people touching food, putting it back down, then I pick it up, I don't know who's had their hands on it,' he says – something I've heard him say a few times before but, as ridiculous as it sounds, aren't buffets just a part of adult life that you have to accept and make the best of, if not – dare I say it – enjoy?

'Just a quick something,' Teddy insists. 'There must be a nice pub close by. I'll buy some champagne, toast our good news.'

I glance at my watch. Well, we are early, and it would be nice to at least raise a toast to our good news, even if it is just the two of us. God, this is all happening so fast.

'Okay, sure,' I reply. 'So long as you throw in some chips.'

'Such a cheap date,' he laughs to himself.

I look at my ring again and smile – I swear the big, stonking diamond smiles back at me. I puff air from my cheeks. God, this is fast.

So fast.

Too fast?

3

'Wow, it's warm,' I say, pulling the front of my dress from my body a couple of times to try to get some air in.

'It is June,' Teddy points out.

'I know, but I am *so* warm,' I reply.

'I still don't understand why you have to take the ring off,' he says, almost sulkily.

'Because it's Dougie and Eden's engagement party,' I remind him. 'It would be the social faux pas to end all social faux pas – and even if it wasn't, Eden would murder us anyway. Come on, it's their night, let's not steal the show.'

'Fine, fine,' he says. 'But I don't think it wants to be taken off – I think it's a sign.'

'It's a sign my fingers are chunkier than you thought,' I joke. 'Nothing more.'

At some point – whether it's because of the heat, the bubbly champagne or the salty chips – my fingers have puffed up and now my engagement ring is firmly stuck on.

'My hands just need to cool down, and some soap will help,' I insist. 'Come on, let's head inside. We can say hello, then I'll slink off to the bathroom.'

Teddy wiggles his eyebrows.

'*Just* me,' I point out with a laugh. 'Grab that present.'

Bluebell House – Mum and Dad's home – sits alone on the edge of their stunning quarter-acre garden. Never in my wildest dreams did I think they would go for something so contemporary to retire in but, I have to say, I love it. It would have been a cool house to grow up in, that's for sure.

The cool mixture of textures – a composition of stone, render, glass and timber – gives the building a really striking, distinctive look. The inside isn't just modern, it's verging on futuristic. My dad always tells us that we should be happy, that this house is an investment, and that when he and my mum die, it will be worth a fortune, leaving Dougie and me with far more money than a savings account would have left us with. I do, of course, point out that it's hard to imagine being 'happy' when both he and my mum die, but he always just laughs that point off.

And speak of the devil...

Dad emerges from the front door to greet us at the car.

'Now then,' he announces. 'We thought you two weren't coming.'

He's joking, although I'm sure that goes without saying, he's a dad of a certain age, he's *always* joking.

Teddy is nearest so he gets one of those manly handshakes that blossoms into a bit of a hug where both men wind up holding hands as their bodies press together. It's funny, because it's always an attempt at keeping a sort of manly distance, but somehow winds up being a lot more intimate.

I just get a regular hug. I keep my hand to my side as much as possible, out of Dad's view. I'm not worried, you know what sixty-something dads are like, I doubt he would notice if I turned up on fire.

Victor 'Vic' Knight is a great dad. He's always been so much fun, so hands-on. He's the kind of dad who, when we were kids, would build us things to play with in the back garden. Huge projects like custom-built playhouses – none of your plastic Wendy houses or pre-bought sheds. Dad built us what was basically a child-sized luxury cabin, complete with a mezzanine level and dormer windows. Of course, with great fun comes a great lack of responsibility, but Mum picked up the slack there.

'How's it going?' I ask him.

'Good, yeah, lots of people here,' he replies. 'Your mother is in her element.'

'She's having fun?' I say.

'No, I mean she's literally on fire with rage – I think Eden's mum is driving her crackers,' he replies, lowering his voice for the second part. 'Anyway, you're staying the night, aren't you?'

I look at Teddy. We've brought our things but it isn't unlike him to leave anyway, if work needs him urgently.

'We are indeed,' he tells Dad. 'I hope you've got the good Scotch open.'

'I've got what I tell everyone is the good Scotch open,' Dad says with a wink. 'Right, come on, let's get inside. The two of you must be starving.'

I could eat – they'll put that on my headstone. I only had chips and I do love a good buffet. Teddy, on the other hand, had steak, chips and onion rings. He must be absolutely stuffed.

Every time I walk into Mum and Dad's house, I can never quite get over how much I love it. The hallway runs from the front to the back of the house, with floor-to-ceiling windows at each end. Through a door to the right is their kitchen-living-dining room and it really is something. I read recently someone saying that in the not-so-distant future, millennials were going to be mortified about the lack of walls in their living spaces, and would be desperately trying to move away from open-plan living. Never mind that my parents are definitely not millennials, it's hard to imagine people abandoning these large, multifunctional rooms, because they're such social spaces. Any time any of us has a birthday, at Christmas – any occasion where you want lots of people in a room, and lots of room to do things – we all pile into here.

The room is full of various people, some I know, some I don't, and some I wish I didn't know.

Probably the coolest part of this room is the quirky mezzanine level that is suspended above the kitchen island, with a black metal staircase that leads up to it. It's like a sort of chill-out area, with comfy sofas, and although it is a part of the same room, it's a fun little nook to escape to.

I glance up and see none other than Heidi, my childhood bestie, staring back down at me.

'Here she is,' she announces excitedly. 'Am I coming up or are you coming down? It might be better if you come up, my dress is a bit short, and those stairs are a bit see-through.'

I laugh.

'I'm on my way,' I call back before turning to Teddy. 'Back in a sec.'

'No worries, I'm going to grab a drink, then I'll see if I can find Dougie,' he replies.

I head up the stairs, where I find Heidi alone.

'Is this the VIP area?' I ask her as she flings her arm around me.

We fall back onto the sofa together. When Heidi releases me, she realises her short red dress has risen up, so she hurriedly pulls it back down.

'No, down there is the VIP section,' she says in hushed tones. 'The very *ignorant* people.'

'Is it bad?' I ask, wincing.

'Eden's lot are awful,' she replies. 'Eden is Eden, so you know, she's "on-brand" as she would say, total nightmare. But her mum and dad are just... awful, but different kinds of awful. She looked down her nose at my outfit because she thinks she's all snooty and high society, and he's rough as a badger's arse, and so vulgar – he said you can see what I had for breakfast in this dress.'

'Why, do you have leftovers in the pockets?' I joke.

Heidi and I have been friends since before we were born. Our mums were pregnant at the same time and quickly became best friends – a friendship that only got stronger after Heidi was born, and then me two months later (and, yes, this 'tremendous' age gap does mean that Heidi can – and does often – play the seniority card). We went to the same schools, the same dance classes, we had a crush on the same boy (and he didn't have a crush on either of us) – we even got the same GCSE results, how weird is that?

We've always felt like two halves of the same *thing*. The only real difference between us at school was that I always felt like the personality, whereas Heidi was the looks. Obviously, Heidi has a gorgeous personality, she's so funny, so witty – she says what she thinks whereas I'm a little more willing to bite my tongue if it keeps the peace. But what I mean is that Heidi is a stunner, she had a decent list of male admirers. I, on the other hand, very much relied on being funny. Teenage girls today somehow manage to pull off Instagram-influencer levels of beauty. Unfortunately for me, I'm from a generation where we all looked awful, looking back. Even the popular girls looked like clowns, with their thick pale blue creamy eyeshadow and blusher that would make a clown, well, blush. Unlucky for me, though, I had glasses, and even though now I have a bunch of super-fashionable pairs that actually do my face many favours, back then I had your basic small, round, mostly lens frames that gave me all the sex appeal of Moleman from *The Simpsons*.

These days, we're both comfortable in our skin and making the most of what we've got. Heidi is an absolute knockout with her pin-straight shoulder-length brown hair, her supermodel long legs, and one of those bodies that looks good no matter what you want to wear. I'm not quite as tall, I painstakingly fry my long blonde hair into big, bouncy curls most days, and while I might not be able to pull off wearing anything, I must be doing okay, to have a gorgeous man like Teddy proposing to me.

Oh, my god, the ring! I quickly – but, ultimately, awkwardly – whip my hand behind my back.

'Right, well, that wasn't subtle at all,' Heidi points out with a laugh. 'What do you have in your hand?'

'Nothing,' I say, technically honestly, but an unusually high-pitched tone to my voice betrays me.

Heidi rolls her eyes before making a play for the right side of my body. I'm ready for her, quickly pulling away from her, but in doing so, I play right into her hands. She knew what I would do before I did it, so, as I pull my right side away from her – and therefore turn my left side towards her – she reaches out and grabs my left hand.

The huge diamond ring on my finger catches her eye in an instant.

'Oh, my god, are you engaged?' she shrieks.

The first thing I notice is the chatter in the room die off to nothing. Then...

'What?'

Uh-oh, that's Eden.

I wince and Heidi's face falls, like she knows what she's done, and I know she didn't mean to do it but... god, Eden isn't going to be happy.

I scoot over on the sofa to peer down to the kitchen below us. Eden's enraged bright red face isn't difficult to spot, although she still has that Stepford-style smile she always wears in public. She's standing over by the open bifold doors with Dougie and a couple of other guests. All eyes are on me as I glance around the room. Eventually my eyes land on my mum. She beckons me down with a waggle of her finger.

'Sorry,' Heidi mouths at me.

'I'll tell you all about it when I come back,' I reply. *'If* I make it back.'

Did you ever drop your plate during lunch at school? Walking down the stairs, with all eyes on me, feels exactly like that – well, without the amused cheering that always followed it, but I feel equally as mortified.

I pause for a second, about halfway down, when I spot Eden walking towards me.

She looks stunning in a white strapless maxi dress with pink floral detail growing upward from the hem. Her long brown locks are always curled with a wand – I've never seen her with any other style, almost as though it's her brand, but social influencing is what Eden does for work, so that makes sense.

Eden is always thinking about the optics. Everything she says, everything she does, everything she posts – it's all been carefully considered to cultivate her brand. She's still at a sort of mid-level, though, so despite preaching authenticity and that she is living her best life, there's something insincere about a social feed where everything is a hashtag ad. I'm sure she comes across well, to her 28,000 followers, but because I know she doesn't have a dog, her posts flogging dog biscuits, or the eyeshadow palette she told me she would only wear if she was trying to get a spot at clown college, make me cringe.

She waits for me underneath the balloon arch, featuring various shades of pink. I hate that I know this but 'May blossom' is what she calls her 'aesthetical theme' at the moment, so obviously she wants her party photos to match everything else on her grid.

Dougie is standing next to her. I'm sure he's relieved she hasn't made him wear a pink suit, although, actually, wait a minute, yes, I can confirm that my brother does in fact have a pink handkerchief in the front pocket of the light beige suit I am certain he didn't choose himself.

I walk over to them with my head held as high as possible, although it is hard not to skulk, just a little. This is exactly what I was trying to avoid. As I approach them, my lips part. Come on, words, come out, but not just any words. The right words, please.

Before I get chance to say anything, my future sister-in-law steps forward and embraces me. She pulls me close and gives me a squeeze.

'Congratulations, I am so happy for you and Teddy,' she says softly, releasing me a little so she can look me in the eye. 'And I can't wait to hear all about *your* engagement at *your* engagement party.'

It's subtle but the emphasis is there on the words that make all the difference. Point taken, Eden, this is your night. See, this is exactly why I wanted to keep things under wraps, because I knew it wouldn't be well received. I never would have intentionally upset her with this today.

'Of course,' I reply reassuringly. 'Congratulations, you look beautiful.'

I turn to hug my brother.

'And congratulations to you too,' I tell him.

'Cheers,' he replies as he squeezes me in that goofball way brothers always seem to insist on when hugging their sisters. 'Typical Knight twins, doing everything at the same time. You couldn't let me have my birthdays to myself, now you're muscling in on my engagement party.'

He's obviously joking. I smile at him.

'Wait, you're not twins, are you?' Joanne, Eden's mum, interrupts. 'I mean, you look a bit alike, but I thought she was older.'

I look left and see that my parents and Eden's parents have approached us. I can tell that my own mum and dad are bursting with pride, itching to celebrate my good news with me. I'd say with me and Teddy, but I'm not actually sure where he is at the moment – hiding in the bathroom, if he has any sense.

'They don't look alike at all,' Eden insists, as though she's almost offended at the concept.

Dougie and I do actually look alike, everyone always tells us that we do. We're both fair-haired, both green-eyed, and our noses and lips definitely came off the same production line. '*She*' isn't older, though.

'Dougie is older,' Mum corrects Joanne.

'We all joke that they're twins because Liv was born on Dougie's first birthday,' Dad tells them.

'Bloody hell, pal, you must've just pushed the doctor out of the way when Dougie was born,' Mick, Eden's dad, jokes.

I can't help but scrunch my nose.

'Ew, Dad,' Eden says.

'Hey, what am I missing?' Teddy says as he slinks up alongside me, wrapping an arm around my waist.

'Oi, you, what happened to asking the father of the bride for permission?' my dad teases him as he slaps him on the back.

'They know?' he asks me.

'They know,' I reply with a smile and a sigh. 'We're really sorry. It was supposed to be a secret, but you know what Heidi is like.'

'We can't believe you told Heidi before us – in our own house,' Mum points out, but she's smiling, I don't think she's all that bothered. 'I don't know how you thought you were going to be able to hide it with a diamond the size of the Rock of Gibraltar on your finger.'

Mum takes my hand and admires my ring.

'Congratulations to you both,' Mum says. 'I want all the details.'

'Listen, this is Dougie and Eden's day, I don't want to take any focus from them at all,' I insist. 'How about we have a mini celebration over breakfast tomorrow and we tell you all about it then?'

'I think that would be for the best,' Eden insists.

I can tell she's annoyed but there's that smile of hers, turned up to full beam. It's terrifying really, when you watch the videos she posts for her followers, and it's just a four-minute compilation video of her frolicking in the park, smiling at ducks, lovingly stroking the trees, and rolling around in the grass. She isn't having fun, she's just trying to look like she is, and that smile is always firmly there, never faltering for a second.

'And rightly so,' Joanne adds. 'This is Eden's day.'

'And Dougie's,' my mum bravely points out.

'Well, yes, but you know what I mean,' Joanne replies.

'Are these marble worktops?' Mick asks as he runs a hand over the kitchen island. This conversation is clearly boring him now.

'Mick, shut up about the kitchen,' Joanne says as she elbows him in the ribs.

It looks like it genuinely hurts him. Oh, what a fine example of marital bliss.

Eden twirls one of her big brown curls and lightly pouts.

'Yes, let's park this until tomorrow,' she says. 'Then you can tell your story and show off your ring and everything else.'

I feel like that's her polite reminder that I shouldn't do any of these things tonight but that's fine by me, it was never the plan.

'Of course,' I say.

'Right, okay, well, everyone back to celebrating us,' Eden replies. 'Dougie, come on, Annabella and Herbie will be here any minute, I want to take photos with them under the balloon arch while my make-up still looks its best, so if everyone else can move away from this area.'

My dad's eyebrows shoot up. I can read his mind, he's baffled that someone is telling him where he can stand in his own house, but he would never say anything.

Eden and Dougie head into the hallway. Joanne hooks her arm with Mick and leads him over to the buffet table. The look in her eyes makes me think she's going to tell him off, although it's hard to say what for, I noticed a couple of corkers, at least.

Mum and Dad stay with me and Teddy.

'I thought it best to keep my mouth shut,' Teddy tells me.

'It's usually the safest option,' I reply. 'But, hey, what did I tell you? I knew she would be mad.'

'Bloody women,' he jokes.

'Congratulations,' Mum tells us in hushed tones. 'I know we're doing it properly tomorrow but, come on, just a quick look at the ring.'

I glance left then right before holding my hand out for her, keen to keep my promise.

'Wow, it's incredible,' she tells me. Then she turns to Teddy. 'It's a beautiful ring.'

'It better be, for the price of it,' he jokes.

God, I really do dread to think. Perhaps it's a good thing that I can't get it off, it means I'm less likely to lose it (although, knowing me, I never could truly rule it out).

'Sorry, we really didn't want to announce it this evening,' I insist.

'Oh, I just want to hear all about it,' Mum replies quietly through a big, bright smile. 'I know, I know, it's their engagement party, but I'm just so happy for you both. It's like I knew, I got everything in to make a big, special breakfast for us all in the morning.'

'Are Eden's parents staying the night?' I ask.

'No,' Mum replies. Her lips lightly purse as she smiles.

Teddy laughs.

'You two are a couple of bitches sometimes,' Teddy teases us. 'Come on, Vic, let's go grab drinks, leave these two to their session.'

'Oi, we're not bitches,' I insist, laughing it off.

'Right after you,' Dad tells him.

'Is she behaving?' I ask Mum once we're alone, but I already know the answer.

I might be able to silently read my dad but with my mum, it's like we've developed the ability to essentially write back. We always know what the other is thinking, all it takes is a look.

Erica Knight is a real lady. She has class, manners, her hair always looks great, and she dresses in a way that, if anyone were to randomly stop her in the street and ask her questions for the news or a TV show in the way they sometimes do, she would be camera-ready. However, like any real lady, she has no time for shit of any description. She'll wear her brave face and she'll hold her tongue when she needs to, but bad behaviour never goes unchecked, and if it gets bad enough, she'll let you know about it. The thing I love the most about my mum, though, is her hidden cheeky side – a side that I'm sure she reserves for when she's only in my company. It's never a shock, when she makes these cheeky jokes, and yet they always catch me off guard.

It's amazing, really, that she lets Eden's mum, Joanne, get away with so much, but it's all in the interest of maintaining good family relationships, and I can appreciate that.

'Oh, she's on top form today,' Mum tells me quietly. 'The WC tiles aren't for her, the ice in her drink was too big, and the food was – let me get this right, because I don't want to misquote her and make what she said sound silly – too nice. The food is too nice, genuinely, she's quite put out by it. She says Mick will alter his expectations – I think it was the brie tartlets that pushed her over the edge, so steer clear of those, unless you want Teddy *getting ideas*.'

'Okay, well, I'm definitely glad they're not staying the night then,' I reply.

'I'm so happy for you,' Mum says again, but then her smile falls and she cocks her head thoughtfully. 'Are you happy?'

'Me?' I reply in a pitch much higher than usual. 'Yes, of course. Why?'

'Oh, nothing, I've had a couple of glasses of champagne already, my radar must be off,' she insists. 'I just thought you seemed a little, well... like you had that look on your face.'

Mum nods, gesturing for me to look behind me.

It's Heidi and her face is trapped in the same wince I left her with. She waves a white serviette at me.

'Is it safe to come out?' she asks.

'Come here,' I insist, grabbing her, giving her a playful shake. 'Of course, you're not in trouble.'

'Excuse me, ladies,' Mum starts. 'It looks like Mick is doing some kind of experiment to find out if he can fit his hand in my Murano Glass vase.'

'Oh, boy,' I say softly.

'Have you seen the new fountain outside?' Heidi asks. 'In the back garden?'

'My parents have a fountain?' I reply in disbelief. 'Dad messages me if he gets a new flower on his lemon tree, I'm sure I would've heard all about a new fountain.'

'Just let me show you it,' she insists.

I follow Heidi through the bifold doors, across the patio and along the cute little pathway that leads to a sort of secret garden area.

Cloaked by trees, Heidi takes a seat on the bench. She pats the space next to her.

'Oh, wow, there is no fountain, is there?' I reply.

I can't help but laugh a little.

'No, there isn't, although I'm going to pitch one to your dad because I think one would look absolutely sick on the lawn next to the decking,' she replies. 'But I just wanted to get you alone, to talk to you about this engagement business.'

'No way!' I say, feigning shock.

'Come on, Liv, let me get this over with,' she insists. 'I love you so much and I just want to make sure you've thought this through.'

'I've been thinking about it ever since he popped the question,' I reply, not that it's been all that long, but it's all I can think about. 'I had no idea he was going to ask me – I had no idea if he ever would, to be honest, I didn't think he was the marrying kind, but I am pleasantly surprised.'

'But there's pleasantly surprised and then there's really, really wanting to marry someone,' she points out. 'Is he good enough for you?'

'Look, Heids, I know you're not his biggest fan, and of course your opinion matters to me,' I tell her.

I don't really know why, and it's not ideal, but Heidi has never really taken to Teddy. When I first started dating him, she told me she thought he seemed stuck-up, and in the early days, when I was finding it hard to process exactly what it meant when Teddy would often be too busy with work to hang out with me, Heidi and I would talk for hours about what it meant. I don't think she felt like he was putting in the effort with me, but I soon learned that, while he's working like crazy for his dream promotion, that's just the way it's going to be. I've always been happy, though, to go a few days without seeing him, because when I eventually do see him, he always takes me on dreamy nights out and gives me gorgeous presents. He really knows how to sweep a girl off her feet.

'Have I had second thoughts since I said yes? Yes,' I admit. 'Is it soon? Yes. Too soon? Maybe?'

'I might not be his biggest fan but I'm not thinking about that,' Heidi insists as she takes my hand in hers. 'The only things I'm thinking about are the look on your face, the tone of your voice, and the words you're saying and, sis, you don't seem sure.'

'I'm not sure,' I admit, lowering my voice. 'Of course I'm not. Are people usually sure?'

Heidi shrugs.

'I know I haven't been with him that long but... I do love him?' I reply.

Heidi narrows her eyes.

'Was that a question?'

It wasn't supposed to be. It did sort of come out like one, though.

'I do love him,' I say, like I mean it this time – because I do. 'I am a little concerned about how fast things are moving but, honestly, I can't believe he's asked, and just imagine what will happen if I say no, surely no relationship can recover from a declined marriage proposal?'

Heidi chews her lip.

'I'm just not sure that's a good enough reason,' she replies.

'I'm so happy with him,' I remind her. 'And this clearly means a lot to him, or he wouldn't have asked. He's taking this commitment seriously, I owe it to him to do the same. You know me, what I've been like in the past when it comes to commitment, I've always worried about things, if I was with the right person, if it was going anywhere, and with Teddy, this is the first time I've allowed myself to relax a little and not worry about that stuff and I really am happy.'

'I mean, it really is a nice fucking ring,' she eventually says through a smile. 'He did good there.'

'I know you're just worried about me, and I love you for it,' I insist. 'But can you just go with me on this one?'

'I suppose,' she says with a smile. 'You're a grown woman, you know your mind. I won't say anything.'

'Thank you,' I reply. 'Honestly, even the proposal itself – the way he did it – shocked me, it was amazing. He took me into the caves, to the wishing well, and he made a wish in it before popping the question. And after he told me how he had originally planned this big, expensive dinner, a string quartet in the park, the works. But his exact words were, "I know how much you love that sentimental crap" – he does know me so well.'

'That sentimental *crap*?' Heidi asks, raising an eyebrow, but she quickly retreats. 'No, sorry, I mean, that's great. That's really nice, he does know you well, and he must love you, to get down on one knee in those dirty caves, because we all know what Teddy is like when it comes to dirt.'

My face falls before I have a chance to stop it.

'He did get dow... no, sorry! Sorry, sorry,' Heidi babbles. 'Blah. Let me start again. Sis, I'm so happy for you, I am excited for your wedding, and I can't wait to see what sort of bridesmaid dress you have for me, but I know I'll look amazing in it.'

'You really will,' I reply. 'Okay, shall we go get some drinks?'

'Yes, I'm astounded you've gone this long without one,' Heidi replies. 'Liv Knight at a party without a drink in her hand is, like, the Halley's Comet of social behaviour.'

'I can't argue with that,' I laugh. 'Come on.'

We link arms as we head back towards the house. I understand exactly why Heidi is freaking out – I've been freaking out myself – but I love Teddy, he loves me, and I know being worried about what rejecting him will do to our relationship is not a great reason to get married, but I think the fact that he asked tells me everything I need to know.

Yes, it's soon, but when you know, you know, right?

God, I hope I'm right. Not just because this is one of the biggest things I'll ever do, but because Heidi would hit me with the biggest 'I told you so' of all time, and I'd say that might be even harder to take, except the doubts are really starting to creep in now.

'I won't be a minute,' I tell her, letting go of her arm. 'Fix me a surprise cocktail, I'll be right with you.'

'No sweat,' she replies.

I hang around on the patio for a second, until Heidi is gone, before sneaking my way along the edge of the house. Something caught my eye as we were walking back, something I must be mistaken about...

I peer around the side of the summer house, where I see Teddy and Eden having a chat. I press myself up against the wall, as close as I can get to it, as though it's going to make my hearing any better.

'Look, at the end of the day, it's not even cheating,' Eden insists. 'And I think, if both parties know and accept that, it's no one else's business.'

I jolt back in horror and knock over a plant. The smash of the pot might just be the loudest sound I have ever heard – or perhaps it just feels like it because that will have definitely given up my position.

Teddy peers around the corner and our eyes meet.

'Oh, *there* you are,' I say. 'Someone said they thought they had seen you heading this way.'

Eden steps out too.

'Oh, Eden, hi,' I say brightly. Far too brightly. I'm so suspicious, which is mad because I'm not the one hiding behind a summer house trying to justify adultery.

It isn't unusual for Teddy and Eden to chat. Annoyingly, but not surprisingly, Eden thinks far more of Teddy than she does of me. When Dougie brought Eden home to meet us all – the first and only girlfriend he's ever introduced to the family (not because he's never had any, I'm sure, but because that's just the sort of guy he is), I got excited. I think any girl with at least one brother, or even only children for that matter, dreams of having a sister, an instant best friend, someone to have girly chats with, to talk boys with and do each other's hair. Well, with Eden, that's not what I got. She has no interest in having a sisterly relationship with me, and the only way in which you could ever consider her having done my hair is the time she gave me a bottle of purple shampoo she had been gifted, because she had no use for it, and she thought I did.

While I might not be all that attractive a friend/family member to her, Teddy, with all his money and connections, is just her kind of guy. She's made a point of forging instant bestie status with him, which is a real kick in the teeth for me. Still, as much as they chat usually, this is weird.

'Babe, Heidi wants to tell you what she thinks of...' I pause. First of all, I never call him babe, second of all, I was going to lie and say she wanted to tell him she liked my ring but I promised I wouldn't talk about our engagement, so... 'the FTSE 100.'

Teddy stares at me for a second or two, completely motionless apart from a burst of baffled blinking.

'The FTSE 100?' he repeats back to me. 'Your friend Heidi? The interior designer?'

He can't believe what he's hearing, which is a coincidence because I can't believe what I'm saying.

'Mad, right?' I say with a shrug.

'Well, I'll leave you two to it,' Eden says as she sheepishly makes her way back to the house.

Teddy waits until she's gone.

'Obviously you're making that up, right?' he says.

'Yeah, *obviously*,' I reply. 'I heard what she said and I didn't know what to do. Teddy, has Eden cheated on my brother?'

Teddy sighs.

'Liv, I know what you're like,' he tells me. 'I know that you'll fly off the handle and get involved but you have to promise me that you won't.'

'But she cheated on him?' I say again.

'It's not that black and white,' he replies. 'And it's between Eden and Dougie.'

'And you,' I point out. 'And when a couple gets married, it's basically a given that anything you tell one person gets told to the other.'

'I'm not sure that's right,' he says, narrowing his eyes. 'I'll only tell you if you promise not to say anything. Can you do that?'

I chew my lip.

'Yes, okay, just tell me because I'm worried,' I say quickly.

'Eden slept with someone before she and Dougie were official,' he tells me in hushed tones. 'I only know because I heard her talking about it at the New Year's Eve party we threw. Obviously I confronted her about it but it turned out Dougie already knew and they had made peace with it. She just pulled me to one side to thank me for not blowing it up in front of everyone at New Year's, because even though Doug forgave her, she knows you guys never would have.'

'And she would be right,' I point out.

'It was very early on, Liv, and Dougie accepts that,' Teddy points out. 'You need to do the same. I know you feel like you have to constantly fight battles for what's right, but you need to let this one go. They're happy. We're happy – we don't have anything like that hanging over us, and we know that we'll never cheat on each other. It's made me feel very lucky, to know that I have you, and to know that you would never do that to me. I'm so lucky you agreed to marry me.'

Teddy takes my hands in his and smiles and, just like that, my doubts and concerns are ejected from my brain. I feel sorry for Dougie but Teddy is right, he's a grown man, and I have to respect that he's happy. All that matters is that I'm happy in my relationship and I am. I really am.

4

I would say Mum had gone all out for our engagement celebration breakfast but, of course, I know that she was planning on serving up a storm regardless. Still, that doesn't make the spread seem any less amazing, and I am happy to claim it in my and Teddy's honour.

We've always been one of those families that is hard to please all at once. So, on a Friday night when we were younger, when we would have a family night eating delicious takeaways and watching movies, everyone would want something different. My favourite was Chinese, Dad's was Indian, Dougie always wanted pizza and Mum much preferred fish and chips. Then, when it came to picking a movie, I would want to watch a romcom, ideally one which stared Matthew McConaughey in the same dreamy role he always played back then; Dad felt a similar way about Clint Eastwood (well, not exactly the same way, but his movies were always his pick); Dougie would usually choose a Quentin Tarantino film or anything directed by Martin Scorsese; and with Mum it was always one of two options: a musical or anything starring Richard Gere. In the end, we had to take it turns to let one person pick the food and the other the movie, so one week it would be chow mein and *Coogan's Bluff*, the next it was pizza and *Pretty Woman*.

It was these differences in taste that made sharing a birthday with

Dougie so difficult for us when we were kids, because obviously we would always have a joint party – and a lot of the time people would buy us the same presents, so whoever opened theirs first kind of ruined the surprise for the other. Dougie wanted a cowboy party, I wanted a princess one. Dougie wanted hot dogs, I wanted sandwiches. He wanted a clown, I wanted *not a clown*. We couldn't even agree on birthday cakes because he always preferred fruity things whereas I'm strictly a chocolate kind of girl. Mum always made it work for us, though, and today, with breakfast, nothing has changed.

The kitchen island is laid out with a breakfast buffet so stunning it looks like the set of a magazine shoot. Not only is there something for everyone, whether you prefer pastries or toast or eggs, but there are options within the options. Different breads, no less than six spreads, scrambled eggs (fried, poached or boiled on request apparently), waffles and pancakes because, even though most people would be happy with one or the other, Mum's motto is why choose one when you can have both?

I'm like a child this morning, in my element, at the make-your-own-sweet-stack station Mum has lovingly put together for her adult children – and her adult children are very grateful. I'm layering up pancakes and waffles, with a mixture of sauces and sprinkles, topping my creation off with a generous squirt of cream. This is all happening much to the amusement of my future husband.

'Are you really going to eat that?' he asks with a chuckle.

'I'm going to eat all of it,' I tell him proudly.

'At least Dougie put fruit on his,' Eden chimes in. 'That's slightly healthier.'

'Yeah, but I have three waffles and two pancakes,' he replies. 'Liv only has half that.'

I smile at my brother. He always has my back.

'As engagement celebrations go, this is amazing, Mum, thank you,' I tell her as she finally sits down with her cup of tea.

'You're welcome, my darlings, I'm just so happy for you both – for all four of you,' she adds. 'How fortunate am I to have both my children getting married? Two weddings, two parties, two big hats.'

'Just wear whatever hat you get for Dougie and Eden's wedding again to

Liv and Teddy's wedding,' Dad suggests – Mum shoots him one hell of a look.

'Have a day off, sweetheart,' Mum claps back.

'To be honest, our wedding will probably come first,' Teddy says between sips of his coffee.

'Really?' both Mum and Eden squeak in unison.

'Yeah, well, you guys are waiting until next year, right?' Teddy replies, although he directs it at Eden.

'Yeah, because a good wedding takes a long time to plan,' she replies, baffled we would even be considering it. 'How will you make all the arrangements?'

'How hard can it be?' Teddy replies. 'We don't care about the wedding that much, we care more about being married.'

I feel almost smug. Listen to him, talking about how the party doesn't matter, it's the relationship that counts. How could I have doubts, when he says all the right things?

'The only thing we need to sort is Porthian Sands,' I say.

'I know that's Liv's only deal-breaker, so the sooner we sort that, the sooner we can do it,' Teddy says.

Eden looks quite put out by this.

'So you're having the same venue as us too,' she points out. 'You know, it's the only place on the Cornwall coast for anyone who is anyone to tie the knot. They don't exactly do shotgun weddings.'

'Oi,' Dougie says with a laugh. 'Come on, you know they're not stealing our idea, it's a family tradition to get married there. It just so happens that, in recent years, it's become trendy.'

'Yes, and how many footballers and reality stars are closely related to the person who built the wedding barn?' Mum adds. 'Alan is always accommodating when we need a date there.'

'Tell you what, why don't I give him a call?' Dad suggests. 'Get you two a date to book in.'

'That would be great, thank you,' Teddy replies.

'Yeah, thanks, Dad,' I add. 'That's the first bit we need to think about, before we can figure out anything else.'

'I'll do it now,' he says almost excitedly.

Eden pouts. She does let the smile slip, when she's amongst family, and there are no cameras pointing at her.

'Well, this is exciting,' Mum says. 'Are you happy if it's a summer, autumn or winter wedding? I always wanted a winter wedding, although we wound up having it in the summer in the end. I just loved the idea of crisp snow, twinkling lights, festive food, hot chocolates by a roaring fire at the end of the day.'

'What happened, did Vic pull rank?' Teddy laughs. 'Did he want drunken grinding on the sweaty dance floor with his tie tied around his head?'

Mum laughs and rolls her eyes.

'Not quite,' she says. 'But, of course, we got married at Porthian Sands too, and the chances of getting all of that on a beach in Cornwall, in a building made mostly of wood... Snow seemed unlikely – slush at best – and we knew everyone would be freezing. Getting married there meant a lot to us – more than the picture I had in my head of the finer details – so summer it was.'

'Well, that rules winter out for us,' Teddy tells me.

'This was decades ago,' Mum reminds him. 'More than I'd care to consider. I imagine – being the wedding hotspot that it is now – they've made improvements to make it a space that can be used all year round.'

I wonder about my dream wedding. Should it be something that already exists in my head? I don't suppose I've ever really thought about it. I suppose it's never been a priority, to plan an event that wasn't on the cards, that might never even happen. I've always known that, if I did get married, it would be at Porthian Sands because it's a family tradition, because my granddad built it, he married my gran there, my parents got married there, Dougie is going to get married there. It's a place that is special to us – after countless weddings and family holidays there – and although we haven't been in a while, it still means as much to us as ever.

Dad takes a seat at the table. He's quiet – too quiet – and the colour has drained from his cheeks. He picks up his tea and takes a sip.

'Well?' Mum prompts him.

He stares back at us over his cup.

'Dad?' I say. 'Is everything okay?'

'Yes, sweetheart,' he replies.

'Okay, something is definitely going on,' Dougie chimes in. 'You don't call anyone sweetheart – especially not Liv.'

I shoot him a look.

'No offence,' he insists with a laugh, holding up his hands. 'I just mean, he calls you Liv, Olive, Olive Oil – never sweetheart. He called Mum "mate" the other day.'

Dad laughs but it's suspiciously sedate for him.

'Come on, Vic, spit it out,' Mum insists. 'We're going to find out eventually.'

Dad grabs a blueberry muffin and takes a big, dramatic bite. He barely chews it before he starts talking.

'Alan is dead,' he mumbles dramatically through his mouthful of muffin.

'What?' Mum replies. 'Oh, no, what happened?'

'He just popped his clogs, out of the blue, last year,' he replies. He pauses for a second to swallow. 'It sounds like it was a big shock for everyone.'

'I'll bet,' Mum replies. 'What was he – sixty? Have his kids taken over then?'

'No,' Dad tells her. 'How long has it been in that family? And they've sold up instead.'

'Oh, that's such a shame,' Mum says.

'Wait, so does that mean no queue-jumping for our weddings?' Eden chimes in.

Wow, Eden, sensitive as ever.

Mum opens her mouth to say something, but Dad gets there first.

'It's worse than that,' Dad says. 'The new owners – they're not going to be doing weddings any more.'

'What, at all?' I say.

'From what I could tell, from the employee I spoke to, it sounds like the new owners simply don't want it to be a wedding venue, just a hotel, so they're just stopping,' Dad explains. 'Just like that.'

'What about the people who have already booked?' I ask.

'They stopped taking bookings a while ago, and they're honouring the ones that had already been made,' he explains. 'But there is one thing the bloke on the phone mentioned. They've just had a cancellation, but it's in just over a month, so in theory someone could take that.'

'Oh, great, well, we did say the sooner the better,' Teddy replies. 'That works for us, get us booked in, will you, Vic?'

'Whoa, whoa, whoa, hang on a minute,' Eden says. She stands up in her place and lays her hands down on the table like she's in a business meeting. 'You can't have that slot – we should get that slot. We've been engaged for almost six months.'

'But we want to get married ASAP,' Teddy replies, very matter-of-factly, and businesslike as ever. 'You guys don't want to get married until next year.'

'*But obviously* that changes if we can't have Porthian Sands,' she points out, as though he were an idiot. 'First come, first served, we got engaged first, we should get the venue.'

I look over at Dougie. He widens his eyes at me.

'*But* we said we wanted to get married this year, and when Vic said there had been a cancellation, we said we would take it,' Teddy points out. 'That is the very definition of first come, first served. Vic mentioned the slot, we claimed it.'

'*But* we've been together for more than a year,' Eden points out. 'Our wedding means so much more.'

'Erm, I don't think that's necessarily true,' I point out. 'Just because we haven't been together for as long as you guys have doesn't mean we love each other any less.'

Also, if I were the point-scoring kind, we've never cheated on each other in any way, shape or form, even if it was fine at the time and forgiven, so that's one in our favour. Not that I'd mention it, though.

'*But* we were first,' Eden whines. 'Dougie, come on, tell them, please.'

'Okay, okay, that's enough buts,' Mum insists. 'It isn't a competition and no one can say either couple is more or less deserving than the other.'

The room falls silent for a second. I don't think anyone knows what to say.

I do really feel for Dougie and Eden because I'm in the same boat. Porthian Sands is special to me and Dougie, and it means a lot to our parents that we want to get married there too. I just hate that one of us is going to be left heartbroken, unless...

'Neither of us could get married there,' I suggest to Dougie. 'It seems unfair that one of us can, and the other can't, and there are plenty of reasons why one of us should over the other, but it just isn't fair. Fair is neither of us getting married there.'

'Or both of you,' Dad chimes in.

'Right, but there's only one day free,' Dougie says. 'Liv is right. We're not going to fall out about it, we can just both find somewhere else.'

'Unless you share the day,' Vic says. 'One of you takes the morning, the other the afternoon.'

'It's a wedding *day*,' Eden replies.

'Unless... no.' Mum pauses for a moment. 'You would have to share the whole day but...'

Her voice trails off again.

'A joint wedding?' Eden says, picking up where Mum left off.

'*That* could be a solution,' Teddy replies enthusiastically.

My jaw tightens. I need to say something, but I can't – what would I say?

'Sharing the day would be a way for us to both get what we want,' Dougie reasons, although he sounds unsure.

'Look, if it means getting married at Porthian Sands, maybe there's a way we can make it work,' Eden says. 'Let's just think about this for a second.'

I can't believe they're considering this!

'If this place is as in demand as you say, we'd better decide fast, before someone else gets in there,' Teddy replies.

I practically force my mouth open so I can speak.

'Wait, this has to be a terrible idea,' I point out. 'I know it means a lot to us, and we all want to get married there, but a joint wedding? Really? And one that we'll need to plan in less than a month?'

'Liv might be right,' Mum says. 'It's your wedding days, you want them to be just right.'

'But we do both want to get married at Porthian Sands,' Dougie reminds me. 'Granddad built it, it's tradition, and if we don't do it at the same time, we won't get to.'

'Surely it will be chaos, though?' I persist.

'We're all adults,' Eden replies. 'I think we can make this work, make everyone happy. We can have back-to-back ceremonies on the beach and then one big party after.'

'So, we'll just be at each other's wedding ceremonies and receptions in wedding dresses?' I say.

'I guess,' she says with a sigh. 'But this means a lot to you both, it's my dream venue, Teddy is clearly dying to marry you as soon as he can... let's make this work.'

Can we make this work? I suppose having one big party would be fun, so long as our ceremonies are completely separate, and the only thing I've ever known for sure about my wedding was that it would be in the barn Granddad built, I don't want to give that up, and I'm sure Dougie doesn't want to either.

Is this a sign that I need to stop and think about things? Does this just go to show that we're rushing into it? But getting married at Porthian Sands is the only part of my wedding day that I've ever been sure of. Perhaps it's a sign that I should take a leap? It's now or never. And, hey, if we can pull this off, then that's surely all the sign I'll need.

'Can we really get this together in less than a month?' I ask.

'I absolutely can,' Eden tells me. 'I live for this stuff. We can do it together. In fact, it might be fun, like a sister bonding activity.'

I smile. It would be nice to feel more like sisters with Eden because, as much time as we've spent around each other, we barely even feel like friends. This could be a turning point for us.

'Maybe we could make it work,' I say, not sounding all that sure of myself, but I'm willing to try if Eden is. 'Okay, yeah. Let's do it.'

'Yay,' Eden says, clapping her hands. 'Oh, my god, I'm getting married in a month!'

'Well, *if* the slot is still free,' Dad chimes in.

'Oh, my goodness, Victor, don't say things like that, get back on the phone,' Mum says with a laugh. 'Quick, quick.'

Dad jumps to his feet and dashes out of the room again.

Teddy looks at his phone.

'I've got to take this,' he tells me. 'It's work.'

'Yeah, no worries,' I reply.

Dougie and Eden are talking excitedly about the idea of getting married this year instead of next year. I turn to Mum.

'Are you sure about this?' she asks me quietly. 'I know you had your heart set on that place but it is just a place. It makes us feel close to your granddad but, you know, this is your wedding day. He would be there in spirit no matter where you had it.'

I smile.

'I know,' I reply. 'But I do love the place, I can't imagine getting married anywhere else, and everyone else is buzzing about it. It's just a shock. Dougie and Eden have been engaged for a while, Teddy knew that he was going to ask me, so it's just me who this is all brand new to. But it could be fun, planning with Eden.'

'Well, we do know she'll be amazing at it,' Mum replies. 'This is very much her thing.'

I nervously get back to my breakfast while we wait for Teddy then Dad to return.

Eventually, Dad pops his head back into the room. He's holding the phone with his hand over the mouthpiece – such a Dad thing to do, when he could just press mute.

'Right, everyone listen up,' he says in a bizarrely loud whisper. 'That date is free, it's ours if we want it, but the hotel is fully booked. Not a single room. The holiday lodges are all full too.'

'We could try and find somewhere,' Mum suggests. 'I know it's quite last minute but...'

'One thing is available,' he continues. 'That big beach house on the edge of the hotel grounds, the one they rent out.'

'Oh, my god, that place is stunning,' I say. 'And massive.'

'Yeah, it could take us all,' Dad replies. 'But it's expensive, and the minimum booking is two weeks.'

'Really?' Dougie says.

'It's probably to deter stag and hen parties,' Mum points out.

'How expensive are we talking?' Eden asks. 'Because we need to plan the whole wedding and that would be so much easier if we were there. You guys are retired, Dougie has flexible hours, so do I. Liv, you're not working at the moment, are you?'

Now isn't the time to explain to her that I only get paid if I work, and therefore always need to be working on or toward something.

'Tell them we'll take it,' Teddy chimes in. 'It doesn't matter what it costs, it's on me, my wedding gift to us all. We can take a two-week holiday, plan the wedding from Cornwall.'

'Oh, Teddy, that's so kind of you,' Eden tells him. 'That would be perfect.'

'That's okay, right, babe?' he asks me.

'My head is spinning,' I say with a laugh. 'But yeah, okay, sure. Even if I do need to work, I can do it from there. Does this overpriced beach house have Wi-Fi?'

'It has a pool and a cinema,' Dad replies with a chuffed smile. 'I'll go get it booked.'

'What if people can't make the date?' I add, throwing another problem into the mix. Of course, Dad still dashes off excitedly to make the call, given that Eden and Dougie are all in.

'Anyone who cares about us will make it,' Eden says confidently. 'But getting married where we want to do it is more important than everyone's second cousins being able to attend. We're going to have to make the best of it.'

'Yeah, who cares?' Teddy agrees. 'So long as all of us are there, and our parents, who else do we need?'

'It's sorted,' Dad calls out from the other room. 'Just finalising the details.'

Wow, that's that then, my wedding is booked. And a double wedding at that. The last twenty-four hours have been a real roller coaster. But I'm marrying the man I love and, even if it's not going to be exactly the way I thought it would, it's happening. Time to just sit back and enjoy the ride.

5

Come on, Heidi, pick up the phone.

'Hello,' she eventually says, out of breath.

'Hey, can you talk?' I reply.

'I am just trying to figure out some of the details on the most high-profile job of my career to date,' she says. 'But I always have time for you.'

'I didn't want to say anything until it was official – and I wanted to tell you quickly while Teddy was in the loo, because we're meeting his mum in a moment to tell her we're engaged, but we just went and gave notice to say we're getting married,' I tell her.

'Wow, congratulations,' she replies. 'That means it's really happening.'

'Well, I was worried we wouldn't be able to do it in time, but we have to, I can tell you...' I pause for dramatic effect. 'We've set a date!'

'Oh, wow,' she replies, her response a little flat. 'So it's *really* really happening.'

'It is,' I say. 'And it's soon, because we really wanted to tie the knot at the place Granddad built, and they're actually stopping doing weddings there, so we have this cancellation. So, first of all, mark 8 July in your calendar, and next to it write that you're going to be not just my chief bridesmaid, but my one and only, because there is no one I would rather have by my side down the aisle. Well, apart from Teddy, obviously, so I guess I mean by my *other* side.'

I laugh like a dork. Heidi stays silent.

'Heids?' I prompt her.

'Liv, I am so, so sorry,' she starts. 'I'm away in Abu Dhabi that week. It's the launch of the new hotel, the one I've just designed all the interiors for, I... I have to be there.'

The thought of not having Heidi at my wedding feels like being slapped across the face.

'Oh, no, I'm so sorry,' I tell her. 'I genuinely mean this, I would change it, but it's not only the last date they have, well, ever, but – you're going to laugh – we've agreed to share the date with Dougie and Eden.'

Heidi goes quiet again.

'That's... wow, yeah,' she says, not really giving much away but obviously, being my best friend, I can read her like a book – she isn't in love with the idea of a double wedding but who is? Needs must.

'I feel so awful,' she continues. 'Perhaps I can get home early, though. It's going to be mad while I'm there, and I'm already super stressed, but if it all goes to plan... the Saturday, yeah?'

I smile to myself. I might not have her blessing, but she has my back.

'Hey, listen, do not worry about it,' I insist. 'And don't worry about the bridesmaid thing. Eden's best friend lives in LA now, she can't make it over until the day before the wedding, so Eden isn't having any bridesmaids either, which makes it less awkward. And we can always celebrate together when you get back.'

'I'll do my best,' she tells me. 'Promise.'

'Oh, Teddy is back, I'd better go,' I say quickly. 'But we'll figure it out, don't worry.'

'Sure thing, speak soon,' she says.

'Bye,' I reply, just as Teddy arrives back.

'Who was that?' he asks me.

'It was Heidi,' I tell him. 'She, erm, she can't come to the wedding, she's in Abu Dhabi for work.'

'Hey, it's all right for some,' he replies. 'Look, I know it's a bit shit, but you're getting married at your dream venue, and all your family is going to be there. That's all that matters.'

'And you,' I reply with a smile. 'You'll be there.'

'I hate to break it to you, babe, but I am your family now,' he says, pulling me close for a kiss. 'Now, come on, Mum is out on the terrace. You know she doesn't like to be kept waiting.'

Teddy takes me by the hand as I take a deep breath. We head through the busy Knightsbridge bar and out onto the sunny roof terrace.

It's busy out here too, as it always is on a hot, sunny day like today. The terrace is packed with so much greenery, you could almost forget you were up in the sky, although when you make your way through the leafy jungle, towards the glass fence around the edges, there is one hell of a view over the rooftops.

We make our way through the tables to find Alicia, Teddy's mum. The place is alive with chatting patrons and cool, ambient music drifting out of hidden speakers. It's a lovely atmosphere and there's just the right amount of breeze. I could easily waste a summer afternoon up here drinking cocktails.

'There she is,' Teddy says, squeezing my hand. 'Oh, and Verity is here.'

My heart stops. Not Verity – anyone but Verity.

'Should we maybe tell your mum the news later?' I ask quickly, before we reach them.

'We can't back out now,' he says. 'Not now the countdown is on.'

If Verity and I had met under any other circumstances, I would probably quite like her. She's tall and slim with glossy auburn hair that flicks under at one side and out at the other. Despite being around my age, she somehow simultaneously looks younger *and* more mature than I do. She's so chic and stylish in her power suits – I didn't think you could feel intimidated by a wardrobe, but I absolutely do. She works for Osa Solutions, in the legal department, although I'm not exactly sure what that entails but it confirms that she has the beauty and the brains, and she's successful in her own right, which is always impressive.

Alicia is only involved in the business in a strange sort of way. I'm sure she has a financial investment in it, given that it's her mum's business, but she concerns herself in what Teddy does in a sort of, I don't know, something between an overbearing mother and a Lady Macbeth vibe, which is as weird as it sounds.

Alicia hangs out with Verity mostly because they're friends (although they always try to style it out as business), which would be absolutely fine, were it not for the fact Verity and Teddy had a very brief fling years ago. Teddy told me about it, just randomly in conversation, around the time we started seeing each other. It came up because we were having a laugh, him telling me all about how his mum was trying to set him up with someone from work, and it being awkward because they'd had a fling that hadn't gone anywhere.

At the time, it was just a funny story, shared in the middle of a series of dating disasters we had both had before we met, but then things got serious between us and I've found myself crossing paths with her, which is great. I don't let it bother me, we both have pasts, and we'd been dating countless other people before we met. I think the reason I find her so uncomfortable to be around is a combination of me being aware of the fact his mum tried her best to push them together, because she thought Verity was perfect for him, but also, I don't know, there's just something in Verity's bright blue eyes, a look that lets me know she got to Teddy first.

Of course, I don't believe for a second that he's interested in her, and the fact that he proposed to me just goes to show that he's serious about me, but I find it awkward nonetheless, and I really, really don't want to do this in front of her right now.

'Edward, darling, come here,' Alicia demands the second she clocks eyes on him. Her tone always baffles me, it's like the warmest greeting delivered in the coldest way.

Alicia is in her late fifties but through a series of, shall we say, age interventions, she has skin that looks decades younger. She's certainly an advert for whatever she's had done because she looks great. Interestingly, though, she very much acts and presents as her real age, if not a little older. It's as though she doesn't want to look younger, just good for her age, which sounds great and normal and fine but, I don't know, with Alicia it feels like it has to be some kind of tactical advantage. She doesn't want to get away with it, she doesn't want to pass for someone younger, and she wants you to know that she has invested in herself. She talks about her new nose like she does her Bentley – proudly, and constantly, and in a way that seems designed to remind you that you don't have either of them. Hey, if I thought a new nose was going to give me some kind of boost in life, I would be all for it, but it's going to take a lot more than that for me.

'Hello, Mother,' Teddy says as he kisses her on both cheeks.

He turns his attention to Verity. She stands up to offer him her cheeks so he can kiss her too.

They both sit back down so we take seats opposite them.

'Hello, Olivia, are you keeping well, dear?' Alicia says.

She picks up her gin and tonic and takes a long, lingering sip.

'I'm really good, thanks,' I reply.

'Oh, really good?' she repeats back to me. 'Edward told me you didn't get your telly job.'

'No, it wasn't a good fit,' I reply, trying not to show any embarrassment – not that I should be embarrassed, people don't get jobs all the time, especially not in this industry, I think it's just having it mentioned here, in front of people, and there's something judgemental yet dismissive in her tone. 'I'm going to write a book instead.'

Alicia turns to Verity.

'She writes romance novels for reality TV personalities,' Alicia tells her and, yep, there's definitely a tone there.

'She's a ghostwriter, Mother, it's a good business,' Teddy says in my defence.

'I mean no disrespect,' Alicia insists. 'Writing books for these people is more befitting the kind of partner I envisioned Edward being with than someone who is one of those people.'

She might not mean any disrespect but that doesn't mean there isn't any to be found.

'Actually, I'm going to try to write my own,' I reply. 'To publish as myself.'

Alicia widens her eyes at me. The needle has swung the other way again. Writing for other people is a job but she clearly thinks writing for myself is some sort of silly dream, and something else I'll fail at.

'I knew you were thinking about it,' Teddy says. 'You're actually going to go for it?'

'Yeah, I had a quick chat with my agent, and with some time off coming up, it seems like a great time to give it a go,' I say.

'I'd love to take time off from work and give something fun a go,' Verity says, and I'm sure she doesn't mean anything by it, but it makes me feel like my job is a silly little whimsical thing we'd all love to abandon our real responsibilities to piss around with.

'Anyway, no offence, Verity, but we thought we were only meeting Mother today,' Teddy tells her. 'I apologise if this seems a little strange but we have some news.'

Alicia glances down at my stomach with a look on her face like she's just chomped on a wasp nest.

'Pregnant?' she asks, practically through gritted teeth.

Incredible.

I remember writing a scene in a romance novel for someone who found fame on a reality dating show, and she wanted this absolute villain of a mother-in-law in there, a real caricature of all the worst characteristics you would hope and pray you would never have to deal with in real life. After it was published, I would check the reviews – I know I shouldn't, but I can't help myself – and I remember someone complaining that the leading lady should tell her mother-in-law to fuck off. That review hasn't changed the way I write but has changed the way I think, when someone in real life isn't being ideal, because I stop and wonder what life would be like if I took their advice. The reality is that, in real life, you can't just tell people to fuck off, you can't scorch the earth with your mother-in-law, because you have a husband who adores her, and if you want to stay with him, you're going to have to find a way to put up with her. So I stop, consider what it might feel like to speak my mind, and then I hold my tongue like a grown woman, because that's the only way to get by in life.

'We're not pregnant, we're engaged,' Teddy corrects her.

I smile, not only to show them how happy I am, but because of all the ways to deliver such wonderful news, that is not how I imagined it coming out. If you don't laugh, you cry.

'Show them the ring,' Teddy insists.

I finally pull my hand out from its hiding place and show them my ring.

'Oh, Edward, you've really outdone yourself with this one,' Alicia says.

Yes. Yes, she is talking about the ring. I imagine this is as close to a 'congratulations' as we're going to get from Alicia.

'It looks a little snug,' Verity points out. 'But it looks stunning – congratulations.'

'Yes, you're going to have to take it to get resized,' Alicia says. 'Made bigger.'

We're all aware that bigger is what it needs to be. I'm not sure what the problem is but, since my finger swelled up, it hasn't gone back down again. It does feel tight on, and it's a bit of a battle to get it off, but it fit me at first. I'm sure it will fit me again, when the summer heat lets up a little, and whatever has caused my fingers to swell calms down again.

'Tell you what, I'll take it in now,' Teddy says. 'Pop it off, and I'll take it on my way to work, that way we can get it back on your finger ASAP.'

'Okay, sure,' I reply.

'Is there, ahem, some sort of rush?' Alicia enquires.

She narrows her eyes at Teddy. I wonder if she's still suspicious this is a shotgun wedding but I'm happy for her to be in interrogation mode, it gives me a moment to struggle my ring off without an audience.

'We are officially getting married on 8 July,' he announces proudly. 'There's this hotel and resort in Cornwall, Porthian Sands, and Liv's granddad actually built their famous wedding barn. I popped the question and then, when we started making plans, we realised that Porthian Sands wasn't going to be hosting weddings any more – going out on a high note, I guess – so we either had to take the only slot they had, or we would've had to find somewhere else, but this is Liv's dream location.'

'I'm sure there are plenty of other perfectly pleasant places,' Alicia offers up. 'Albeit without the family connection, but it allows you to take your time, enjoy your engagement, shop for a dress from somewhere divine, not the first thing off the rack you can get in time.'

'Well, I actually have that sorted,' I inform her. 'My future sister-in-law, Eden, has all these connections, and she's got us an appointment at Evera, in South Kensington, so we're going to pick out dresses this afternoon, and they've said they'll be ready in time for the eighth.'

'I've heard of Evera,' Verity says, a glimmer of envy in her eye. 'One of the royals got her dress there. I forget which but it was big news at the time, it really put them on the map.'

'Your dresses?' Alicia repeats back to me. 'Is she your bridesmaid?'

'No, I'm not actually having any bridesmaids,' I reply.

Alicia waits impatiently for an explanation.

'Dougie, my brother, and Eden also wanted to get married at Porthian Sands,' I explain. 'So... so we're having a sort of joint wedding.'

'No!' Alicia gasps. 'Edward, no, tell me you're not having a joint wedding – it's like something out of a soap opera.'

I bite my tongue. You can't tell people to fuck off in real life, you can't tell people to fuck off in real life.

Teddy just laughs.

'Mother, this is the compromise, and we're really looking forward to it,' he tells her, unbothered by what she thinks. 'We're renting a beach house at the venue for a couple of weeks so we're going to make a bit of a staycation of it, and all go and spend time there, I would love it if you were to join us, but you have to lighten up.'

I smile. I really do feel like he stands up for me.

'I am light,' Alicia insists. 'And I am, obviously, very happy for you both, it's just so sudden, it's a shock.'

'It's a good shock, though,' he reminds her.

Alicia visibly softens.

'Of course it is,' she says with a smile. 'Where are my manners? Edward, darling, congratulations. Olivia, as my gift to you, I want to buy your dress.'

'Oh, Alicia, that's so generous of you,' I say. 'But, honestly, you don't have to do that.'

'No, no, I'm going to have to insist,' she says. 'Edward, tell her, darling, won't you?'

'Go on, Liv, let Mum buy your dress,' he says encouragingly, like this is some sort of olive branch I should accept. 'You appreciate the offer, don't you?'

'I really do,' I insist.

'Wonderful, that settles it, I am buying your dress,' she replies. 'I tell you what, let's make an afternoon of us, just us ladies, wouldn't that be nice?'

'I really appreciate the offer,' I say, as convincingly as I can, because it would be true if she were anyone else but, from Alicia, I don't know. It doesn't feel genuine. 'There's no need to come. It's just going to be me and Eden.'

'All the more reason,' she insists. 'You need as many opinions as you can get, no?'

God, the thought of her giving her opinion on my taste in dresses sends me cold. But what choice do I have, if I want to keep the peace?

'Okay, sure,' I say. 'Thank you.'

'Marvellous,' she replies. 'Between me and Verity, we'll make sure you find something truly special.'

What? No! She's bringing Verity too? That's so, so weird.

'Lovely stuff,' Teddy says. 'Right, let's get lunch ordered, I've got to drop this ring at the jewellers on the way back to the office.'

As everyone fusses with their menus, working out what to have to eat, I silently seethe. I don't want Alicia coming with me, but I definitely don't want Verity along for the ride.

Oh, god, this is going to be awkward. So, so awkward. I suppose I should just be grateful we have her blessing – well, that we got it eventually. Otherwise, well, that really would have been awkward.

6

Evera Bridal Boutique is like something out of a movie – unfortunately, so is turning up with my future mother-in-law and my future husband's former fling.

The first thing that strikes me as I walk through the door is the sheer grandeur of the place. It's a stunning old building with large windows and high ceilings. The walls are painted a very slight, very muted shade of soft pink but all other surfaces and furnishings are white and spotless. Powerful bursts of colour come from the flower displays that cram every window, every doorway, every archway, and sit atop any surface that isn't being used for anything else. The air smells sweet, like roses and vanilla, and feels so nice and cool on my skin on a hot day like today.

The second thing that strikes me is the fact that Eden, who is already here, has brought Joanne with her.

'I thought we said we weren't bringing mums,' is the first thing I say to her, after pulling her to one side, of course.

'I know, but my mum was so excited to come and I didn't think having an extra person to give us their opinion would hurt. And anyway, you've invited people.'

'Technically Teddy's mum and her bestie invited themselves,' I reply, but I can't say much else. I just feel so bad that Eden's mum is here, Teddy's mum is here – my mum is the only person who isn't here, and obviously I would like her here for me, but I feel so bad that she's the only one who has been left out, and I probably feel the worst of all because I know that she won't kick off or get upset, she will be so understanding about it all.

'Look, Liv, we need to crack on,' Eden says as she ushers me back towards the crowd. 'This place is super exclusive, appointments are like gold dust, we only have a certain amount of time.'

'Okay, sorry,' I reply. I should be grateful that she's got us in here. Lord knows I wouldn't have got an appointment without her influencer connections, and if I'm being perfectly honest with you, I hadn't even heard of this place until Eden told me about it, despite it being a place where royalty come to get dresses for their big day.

'I've told them which brands we're interested in and which ones we aren't,' Eden informs me. 'That will save us some time.'

I hadn't realised there were brands I was interested in and brands I wasn't interested in – I can only just about confirm there are brands, I can't say wedding dresses are something I've thought all that much about, because why would I? This is my first wedding and it's not like I work in the industry. I suppose people who plan their weddings already have this sort of thing in mind, but I could never be so presumptuous, to feel so certain someone would want to marry me, to me that would be like picking out the interiors for a car I don't own, knowing full well that I can't drive.

A woman who is somehow enthusiastic and aloof shows us into a separate room just as beautiful as this one. We've all been given glasses of champagne that seem to be topped up the instant anyone so much as takes a sip, which makes it really difficult to keep track of how much you've actually had, but really easy to take the edge off all of this.

Eden has gone first – because she was engaged first which, yes, she did cite when she opted to go first – so all I've done so far is drink and watch her try on dress after dress. Eden definitely knows what she wants because all of her dresses have a similar vibe. She's opting for floor-length, strapless, backless white gowns with lots of lace and twinkling little stones. Very complicated but stunningly beautiful, show-stopping gowns.

'Oh, my god, Eden, you look a million dollars,' Joanne tells her. 'Is that the Eliza Crawford gown?'

'It is,' Eden says as she twirls around in front of a series of mirrors. 'Do you think it's eye-catching enough?'

Jill, the woman who is assisting us today, almost smiles.

'You look divine,' she tells Eden. 'Classic Hollywood glamour at its finest.'

'I love it,' Verity adds.

'Yes, very sophisticated,' Alicia says, almost reluctantly.

'Do you think you're going to say yes to the dress?' Joanne asks, clearly on the edge of her seat, so bursting with pride at how fantastic her daughter looks, even if Eden looks unsure.

Jill shoots daggers at Joanne.

'We don't say that in here,' she tells her angrily. 'It isn't that sort of establishment.'

Eden looks to me for the final word.

'You look beautiful,' I tell her. 'Like that dress was made for you.'

Eden exhales deeply and twirls for the mirror again. She smiles at herself, as though she has just bumped into a much-loved friend she hasn't seen for years, and a couple of tears form in her eyes, ever so slight ones, just enough to catch the light and twinkle like her dress.

'I can't believe it. I've found my dress,' she announces. 'I'll take it.'

Jill appeared to be opening her mouth then, as though she was ready to slap Eden down if she dared to utter a sentence that might rhyme the word 'yes' with the word 'dress'. It doesn't seem like something I would say anyway but I'll be sure to avoid it.

As Eden goes to take her dress off, people talk among themselves – well, I look at my phone, because no one is really saying much to me. Eventually, Eden reappears and I'm sent behind a curtain where a rail of dresses awaits me. This will be the brands Eden has hand-selected for me. Hmm, let's see, what do we have here? I'm looking through them one at a time for something that would suit me. I may not know what I want my wedding dress to look like, but I know what styles I like generally. But all of these are just more of the same, similar to Eden's dress, with a lot of skin on show – something I know I don't want from a wedding dress.

'Are there any others to look at?' I call back.

'What?' Eden squeaks. 'You must like one of those.'

It's like she can't quite believe her ears.

'I'm thinking, with it being a beach wedding, something a bit more...' I pause. Do I even have the words to describe what I mean? 'Boho?'

Nice. A term I can only recall being used to describe Sienna Miller in *Starstruck* magazine when I was younger. I'm so fashion.

'You'll struggle to find anything remotely bohemian here,' Jill replies. 'What is it that you had in mind?'

She joins me behind the curtain.

'Erm, something simple, kind of floaty, with sleeves,' I reply.

'Sleeves,' I hear Eden practically sob.

'Olivia, you don't have sleeves for a summer wedding,' Alicia calls out, very matter-of-factly, as though I were an idiot for not knowing.

'Not like sleeve-sleeves,' I clarify unhelpfully. 'Just some, like, lacy ones. I just don't fancy having my arms out, a low back, a low front – save something for the wedding night, right?'

Oh, good lord, I'm trying to make jokes, at a time like now, with this audience.

'Try this one,' Jill suggests. 'And we'll take it from there.'

The dress Jill has selected for me is long and lacy, and while it isn't dripping with diamonds like Eden's was, or nipped in as tightly at the waist, it is strapless and backless and low-cut – and oh, my!

I step out in front of everyone and take my place in front of the mirror. I feel awkward – and I must surely look it too – I'm shuffling like I'm wearing a hospital gown, or like someone has tied my shoelaces together.

It's a beautiful dress – they all are – but it's not what I want, I don't know if it suits me, and I definitely don't feel beautiful and confident in it.

'Well, I can't wear this dress, I'm missing something vital,' I say as I look at myself.

'A rounder bum?' Eden suggests thoughtfully.

Wow, shots fired, and she doesn't even realise she's holding a gun.

'The audacity,' I correct her. 'This dress is so beautiful... but it isn't me.'

'You're not supposed to be yourself on your wedding day,' Joanne informs me. 'You're supposed to be someone better.'

I don't think she means that as offensively as it sounds.

'You're supposed to look beautiful on your wedding day,' Alicia pipes up. 'This dress is your best shot at turning heads.'

Okay, now *she* probably does mean that as offensively as it sounds.

I look at myself in the mirror again. It is a beautiful dress – it's not what I had in mind, but it is incredible, and if I can just find the confidence to wear it...

'You have to get it,' Eden insists. 'It's perfect.'

'I agree,' Verity adds. 'Edward will love it.'

So, so gross that she's sitting there telling me what Teddy will like, even if she means well. I just don't need it from someone I know he's slept with.

I look in the mirror again. I'm really, really not sure about this one.

'Are you certain I look okay?' I ask no one specific.

'It's perfect for the wedding,' Eden says.

'Yeah, it's really classy,' Joanne adds.

'It *has* to be that dress,' Alicia says with a firm finality. 'No other dress is good enough.'

It is a beautiful dress, without a doubt, it's just not really what I had in mind. But I suppose, if everyone else thinks it's the best dress for the job, then what do I know?

'Okay, yes,' I say – but then I see the look on Jill's face. 'Sorry, I mean I'll take it. I choose this one.'

'Wonderful,' Jill says. 'Let's sit down and go over the details.'

I chew my lip thoughtfully as I look myself up and down in the mirror. It's a great dress, it will be fine. I'll wear it around the house a bit, get myself used to wearing something so... so... magnificent. I was probably going to feel this awkward in any wedding dress because they're just so unlike anything people usually wear from day to day. Big, white and with intricate detail. I usually steer clear of anything I could stain with tea or catch on a door handle. But it's beautiful, it's going to be great, and even if I wasn't actually allowed to say it in as many words, I have said yes to a dress. And under the watchful eye of my future mother-in-law and my fiancé's ex-fling, no less. Surely that's the most difficult part.

7

'Are we there yet?' I whine, half-joking, half-serious. I really hope we are.

'Gosh, you and your brother used to sing that all the time when you were younger,' Mum says with a laugh. 'Sometimes it doesn't feel like either of you have grown up.'

It's funny she should say that because today, travelling in the back of the car, with Mum and Dad sitting in the front, it has very much reminded me of childhood trips – just without the annoying brother winding me up, or playing games with his DS volume cranked all the way up, or insisting we listen to power ballads on repeat.

The reason I'm travelling with Mum and Dad is because, right at the last minute, Teddy was called into the office. He insisted I still go today, and that he'll join us tomorrow, but I can't help but worry turning up without him (and without my ring, because he hasn't picked it up yet) foreshadows something awful, although if signs like that were a true indicator of how things are going to turn out, then this wedding is screwed from the get-go, because this trip hasn't been all that plain sailing since we set off.

As if it wasn't bad enough that Teddy wasn't able to make it today, leaving me to get a lift with my mum and dad, the only break I've had from my mum telling my dad stories about people they know that he has absolutely no interest in (unless he can think of a joke to crack, of course) was when we stopped at a service station and briefly lost my mum. We can certainly see the funny side of it now that we're safely back in the car and almost at our destination but at the time it was genuinely horrifying. The three of us separated, my mum and dad to go to the toilets while I ordered us some drinks, but when it came time to meet up – outside the WHSmith, where the random selection of junk from garden ornaments to intense-looking cuddly toys are on sale – Mum never showed up. Dad and I chatted while we waited, eventually realising she had been longer than expected, so we called her.

'Where are you?' she asked me.

'Outside WHSmith,' I replied. 'Where are you?'

'*I'm* outside WHSmith,' she insisted.

I paused and looked around but there was no sign of her.

'We're at the Burger King side,' I told her, hoping she would come to us.

'I can see Burger King and you're not there,' she replied. 'Come on, stop playing your dad's silly games and let's get back on the road.'

'Okay, listen, walk over to the Starbucks by the door, we'll meet you there,' I said.

I stayed on the line with her, thinking it would be for the best while we found each other again.

'Right, I'm by Starbucks,' she eventually said.

'*So are we*,' I replied in disbelief.

It was like in a science fiction movie, where someone is transported to an alternate universe – well, how else would you explain Mum standing in the exact same spots as me and Dad, but being nowhere to be seen? It turns out she had wandered over the bridge that crosses the motorway, to the service station on the other side, which has all the same shops as the side we started at. Eventually, we were able to find her and get back on the road, and thankfully I think we're almost there, but it's been one hell of a journey.

'I think it's so lovely that you and Dougie are both so keen to get married in Granddad's barn,' Mum says. I can't see her face but I can hear her smile.

'Of course,' I reply. 'It's tradition.'

Weddings at the Porthian Sands Resort take place in a gorgeous wooden barn that sits just outside the hotel, on a terrace that looks out over the beach below. We say it's Granddad's barn – of course, it isn't actually his, but he did play a big part in the planning and building of it. He actually proposed to my grandma just before he started working on it, and apparently he would always say he was building it for her, so that they could get married in it. She would always tell us how she dreamed of looking out to sea while she said her vows, almost as though she was looking out to her future and all the places they would go together. So Gran and Granddad got married there, my great-auntie and uncle did too, and in later years my parents and my cousins tied the knot there. It felt like our place.

It's only in recent years that it has become this boujee wedding venue, resulting in the barn being super in demand (which is why Eden is so keen to tie the knot there), but ever since we were kids, Dougie and I have always just known that if and when we had our own weddings, we would follow in the family footsteps. Well, why else would we agree to a double wedding, if it weren't so important? Plus, every couple in our family who have tied the knot there have been together forever – or to this date, at least, although if you ever flag that to my mum, she jokily tells my dad not to count his chickens just yet.

'It's funny how things work out sometimes, isn't it?' Mum says. 'They do say Porthian Sands is the place you go to find true love. It must be something in the Cornish air.'

'I suspect it's more likely something that's in the Cornish cider,' Dad jokes.

'Cynic,' she ticks him off. 'I'm not saying I believe it, it's just urban legend, isn't it?'

'A marketing ploy,' Dad adds.

'Maybe it is,' Mum continues. 'But I like the idea that it's a place for lovers, a place where something just tells you that you've found the person you're going to spend the rest of your life with. And it can't be a coincidence that Liv's boyfriend proposed to her when he did, meaning you called the hotel when you did, and we found out that they weren't going to be hosting weddings any more, but that there was just one slot left… it's meant to be.'

'I can't argue with that,' I reply with a smile.

Sometimes I believe in fate, in signs, in those inexplicable messages from the universe, and I love the idea that in Porthian Sands this magical energy is supposedly so much more powerful. But I do also try to be quite a realistic person, and the idea that a tidal wave might wash over my wedding ceremony if Teddy isn't the right one for me, or that Eden will be carried off by a flock of seagulls (oh, imagine!) if Dougie and her aren't meant to be – come on.

I've seen Porthian House many times on my various trips to Cornwall, but I have never set foot inside until just now.

A stunning white contemporary beachfront mansion sits at the top of a long driveway, just up from the hotel. It looks more like it belongs abroad, in the Med somewhere, with its flat roof and gleaming white walls – well, what you can see of the walls, because a larger proportion of the building is glass. It has all these huge anthracite-grey framed windows, most of them floor to ceiling – in fact, I think many of them are doors, not just windows. The upstairs floors boast multiple balconies coming off the bedrooms, with clear glass fences so that you can enjoy the view, from all angles, uninterrupted.

Approaching it from the side, you can see that it doesn't just face out on to the beach, it's sitting on it, with a patio and a bit of a garden leading right out on to it, like its own personal patch of beach for guests to enjoy.

'You wouldn't get much change out of five mil for this place,' Dad announces.

'Careful, Vic, I'll be getting ideas,' Mum says.

'Ideas?' he replies.

'Yes, ideas about selling up and finding somewhere on the beach to live,' she replies. 'I may have been born in Oxford, but this is where my family is from, I feel a deep connection with the place. Gosh, I'd love nothing more than to live on the coast. Here would be perfect.'

'Yes, the five-million-pound beach house would probably be perfect for most of us,' I tease. 'Are we the last ones here?'

I notice multiple cars parked on the driveway.

'Not exactly,' Dad replies as he takes cases from the boot. 'That will be Teddy, eventually, unless he stands you up.'

'Oh, do behave, Victor,' Mum ticks him off. She turns to me. 'I should've bloody stood him up.'

'Ah, but then you wouldn't have me,' I reply.

'There is that,' she replies with a smile. 'And I suppose I could always divorce him.'

'She's joking,' Dad tells me. Then his face falls playfully. 'I'm pretty sure she's joking.'

We take our cases and walk up the pathway to the house. All of the pathways and flower beds have the same little white walls running alongside them, tying them to the house, making the place appear even bigger, even more spectacular than it is.

'It's been recently renovated apparently,' Dad tells us as we approach the front door. 'Remodelled, actually. I'm interested to see if they've done a good job.'

A large black front door sits between two floor-to-ceiling windows. Dad presses the smart doorbell. Eventually we're greeted by Eden and Dougie.

'Oh, my gosh, hello, come in,' Eden insists.

She welcomes us warmly, but it very much feels as though this is her house, there's just something about the way she lets us in, gesturing where we should put our bags down so we can all hug.

'Bloody hell,' Dad practically cackles. 'Look at this place. Whew.'

Dad admires the glass atrium in the centre of the entrance, following it up through the floor above us, peering up until he can see the sky.

'Isn't it gorgeous?' Eden coos. 'So, this is the open-plan living space.'

It's an enormous room. Light and bright with floor-to-ceiling windows everywhere, apart from the side that faces the beach where bifold doors are open, taking the inside space outside.

In the heart of the living area, there is a large, inviting-looking sofa with soft beige cushions – it must seat at least twenty people, and so does the long dining table. This certainly is a party house, although, with all the fancy artwork and sculptures (not to mention all the glass), I can totally understand why they don't want stag or hen parties here.

Beyond the lounge area, which looks out over the beach, there's an almost entirely white kitchen. It's so minimal – which doesn't check out for a place like this – so I can only imagine all the bells and whistles are thoughtfully hidden away. I can't wait to see what it does have.

'Let's show you to your rooms first, shall we?' Eden suggests.

'Let's,' Mum says excitedly.

'Hey, this is a bit of all right, isn't it?' Dad says as he pats Dougie on the back.

'It's unreal,' he replies. 'Liv, where's Teddy?'

'He's going to be late,' I reply. 'Maybe a day.'

'Oh,' he replies. 'Well, I'll say it again when I see him, but thank him again for this place, won't you?'

'Of course,' I reply.

What feels weird about all of this – well, weirder beyond the expected amount when you're moving into a beachfront mansion with your family ahead of the double wedding you're having, that you've only partially planned over the last two weeks, of course – is being here alone. I know this isn't how it is, but I feel like I've just turned up to my wedding without my groom. I know, I know, he hasn't stood me up, but this feels stood-up adjacent, perhaps. I was so excited but now, turning up here without Teddy, it's just taken the shine off, knocked the wind out of my sails a little. But he'll be here soon and then perhaps it will start feeling real. Right now, I don't feel excited, I just feel anxious.

We climb the stunning curved wooden staircase that wraps around the atrium until we're on the first floor.

'This is your bedroom,' Dougie tells my parents.

'Check it out then meet us out on the patio,' Eden instructs them. 'My parents are already out there. We'll show Liv her room and then we can all have a chat. I'll show you the pool, the cinema and the games room later.'

'The pool, the cinema and the games room,' Dad repeats back to her. 'Oh, my!'

That joke gets about as much laughter as it deserves, but I can't blame him for being excited about the house. Houses are very much his thing and this is one hell of an example of how to get it right.

'See you down there,' Mum says. 'Unless I get distracted by a big bath with a view.'

Mum and Dad wander into their room and soon enough, yes, I hear Mum squeak, confirming her suspicions about the bath of her dreams.

'Okay, so, this is the master bedroom,' Eden says.

I follow her into a large room with white walls, a gigantic bed with perfect white sheets, and not only is there a massive free-standing bath in front of the floor-to-ceiling windows but there's a telescope for looking out over the view, out to sea, up at the stars – my god, it's just amazing.

'Wow,' I blurt. 'This is just... wow.'

'There's a gorgeous en suite and one of the windows is actually a door that leads out onto the balcony,' she tells me. 'And if you follow it along there's a little gate that leads to a sun terrace on top of the pool room.'

'This is just amazing,' I blurt. 'And this... this is my room?'

'Ah, well, here's the thing,' she starts.

I should have known this was too good to be true.

'Obviously there's only one master suite, and two couples, so we thought the fairest thing to do would be to share it,' Eden announces.

'I take it you don't mean the four of us sleeping in that bed,' I half joke, because as daft as it sounds, I can't quite find the faith required to truly rule it out.

'Obviously not,' she says with a roll of her eyes. Eden never gets my jokes, so I'm not sure why I'm expecting a half-joke to land.

'We thought we could have a week each,' Dougie chimes in.

'And we thought we could go first, because we got here first, but with Teddy not being here yet, that's perfect,' Eden adds. 'We'll take it this week, you and Teddy can have it next week.'

'Right, okay,' I reply. It's hard not to be a little disappointed but, if we're taking it in turns to sleep in the master suite, I would obviously much prefer to sleep in it when Teddy is here to enjoy it too.

'So, where is my room?' I ask.

'Back downstairs,' Eden announces excitedly.

Back downstairs, if you don't head for the living space, you can walk down a small corridor with three doors off it.

'This one is a cupboard,' Eden tells me. 'This one is your bathroom.'

I notice my bathroom door is outside my bedroom, so no en suite for me.

'And this is your bedroom,' she announces.

It should have occurred to me, considering the geography of the house, that this room is the only one so far that doesn't look out over the beach, it faces the driveway, with the road to the hotel just beyond it.

'Oh,' I blurt flatly.

'I know, it doesn't exactly have the grandeur of the room upstairs,' Eden says. 'But that's why we thought the fairest thing to do would be to swap halfway through.'

It's not that there's anything wrong with this room. It's not exactly small, the walls are white, the bed looks nice, and it does have floor-to-ceiling windows but... I don't know. It's nothing special, not like the one upstairs. Even something as simple as not having a sea view – and living in Oxford, then London, a sea view is not exactly something I'm accustomed to – feels like I'm really missing out on something.

'I'll go get started on some drinks,' Dougie says. 'So long as it's all right?'

'Yeah, it's fine,' I reply. 'I'll just look forward to swapping.'

'So glad you're cool with it,' Eden says. 'Come on, let's go outside and see my parents, we're just talking wedding plans and obviously I need the input of my co-bride.'

Before I get the chance to open my mouth, a very loud rumbling, almost rattling sound fills the room. It sounds like it's coming from the next room, like someone is taking a chainsaw to the furniture.

'What's that?' I ask, raising my voice a little, just to make sure Eden can hear me.

'Oh, there's a bit of a noisy flush in your bathroom,' she tells me. 'I guess, because it's down here, it's used as a sort of downstairs WC too, but don't worry if you want a long shower or anything, people can always go use one of the ones upstairs.'

'Great,' I reply, trying not to sound too disappointed but, my god, this is far from ideal.

I perk up a little when we head out onto the patio where Dougie and both sets of parents are waiting, all sitting on comfortable-looking outdoor furniture.

Looking out to sea, you can see for miles. I love the way the sea just starts where the sand stops and then fades away to absolutely nothing, just the flat line of the horizon. It makes me want to get in a boat and chase it, although I know that's not how it works, I'd just end up in France if I didn't die somewhere along the way.

The table is laid out with various drinks and snacks. The parasol above is lightly blowing in the breeze. Honestly, this patio is heaven. I wish Teddy were here but it's so nice that even being here alone far from sucks.

'Right, sit down,' Eden demands. 'This wedding isn't going to plan itself and we have less than two weeks to go. It's so crazy that we think we can do this.'

'If anyone can do it, you can,' Dougie tells her. 'This is your thing.'

'Yeah, plus, with your and Teddy's money, I'm pretty sure we could get Michael Bublé here to serenade us, if we wanted to,' she replies. She thinks for a moment. 'Nah, that's probably tacky, isn't it?'

I am so glad she walked that one back on her own.

Eden places two scrapbooks on the table in front of her. One is blue, the other is white, but both are stuffed to the brim.

'Wedding planning scrapbooks,' she says with a self-satisfied sigh.

'Which one is yours and which one is Liv's?' Dad asks.

'Oh, they're both mine,' she quickly corrects him.

'I'm amazed you've found the time to do two,' I tell her. 'These last couple of weeks all I've done is google things and then forget everything I saw, only to need to google it all again later.'

'I haven't done them over the last fortnight,' she points out with a scoff. 'I've been working on these since I was teenager. One for a summer wedding, one for winter. I thought it helpful to bring both, just so you can really get a sense of what I go for.'

Eden lays the summer wedding scrapbook in the centre of the table and starts turning pages while everyone looks on in (whether it's good or bad) amazement.

'So, for the colour palette, for a July wedding at the beach, I'm thinking peach, blush and gold,' she says.

'Pink?' I reply.

'Summer pink,' she corrects me. 'May-blossom pink is over, we're moving into more summery shades.'

I pause for a second. Oh, my god, she's doing a colour palette to match her Instagram feed *again*.

'Blush could be the main colour, gold for the accent, and peach for the guests – pretty in peach,' she says excitedly. 'That's what we can tell everyone.'

'Sorry, the colour for the guests?' I reply.

'Yes, for their outfits,' she replies.

I pause, which prompts Eden to scrunch her face up. She thinks I'm daft.

'That's not a thing, is it?' I ask.

'It's very much a thing, to have the guests match the wedding aesthetic,' she points out. 'Anyone who is anyone is doing it.'

'It's in less than two weeks' time,' I remind her before turning to my dad. 'Did you pack your peach suit, pops?'

Dad laughs.

Obviously I'm only trying to prove a point but come on, that's not a reasonable request.

'People will make the effort if we ask them to,' she says.

'If I tell Heidi she needs to buy and wear a peach dress, she's going to laugh in my face,' I reply.

Eden shows her teeth as she frowns.

'Oh, I thought Dougie said she wasn't coming,' she replies, turning to Dougie for confirmation.

'Well, that's what you said, right?' he checks with me.

'She's coming, she just might not be here until the day before,' I say confidently, but I'm still little more than hopeful at this point. It didn't sound likely, despite her saying she would try, but I'm not ready to admit it to this lot yet.

I allow Eden to carry on talking about the wedding she's been planning since she was thirteen, and how she's going to carry her brand throughout the day.

Now, more than ever, I really hope Heidi can come. I hope Teddy turns up soon because he's like me, there's no way he's going to go in for all this stuff with the colours, I just need someone on my side. Heidi would hate it just as much as I do, though, so much so that, as hopeful as I am that she can make it on the day, one way to make sure for certain that she doesn't show is if I tell her she has to wear peach.

I need to find a way to nip this in the bud, fast.

8

My plan, as I walked to the hotel bar, was to lose myself in a glass of wine. Now that I'm here, with the glass in front of me, it is probably big enough to get lost in, it's huge. The young man behind the bar actually apologised for pouring it so big, explaining that it was his first day. But as he reached for another glass to get the measure right, and make less of a sloppy job of it, I was very quick to insist that it was fine.

If the beach house is a perfect example of cool and contemporary, then the hotel bar is the exact opposite. Far from being modern, it's like travelling back in time, but in a way that is so charming.

We would mostly stay here when Dougie and I were kids, so we never had cause to visit the bar. It's a dark room with soft lighting. The heavy curtains surrounding the windows – despite being open – obstruct a lot of the natural light from outside. The bar is made of a stunning dark wood, with hand-carved details, and all the tables and chairs match. All soft furnishings are dark red or dark green, patterns come in the form of plaid and nothing else, and the art on the walls features a series of landscapes and portraits. It's old and stuffy but in a way that feels completely appropriate for the space, there's something comforting about it. Funny, really, because it still feels like the kind of place that would have a 'no women allowed' rule but here I am, with my giant glass of white wine, wondering how the hell I've got myself into a mess like this.

I'm sure there is someone, somewhere, probably lots of people, who would have screamed at me from the top of their lungs to warn me just how terrible an idea a joint wedding would be. Yes, it's probably more cost-effective, and it's easier to have everyone turn up to the one big day, rather than trying to get everyone to turn up to two – I guess there's that. You might even say that having two brides – two people pushing to make their big day special, working together – would be a huge bonus, but that might actually be our biggest problem. It's not that Eden wants this and I want that, it's that Eden has been planning this wedding since before her GCSEs, she knows exactly what she wants, whereas I don't have this clear idea of colours or flowers or first-dance music. For me it's all to figure out, for Eden it's sorted, so when we come to making decisions together, Eden has her ideas, but I don't know what mine are yet, so even if we try to compromise, it always leans Eden's way.

Take the colour palette. Yes, the wedding has to have a colour palette, apparently, and it has to be decided in advance. So we're all sitting there, and Eden has these very specific colours in mind – colours she's always dreamed of, colours that match her Instagram grid or whatever. I, on the other hand, don't already have colours, I would need to pick colours before I could negotiate with her. This means that as we chatted, and tried to reach a compromise, I didn't have any of my own ideas to push forward, just Eden's to try to shoot down, and it turns out this makes you look and feel like a total villain. So the compromise wasn't Eden chooses one colour and I choose another, the compromise was Eden chooses the colours and I win the battle over whether we will force guests to wear one of these particular colours. Yep, that's the compromise, Eden's wedding colours and a suggested dress code colour for guests, but not an enforcement. Eden is hopeful people will still feel obliged to wear peach and, if they don't, well, she'll crop them out of the photos or 'tweak them in post' apparently.

I sigh and take another sip from my gigantic drink. Geez, even this isn't hitting the spot. Then again, did I think wine was going to solve my problems? It's just wine. It can give me a little buzz, but it can't make my wedding better, can it? *Can* it? Another sip, just in case.

I feel my phone vibrating in my pocket. I take it out and see that Mum is calling.

'Hello, sweetheart, are you okay?' she asks. I think she probably knows the answer.

'Oh, you know,' I reply. 'I don't feel like that went very well.'

'No, it was a little bizarre,' she replies. 'But Teddy will be here tomorrow and you know he's not going to go in for too much... Eden stuff.'

'Yeah, I know,' I reply. 'I just wish he was here now – or that he would answer his phone, so that I could tell him about it.'

Perhaps when Teddy does arrive, it will finally feel like my wedding too, and like I do in fact have a say in it.

'I know, sweetheart, but listen, I'm just at the shop,' she tells me. 'We thought it might be nice to cook tonight and eat at the house, it really is so lovely there, and where else are we going to get our very own private dining terrace on the beach, hey?'

'Yeah, that would be great,' I reply, trying to muster up a little enthusiasm, but it's hard not to feel down in the dumps. I really need to let this colour business go.

'I've offered to cook so I just wondered if there was anything you fancied?' she asks.

'Oh, I don't know, maybe some sun-blushed tomatoes, and something peach for dessert,' I reply.

Mum laughs.

'Sorry, sorry, I'll let it go now,' I insist. 'I appreciate you asking me. You know I love everything you make.'

'Maybe some pasta?' she suggests. 'And I'll make a salad, just in case Eden isn't eating pasta at the moment, I know sometimes she's gluten-free.'

'Oh, of course,' I reply. 'You never know with Princess Eden.'

'Try not to let her get to you, sweetheart,' Mum insists. 'But I'll buy lots of chocolate just in case. Love you, see you soon.'

'Love you too,' I reply.

As I hang up the phone, I huff and drop it down on the table with a bigger thud than I intended. As I exhale so deeply it almost knocks what is left of my wine over, I notice I've caught the attention of a concerned-looking man.

'Is everything okay?' he asks me. 'Tell me if I'm intruding, I can go away, you just seem really upset, so I thought I'd better check.'

'Sorry for the dramatics,' I say, a little embarrassed. 'I'm just... having a bad day.'

'No, it's fine,' he replies. 'It's not every day you hear someone say "love you" and then slam the phone down.'

I don't feel like the man is prying, more like he's delicately trying to work out if I need help. Oh, god, I hope he doesn't think I'm in some kind of domestic crisis.

'It was my mum,' I tell him. 'And I'm not mad at her, it's my future sister-in-law, she's being a real bridezilla.'

'Ah, wedding rage,' he replies. 'Well, that makes sense. In fact, your reaction seems quite muted. What is it – NDAs for all the guests? No one else is allowed to wear lipstick?'

'You're not far off the mark,' I reply. 'All guests have to wear peach.'

'Oh, god, not peach,' he jokes. 'Sage, fuchsia or even vermilion. Not peach, though.'

I can't help but laugh.

'I have to admit, I'm not sure I know what any of those colours are,' he confesses.

'I'm pretty sure sage is green,' I reply. 'Green would be nice for summer wedding colours but she's insisting on blush and peach. Anything I suggest just isn't good enough, and a lot of the wedding planning is happening last minute, so there's still so much to figure out, and she clearly doesn't think I'm qualified. And, to be honest, maybe I'm not. I don't know where I'll find flowers or photographers.'

'I might be able to help you with that,' he replies.

He doesn't have a local accent, in fact he sounds more like he's from closer to my neck of the woods. He's rocking a scruffy-chic kind of style, sort of like the look that Robert Pattinson makes work for him, but with his longish brown hair and beard, he looks more like a mid-thirties version of Bradley Cooper in *A Star is Born*. It's a good look, it suits him. I can't help notice him getting some dirty looks from the man behind the bar, though.

'Oh, really?' I reply.

'Yeah, I don't know if you're free tomorrow but it's the first day of an events fair one of the hotels down the coast holds each year. It's a big deal, it goes on for about ten days, but they have a bit of everything there, so if you're looking for florists or photographers, there might be someone who can help you out.'

'Oh, my gosh, that sounds perfect,' I reply. 'Between you and me, random man I just met in a bar, pretty much everyone I'm here with has expensive taste. Is it a boujee kind of thing with prices that are going to make me cry?'

'There's something for everyone,' he replies with a laugh.

'Thank god,' I reply. 'It's no fun, being the only one who isn't rolling in it. They're my family and I love them but sometimes I get so sick of people who forget what it's like to have to consciously pay for things, so here's to finding a cheap photographer.'

I jokily raise my glass before taking a sip.

I know, I know, I might not be able to afford things, and Teddy is really well off, but the last thing I want to do is ask him for money. Yes, it's our wedding, but I really want to feel like I'm contributing something. I want to pay for something with my own money.

'Excuse me, sir,' the barman interrupts us. 'I'm going to have to ask you to leave.'

'It's okay, stand down,' the man replies with a laugh.

'Your attire falls short of the standards we choose to uphold in the bar,' the barman insists. 'Shorts, trainers and, well, shirts with holes in them are not allowed.'

The barman tries to toughen up with each word that he says.

'Okay, but—' the man at my table begins, but the barman doesn't give him a chance.

'Sir, you aren't the kind of clientele we allow at the bar,' the barman insists. 'I'm going to have to insist you leave right now or I'll call the manager.'

Wow, I'm gripped. Okay, fair enough, the man isn't wearing the smartest outfit, he looks like he's just come in from a walk on the beach, or (I don't know why on earth he would have been doing this, but) chopping wood. It's late afternoon, it's not busy. I'm sure he could cut him some slack, and telling him he's not the right kind of clientele seems quite harsh.

'Are you new here?' the man asks him.

'Yes, but you still have to get out if I tell you to,' the barman insists.

He's starting to lose his cool, now that he knows the man isn't going to be obliging.

'You've been warned,' the barman insists, although it kind of comes across like when you're a kid and your mum tells you she's going to count to three, but you know nothing really happens at three, so you call her bluff.

'I'm going to call the bar manager,' the barman insists. 'And he's going to call for security and you're going to feel very silly.'

'I'm sure I will,' the man replies with a smile.

Clearly not getting anywhere, the barman takes his phone from his pocket and a scruffy piece of paper from the other. He punches a number into his phone before raising it to his ear.

Right on cue, the man at the table's phone starts ringing. He removes it from his shorts and answers.

'Hello?'

The barman looks stunned.

'Hello?' the man at my table sings, as though he can't understand why the person on the other end can't hear him.

'I, er, I... I, er...' the barman stutters.

'I think you're breaking up,' the man at my table replies, but then he hangs up the phone and stops toying with him.

'I'm so sorry,' the barman says. 'I thought...'

'It's okay,' the man who I now know is the bar manager says with a laugh. 'This is supposed to be my week off, you were given that number for emergencies only.'

'I know, again, I'm so sorry,' the barman replies.

'You're okay, kid, you're not in trouble,' the man at my table insists. 'But next time, don't worry too much about it, and don't say anything that might make people feel bad. If someone comes in wearing shorts, hey, I don't care if you don't, okay?'

'Okay, yeah, sure, cool,' the barman babbles.

'I actually feel bad for him,' the man at my table tells me once we're alone again. 'So, this events fair, it's at the Maelstrom, it's not far down the road. Are you staying here at the hotel?'

'Perfect, I'll go tomorrow,' I reply. 'We're staying in the big beach house. I should probably head back there soon, my mum is making dinner.'

'Oh, nice,' the man replies. 'I actually live in the garden.'

My face must say it all.

'Well, not in the garden,' he backtracks. 'If you venture beyond the patio, and up the hill, I live in the cute little one-bed cottage. In fact, just as an FYI in case you don't know, your hot tub is up there. It's great when I can't sleep.'

I laugh.

'You want to talk about plumbing, I'm in the downstairs bedroom in the house, and when someone flushes the loo next door, it sounds like the world is ending,' I reply.

'Ah, yes, the macerator,' he replies.

'The what?' I reply.

'If you don't know what a macerator is, I don't recommend you go out of your way to find out,' he replies. 'But, yes, they are noisy.'

'Well, thanks for the tip about the wedding fair, and the hot tub,' I reply. 'Maybe I'll see you around, neighbour.'

'I'm Hugo,' he says, offering me a hand to shake.

'Nice to meet you, Hugo,' I reply. 'I'm Liv.'

'See you around, Liv,' he replies. 'I'm going to go make sure the barman knows he isn't in trouble.'

I can't help but smile. Hugo seems nice. Nice and useful because this events fair tomorrow could be a huge help. Finally, I feel like I'm actively doing something.

I just wish Teddy was here with me to help too.

9

Mum was right, why would we ever want to go to a restaurant when we have our own private beachfront dining area right here? Plus, of course restaurant food is great (most of the time), but I don't think there is a chef in this world who can beat my mum's cooking.

We're having pasta tonight – macaroni with meatballs – and I'm sure there are award-winning chefs making this exact dish in Italy, but they can't even begin to compete with the comfort that comes from my mum's tomato sauce. It's not just the texture, or the sweetness, it's the way it reminds me of getting through a difficult day at school or being dumped by some silly teenage boy who didn't deserve me. I would go home, Mum would make dinner, and everything would feel better. Perhaps that's why she's made her practically medicinal meatballs tonight.

Eden is the last person to sit down at the table. As I look up to greet her, I notice the cottage Hugo said he lived in. The beach house is next to a small cliff which is part of the garden. If you head up the steps, through the trees, you can just about see the cottage. It's very cute and more traditional – it looks positively old-fashioned in comparison to the house. I suppose it's intentionally kept that way, though, like a quaint little cottage off the main house. I suppose it's more valuable to rent it out as a house for staff than it is to tag it on as an extra few rooms for a house that already has a lot of rooms. Then again, if it doesn't have the world's loudest toilet, then I wish it did come with the house, I'd happily go stay there on my own. Well, on my own or with Teddy when he gets here tomorrow.

It's later than we would usually eat so it's starting to get dark. This house lights up like a Christmas tree at night, inside and out. Out here, there are all sorts of lights, from the up/down lights on the side of the house to the festooned lights that stretch across the patio.

Cute little lights dotted around the trees lead the way up to the cottage. I am reminded that Hugo said we had a hot tub up there – no one mentioned that to me when we booked. I might go see later.

The cottage is so cute, I can't stop looking at it. I need to snap out of it, and focus on what's going on at the table. I guess I just can't face a repeat of earlier.

'Just the balls for me,' Eden says, dragging me back.

'Of course,' Mum says, stifling a smile.

'Liv, you'll be pleased to know that, while you were out, I organised all the things for the table stylings – in our now agreed colours,' Eden tells me proudly.

Is there a dig in there? Does she think I was out having fun? Because I wasn't having fun at all, I was trying to drown my sorrows in a bar, when really the only place that could be truly up to the job is the sea.

I've decided that I need to change my attitude. This wedding is happening and if I don't make an effort, then it's all going to be planned without me having a say in any of it. It's not going to be my wedding, it's going to be Dougie and Eden's wedding, and if I'm lucky, they'll let me and Teddy do a bit of paperwork.

If I want to see myself in this wedding, then I need to put myself in this wedding.

'I've been thinking, seeing as though you've figured out the colour scheme and organised the – *table stylings?* – for us, perhaps I could organise something,' I say. 'This shouldn't be all on you, as great as you are at organising these things.'

I wait calmly and patiently for a response, hoping I didn't overcook it.

'Well, like what?' she asks.

'I could sort the flowers,' I suggest.

'I've already made us an appointment at a local florist,' she replies.

'The music?' I say.

'Hmm, no, I think that should be more of a collaborative decision, if we're going to have to listen to them all night, you know?' she says, shooting that one down too.

'Okay then, how about I sort out a photographer?' I eventually offer up.

'Do you think that's something you can do?' she replies.

'Of course she can,' my mum insists, jumping to my defence.

I was just about to tell everyone about the events fair – Hugo said there would be photographers, among other things – but with Eden's complete lack of faith in me, I want to go, sort us a photographer, and do it all unaided. I'm going to show them all that I can organise the best wedding photographer (my) money can buy.

'Well, okay, see what you can find,' she tells me, unable to hide her uncertainty. 'The photographer is a big deal – you only get one shot at good photos.'

'It's my wedding too,' I remind her politely. 'I want good photos too.'

'Of course,' she replies. 'Just make sure it's a photographer and videographer service – we want videos too, don't we?'

My face betrays me for a split second.

'Unless you want me to handle it?' she offers again.

Wow, she really doesn't have any faith in me at all. Luckily for all of us, nothing motivates me more than proving people wrong.

'Perhaps Eden could look into a backup photographer?' Joanne suggests ever so helpfully.

'If Liv says she's going to sort a photographer, then she's going to sort one,' my mum insists.

I smile at her. She always has my back.

'It will be fine, Eden,' Dougie reassures her, giving her arm a loving pat.

I feel like my brother has my back too, he just has a very demanding fiancée he has to contend with at the same time.

Dad would have my back if he was paying attention, but I just spotted him out of the corner of my eye, trying to dip his serviette in his water before dabbing it on his white shirt to try to get rid of the pasta sauce he must've spilt.

Lucky for him, all eyes are on Eden. She hasn't touched her food yet – well, she hasn't eaten her food yet. She's been arranging it, moving it around her plate, and handling the bread to get the composition just right. Now she's kneeling on her chair, taking a flat-lay picture of the table.

'Dad, move your arms,' she practically snaps.

Mick, ever the joker, starts doing the 'Macarena'. This goes down a treat with my dad. Why is it that dads are like kids? If you put them together and leave them to amuse each other, they'll be distracted and (hopefully) will stay out of trouble together.

'Save it for the wedding,' my dad tells him with a laugh.

'Oh, god, there'll be none of that at my wedding,' Eden insists.

'No disco?' Mum replies. 'Aw, I love a disco.'

'So do I,' I add. 'So does Dougie, don't you, Doug?'

Eden turns to him.

'You know me, I can dance to anything,' he says tactfully.

'Just you wait until the night do. We'll have his trousers off and he'll be tied to a chair getting thrown around the dance floor, even if it's Beethoven,' Mick jokes.

'No, Dad, seriously, don't even joke about it,' Eden insists. 'It's not going to be that sort of wedding. Dougie's trousers are 100 per cent staying on, on our wedding night.'

I purse my lips, lest I laugh and lower the tone.

'Anyway, what time is Teddy coming tomorrow?' Eden asks me. 'Because I've got us in with a florist potentially late tomorrow afternoon or the morning after. She's going to confirm with me, so I'll let you know.'

'Okay, sure,' I reply. 'Well, hopefully he'll be here in the morning. I'm going to give him a call after dinner.'

'Is it a bit strange that he isn't here?' Joanne dares to ask.

I notice my mum's eyes widen.

'No,' I quickly insist. 'He's very busy at work.'

'We're all busy at work,' Eden adds.

We're really not. Both sets of parents are retired, Dougie has set himself up for life so it's only a matter of time before he retires – not that he works all that much at the moment anyway – Eden's work is genuinely just posting photos of her day (and I'm not saying influencing isn't a job, but taking photos of what you're doing anyway doesn't get in the way of what you're doing), and as for me, well, chance would be a fine thing.

'He's on track to take over the company, once he proves himself worthy to his grandmother,' I inform them. 'He's working so hard to show her that he's up to the job, that the company will be safe in his hands.'

Joanne just pulls a face.

'Different people have different priorities, Mum,' Eden tells her. 'He'll get here when he gets here.'

Mick, clearly tired of this conversation, begins telling the tale of how he saw a seagull steal an entire sausage from a girl on the beach today. It flew up to her, grabbed it and swallowed it whole – apparently.

My dad is, of course, positively charmed by this story, in particular Mick's surprisingly graphic mime of a seagull swallowing a whole sausage.

Looking up towards the cottage, where you can just about see part of it poking through the trees, I notice there is now a light on, so Hugo must definitely be home. I'm tempted to wander up there, to see what it looks like, to check out the view, and a dip in the hot tub would be lovely.

I need to sort out all my drama, though, first – and a dip in the hot tub with Teddy would be so much better than going in alone or, worse, going in with a member of my family, or Eden's. I'm not sure who I'd least like to take an awkward outdoor bath with.

I'll call Teddy after dinner, see what time he's getting here in the morning. He's a strong person, very assertive. There is no way he's going to take any crap from Eden and he's not going to let her boss me around either. Sure, I'll feel like a kid, hiding behind her dad – well, *a* dad, my dad isn't someone I can hide behind, he's currently repeating Mick's seagull mime back to him so he can see how funny it looks.

Everything will be better once Teddy is here. Then perhaps we can turn this wedding into something we want, rather than just something we're going to be attending (breaking only to sign a bit of paperwork).

I may have lost the battle when it comes to blush and peach, but there's no way Teddy is going to let her get away with getting her way on *every single thing*.

He just needs to get here first.

10

I tap my nails anxiously on the bedside table as I wait for Teddy to answer his phone.

'Hey, babe,' he eventually answers. 'How's it going?'

'Hmm,' I practically squeal, my eyes open as wide as they can go.

'That bad?' he replies. 'Is it Eden? Is she trying to commandeer the whole thing?'

'Was it ever in doubt that she would?' I reply.

I'm hiding in my room while everyone else continues to hang out on the patio, under the stars, chatting and drinking. I know I would be having way more fun if Teddy were here too so I decided the best thing I could do would be to retire to my room early and give him a call.

Someone must have just used the loo because the macerator – which I'm very upset to say I did google, and now I know exactly what that noise is, unfortunately – goes into overdrive.

'What's that?' Teddy asks.

'It's the lav in the room next to mine,' I reply.

'Christ, has Eden been doing the cooking?' he jokes.

Eden has cooked for us once and only once. No one felt well after her chilli *at all*. It was her first and only cooking video tutorial, let's put it that way.

'I've been given the worst room,' I tell him. 'Not only does the toilet flush sound like an earthquake has hit, but I'm in the only bedroom that doesn't face the beach, which wouldn't be a big deal, but the white blinds do nothing to block out the light. We're at the end of the road that leads down to the hotel so, every time someone drives down it, my room lights up like it's daytime.'

'Hmm,' Teddy replies. 'That doesn't seem very fair at all – especially given that I'm paying for it.'

'Oh, no, it's very fair apparently because they're going to take the master suite for the first week and then we get it for the second week, when you're here to enjoy it too,' I tell him.

'Presumably with clean sheets,' he says hopefully.

'That's why you need to get here as soon as possible,' I tell him. 'And I don't know if this speeds things up or not, but I just found out there's a hidden hot tub in the garden, so there's that.'

'Oh, really?' he replies – I have his interest now. 'Do tell, Olivia Knight, what would we get up to in this hot tub?'

'If you come here, I'll show you,' I reply in my sexiest voice.

Teddy groans, just a little.

'I'm alone right now,' he tells me. 'I take it you are too. Why don't you tell me what we'll do, let's have a little fun.'

'Oh, no, you're not getting off that lightly,' I tell him. 'Literally.'

'Come on, babe,' he moans. 'You're killing me here. I can't wait until I see you.'

'You can't wait until morning?' I reply in disbelief.

Teddy falls silent for a second.

'You are coming in the morning, right?' I ask.

'Liv, listen, I don't think I'm going to make it there tomorrow at all,' he confesses.

'What?' I squeak.

'I want to be there – of course I do, I want to plan this wedding with you,' he insists. 'But you know what Grandmother is like. She won't hand control over to me unless she believes I'm perfect. You know how important work ethic and good values are.'

'One thing I know about your grandmother is that family values matter to her the most,' I remind him.

'Yes, how they look,' he corrects me. 'It's all optics with Grandmother. Family values don't matter as far as handing over control goes. For that, I need to show her that I can do this. I have a big client – big money changing hands, I don't expect you to understand how it works, but I do expect you to understand that this is important to me.'

When I mentioned family values, I meant Teddy being allowed time off to plan and attend his own wedding, not his grandmother handing over the business without thinking it through first.

'So, when will you be here?' I ask.

'I can put it to bed tomorrow, be there the next day,' he tells me. 'Is that okay?'

What can I say? What choice do I have?

'I'm doing this for us,' he reminds me. 'Imagine the life we can have together, if I secure my position at the top.'

I wonder what our life together will be like. If Teddy is running the company, is he always going to be this busy? He's busy enough as it is. Does running the company mean he'll have more free time or less?

'You know work is important to me,' he says.

I do know that work is important to him – I just hoped that our wedding would be important to him too.

And right on cue, the macerator fires up again.

Wow, what a fairy-tale wedding this is shaping up to be so far.

11

The Maelstrom Hotel and Spa sits on the top of a cliff, on the edge of the beach, not too far from the Porthian Sands Resort.

While Porthian Sands is a more traditional place in the main building, the Maelstrom Hotel has been renovated into something modern. I think I prefer the classic look. There's something so charming about the old building Porthian Sands has always operated in. Here, I don't know, it's nice, but you get what you get from a decent chain hotel. Neutral colours, simple design, a layout that – even if you don't know it – you can just figure out as you go. I went from the car park to reception to the function room in a matter of seconds, like I'd been here a thousand times before. It's great, it's practical but... I don't know, you can't put a price on charm, even if the stairwells do make a bit of a labyrinth, and it's a real learning curve, working out which doorways have steps and which ones don't – of course I'm living it up in the beach house this trip, so I haven't had to worry about it too much.

The function room here is massive – in fact, it looks like two separate function rooms with a partition removed to make one enormous space that opens out on to a big terrace, so the event spills outside too.

It's a much bigger fair than I imagined – busier too. I suppose in a stunning county like Cornwall, so many people want to come here to have their events, and with so many gorgeous hotels and big holiday rentals, the events market must be booming.

A large pop-up stage sits in the heart of the room with a series of stalls set up around it. Honestly, I don't think there is any kind of party you couldn't throw only using the businesses in this room. One minute, you're passing a balloon company – their stalls framed with the most stunning balloon arches – then florists with equally gorgeous displays on show. But, for the party with a difference, there are companies who specialise in other sorts of inflatables (from bouncy castles to, shall we say, more grown-up things for adults to bounce up and down on), an agency that provides basically any sort of stripper your heart desires, and there's even a very intense-looking man with a long white beard and some sort of bird of prey sitting eerily still on his arm who has a sign claiming: 'Most animals available for hire'. A small part of me wants to try to find out just how true the claim is, but I don't think Eden would be impressed if I wound up hiring a dolphin for her wedding – not unless we could have it painted peach, anyway.

The fair is in full swing now. I'm here a little later than I planned to be because I made a big effort to miss breakfast back at the house. I couldn't face the thought of sitting down with everyone, talking about the wedding and, let's face it, being told how it's going to go. More than that, though, if I'm being honest, I'm a little embarrassed about the fact that Teddy isn't going to arrive today. I know that he's busy but I'm worried that, to others, it might look like he doesn't care. So long as we're happy, that's all that matters, I'll just have to suck it up and tell them.

'Would you like to try a cake sample?' a young woman running a cake stall asks me.

'Does anyone ever say no?' I reply with a laugh.

'Not often,' she admits. 'We've got fruit, vanilla, or chocolate.'

We don't have wedding cakes sorted yet so this could potentially be useful. I'm sure Eden has her ideas about what she wants but it would be good to have suggestions of where we can try. After all, with the tight time frame, it's not going to be easy finding someone with availability, although Eden seems confident that somehow you can get anything done in any amount of time.

'It's got to be chocolate, right?' a familiar man's voice says behind me.

'Oh, got to be,' I reply.

'Can I try one of those, please?' Hugo asks.

'Of course,' the woman replies.

We both take the last two samples of chocolate cake. The baker leaves us to eat them while she goes to replenish her plate. It's probably for the best that she takes them away from me because it's delicious.

'Oh, my god, this is heavenly,' I blurt, my eyes practically rolling into the back of my head. 'Tell me there's a stall giving away cups of tea?'

'Not giving them away, but there's one where you can buy them, if you fancy joining me?' he suggests. 'You can't eat cake without a cuppa.'

'That's what I always say,' I say excitedly as I polish the last of my cake off. That's the only problem with sample sizes – they're too small.

'Well, fancy meeting you here,' Hugo jokes.

'Fancy that, huh?' I reply with a smile. 'Thanks for the—'

'Oh, just a sec,' he interrupts me.

Hugo reaches forward and lightly brushes the side of my mouth with this thumb.

'Tell me I didn't have chocolate on my face,' I reply through a cringe.

'Okay, you didn't have chocolate on your face,' he replies. 'I'm just a creep who likes to touch women's faces.'

I can't help but laugh until I notice a man staring at us. He's holding a camera up, waiting for our conversation to pause, before he interrupts us.

'Can I take your photo?' he asks us. 'It's for a competition.'

Hugo looks at me.

'Okay, sure,' I reply.

I'm not sure how a photo of me with someone who is only one step above a stranger can help him win a photography competition, but he's welcome to try.

Hugo and I lean in slightly, our heads almost touching, as we smile for the camera.

Once the photographer has gone, we get back to our conversation.

'So, you were saying thank you for something?' Hugo prompts me.

'Yes, thank you for recommending I come here,' I reply. 'It's got everything. Like, actually everything.'

'It really does,' he replies. 'There's a stall near the terrace where you can hire guests.'

'Wow, I hope it never comes to that,' I muse. 'Anyway, fewer guests means more cake for me.'

'That's true,' he replies. 'That was a seriously good chocolate cake. Do you think your future sister-in-law will approve?'

'Oh, no, I'm sure chocolate will clash with her colour scheme,' I joke. 'Honestly, she's driving me mad. She has reluctantly given me the task of finding a wedding photographer. I don't think she thinks I can do it, but I insisted, and I'm insisting I pay, but that means I need to find someone affordable. The problem is that when Eden – that's the girl my brother is marrying – did reluctantly give me her sign-off to arrange a photographer – for a wedding which is in less than two weeks, by the way – she started barking requirements at me. They have to be amazing, they have to be a videographer too. So now, you know, no pressure, I just have to find the cheapest best photographer... or the best cheapest photographer is probably more the case.'

'Wow, that sounds like a tall order,' Hugo replies. 'But there are lots of photographers here. I'm sure we can find you one.'

'Oh, don't let me distract you from whatever you're doing,' I insist.

'Ah, it's fine, I come to these things all the time for work,' he replies. 'And it is supposed to be my week off. To be honest, I'm just here for something to do, for a bunch of free cake and sugared almonds, and one of the best cups of tea made by someone other than myself. Interested?'

'I could certainly go for the tea,' I reply.

'By the time we've got a drink, and hit up all of the other cake stalls, the first one might have had a staff change, so we can go again,' he suggests with a cheeky smile. 'If you work the room long enough, you can consume a whole cake. Oh, and you can browse for photographers on the way, of course.'

'Now that sounds like my kind of afternoon,' I reply. 'I'm in.'

'Okay, this way,' Hugo instructs, gesturing down one of the aisles formed by all the stalls.

'It doesn't matter how warm it is, I'm always in the mood for a nice, hot cup of tea,' I confess. 'My mum swears blind it isn't true, but I remember drinking cups of tea when I was a kid. She reckons I was a teen when I started but I'm certain I can recall drinking it with sugar from a sippy cup. I think I'm right and my mum is just worried letting your kids have caffeine constitutes some form of child abuse.'

'Well, I was pretty young when I started drinking it,' Hugo replies. 'My mum isn't with us any more, but she was a hardened tea drinker – she must've had at least six cups a day. So, me being the mummy's boy that I was, I would chain-drink tea with her, but now, if I don't drink it, I get a headache. No one warns you about the headache.'

'Oh, my gosh, so do I,' I tell him, oddly excited. 'When I wake up on a morning, that's it, the timer starts ticking, I've got until the evening before the headache kicks in.'

'Do you know why it happens?' he asks. I shake my head. 'I looked it up and apparently it's because caffeine narrows the blood vessels in your head. When you drink it often your body learns to adapt but, if you skip your usual cups, you end up with enlarged blood vessels, which has a knock-on effect that ultimately leads to a headache.'

'I feel oddly ashamed of myself,' I reply with a laugh. 'So, I'm doing this dance forever, basically?'

'Well, you could give up drinking tea,' Hugo replies.

We both snort with laughter.

Hugo stops in his tracks.

'Oh, did you hear that?' he says. 'An announcement, about the photography competition.'

'Do you think our guy won?' I reply.

'With a picture of me?' he jokes. 'Doubtful.'

I smile at Hugo's self-deprecating joke. He's dressed smarter today than he was yesterday. He's wearing shorts – it is summer, after all – but today's brown T-shirt doesn't have any holes in it. He has the sleeves rolled up once or twice, to make them shorter, showing off his biceps. I don't know why I'm so fixated on the idea of him chopping wood, but his guns are further evidence of the idea. His longish hair is neatly brushed back, but in an unstyled way. I'll bet it falls forward, in that rugged manly way, when he chops wood – again with the wood.

'Are the sleeves not a look?' he jokes, catching me staring at his arms.

I quickly look away, only to clock one of the screens dotted around the room and there it is, the photo of me and Hugo that we posed for, up there next to a snap I didn't realise had been taken of him wiping chocolate from my mouth and me looking back at him bashfully. I am so relieved you can't tell it's chocolate – it really does just look like he enjoys touching women's faces.

'And that is our final couple, couple number three,' the man on the stage with the microphone announces. 'Just a reminder that our Cornwall's Cutest Couple competition is sponsored by Calimeris Photography, and that the winning couple will win a voucher for free photography by Cris Calimeris himself, at an event of their choosing – dates permitting, of course.'

'Did he just say the cutest couple?' I say.

'He also said free photographer,' Hugo replies excitedly. 'And Cris Calimeris – I think I've heard of him.'

'Our three favourite couples will be invited to take part in three rounds so, if you see yourselves on the screens, please make your way to the stage,' the announcer continues. 'Just three simple challenges stand between them and the fantastic prize of wedding photography, a snapper for a big birthday bash, or even a sexy couple's photo shoot. And remember, folks, these rounds will be taking place over the course of the fair, so all the more reason to come back again and again.'

'Liv, this could be the answer to your prayers,' Hugo tells me. 'Three rounds and you've bagged yourself a wedding photographer that even your fussy future sister-in-law couldn't turn her nose up at. And not just a great one, but a free one!'

'I...'

My words don't come out.

'I know it's kind of strange, and that we didn't actually enter the competition to begin with, but they don't know that we're not a real couple,' Hugo tells me. 'I'll happily take part, if you want, maybe we can win?'

I feel all the colour drain from my cheeks before that heavy feeling, the one that feels like being hit by a train, sets in. How is it that I am only now realising I have so far neglected to tell Hugo not only that I am engaged, but that this is my wedding too?

'Hugo, I can't,' I insist.

'How hard can it be?' he replies. 'They do these sorts of things every year. Something funny to gather crowds. It's never anything hard, or awful, just fun-to-watch challenges. I'm sure we could win.'

'Hugo, I'm engaged,' I blurt. 'And this is my wedding too. We're having a joint wedding, I can't believe I haven't mentioned it. What was I thinking?'

Hugo just stares at me for a moment.

'Wow,' he eventually blurts. 'Sorry, I didn't think I... sorry. I didn't know. How could I?'

He looks down at my hand.

'My ring is getting altered,' I tell him, assuming that's what he's looking for. 'Oh, my god, is it warm in here?'

'Yeah, it's like twenty-seven degrees outside,' he replies. 'Come on, let's sit down for a second.'

Hugo, ever the gentleman, leads me to a seating area that is, coincidentally, next to the stage where the three other couples who were selected are waiting to give their details.

'I am so sorry,' I tell him once we're sitting down. 'I promise you, I never meant to keep it from you.'

'Hey, listen, it's okay,' he insists. 'Look, you're engaged, you're getting married – that's great. It's good news, I'm happy for you, he's a very lucky guy. I'm just... surprised. And a little embarrassed that I just suggested we pretend to be a couple. But don't worry, okay? It was an honest mistake.'

I sigh with relief.

'I know this isn't anywhere close to cheating, but I feel so bad for not mentioning it,' I tell him. 'And I can't believe it, because winning the competition would have been the answer to all my problems, but yeah.'

Hugo stares at me thoughtfully for a second. I can see the cogs turning in his brain.

'Look, whether you're single, engaged or married, it doesn't matter, that's not why I offered to help you,' he tells me. 'You said you needed a photographer for a wedding and I said I'd help you get one, so what do you say?'

'What?' I squeak.

'I can't believe I'm saying it either,' Hugo replies. 'But if I don't offer now then it seems like before I was only doing it to try and woo you, so my offer still stands, I'll help you try and win your photographer if you want.'

Hugo laughs to let me know that he's joking about the wooing part.

I think for a second. Is it weird, to enter this competition with Hugo, when we're not actually a couple? I'm sure it is. But the important detail is that we're not a couple, we're just going to pretend we are, to win a wedding photographer – an amazing one, that I couldn't ever possibly afford to pay for with my own money. Hell, I was worrying about how I was going to afford a cheap one last minute.

'The wedding is really soon,' I tell him. 'On the eighth.'

'Wow, that is soon,' he replies. 'But you heard what the guy said, you can check dates before you enter. Maybe Cris Calimeris is free?'

'Are we really going to do this?' I ask through an awkward smile.

'Well, I'm game if you are,' he replies. 'And I'm not being totally selfless. I could drum up some local business for the bar, it's been so quiet lately.'

'Okay,' I say, not sounding all that sure of myself. I try again. 'Yeah, okay, let's win this bitch.'

Hugo laughs.

'We can make a mockery of the whole competition by winning, despite not even really knowing each other,' he jokes. 'Potentially unethical, but it is for you, and for a real wedding, so I think that's okay. I'm just a means to an end.'

'Thank you for doing this,' I tell him. I think for a moment. 'Listen, I doubt it will come up, but if you happen to bump into anyone I'm here with, can you not mention it please? Just, partially because I really want them to think I've done this on my own, the normal way, not through some kind of elaborate scam or fluke. But mostly because this is really weird and I'm not sure they would understand.'

'Yeah, that makes sense,' Hugo replies. 'Right, come on, before I come to my senses and change my mind. Let's go see if Cris Calimeris is free on the eighth.'

'I can't see it,' I reply. 'But let's try. And Hugo, again, I'm sorry. I'm mortified, I'm an idiot, I'm... yeah. I'm just sorry.'

'It's not a problem,' he insists. 'Don't beat yourself up, we just hadn't got around to that part of the conversation yet.'

'Thanks,' I tell him. 'Okay, let's make this weird.'

Hugo laughs as we make our way to the stage.

Am I doing this? Am I really doing this? It's so good of Hugo to say he'll help me out, even though it's me who is getting married. I feel so, so embarrassed that I didn't mention it – that it didn't occur to me to mention it. Then again, I have only been engaged for a matter of weeks.

I know this is strange. So, so strange. But imagine if I pull it off? Imagine if I get not just any wedding photographer, but the best wedding photographer going, and for free too. Teddy will be impressed, Dougie will be happy, Eden will be ecstatic.

But, best of all, I will be bringing something to the table, planning something for the wedding, and it will be all me.

Well, and Hugo, of course. But no one else needs to know that.

12

In a room, just off the kitchen, is the house games room, cinema and swimming pool.

Arriving back at the house, I eventually find Eden, Dougie, Mick and Joanne having a swim.

'Hello,' I say brightly as I approach the edge of the pool.

Having a house with its own pool must be nothing short of amazing and, if you're going to have a pool in your house, have one like this. The shape of the pool is nothing special, just your standard rectangular pool, but it's inside some kind of party room. It's all turned off at the moment, given that it's still light out, but the room is full of mirrors and lights, and there's a disco ball hanging from the ceiling. I'll bet this is one hell of a place to throw a party.

'Hey, Liv, fancy a swim before dinner?' Dougie calls out as he smacks a beach ball towards Mick.

'Maybe,' I reply. 'Where are Mum and Dad?'

'They've gone shopping,' he tells me. 'Clothes shopping, I think. They said it was a bit of a drive.'

I don't need to ask why my mum and dad have gone clothes shopping because I know – they will be out in search of something peach, as per Eden's dress code.

'I daren't even ask but did you spend today sorting a photographer?' Eden asks.

With the team running the competition confirming that, yes, Cris was available on 8 July, Hugo and I threw our names into the hat. We are officially a fake couple.

'I actually have something in the works,' I reply.

I'll know more about the competition tomorrow in the morning – they said they would email Hugo the details. It sounds like they make a real spectacle of it, I guess it's to draw a crowd for the fair, and to entertain people, but who knows if we can win? I'll know how doable the plan is when I find out what's involved. Obviously I'm not going to leave it until the last minute, I can't afford to be reckless with less than two weeks until the wedding, and it isn't just me and Teddy depending on my sorting it, it's Dougie and Eden too.

'I had a feeling you weren't going to sort it,' she says with a sigh.

'It hasn't even been a day,' I remind her. 'And everything we're doing is already last minute as it is.'

'I know, but it doesn't look good,' she replies. 'Especially with you not turning up at the florist's today.'

'What do you mean I didn't turn up at the florist's?' I ask.

'I told you we were meeting the florist today,' she replies. 'But you never showed up.'

'You told me you would confirm with me when and where,' I point out, starting to get a little ticked off.

'And I did,' she insists.

'No, you didn't,' I reply.

'Okay, ladies, let's calm down,' Dougie insists. 'Someone has obviously made an honest mistake.'

'So, you've chosen my flowers?' I say.

'*Our* flowers,' Eden reminds me. 'But yes. Someone had to. Look, it's not a big deal, they only had so many flowers available in our colours, so we were quite limited anyway.'

'We did the best with what we had,' Joanne adds. 'We had to make the decisions we were faced with.'

I open my mouth to say something. I'm not sure what the words are going to be yet, but I get a feeling Eden isn't going to like them.

I feel my phone vibrating – it's Teddy.

'Teddy is calling,' I tell them. 'I'll be back in a minute.'

With the house otherwise free, I answer my phone in the lounge area.

'Hello,' I say with a sigh as I kick off my shoes and curl up in the corner of the sofa.

'Uh-oh,' he replies playfully. 'That's not a good hello.'

'No, it's not,' I reply. 'How are you?'

'I'm good – work is going really well, I feel like I'm getting closer,' he replies. 'How's wedding planning?'

'Well, Eden doesn't trust me to hire a photographer, so I'm doing my best to prove her wrong,' I tell him. 'But otherwise, she's pretty much taking over. You know she chose the colours and now she's chosen the flowers – but this time, behind my back. I don't even know what they are.'

'Try to see the positives, babe, it's one less thing to worry about,' he says. 'Don't let it bother you.'

'I know, it's just... I'm seeing a whole lot of Eden and Dougie in this wedding but not very much us,' I reply. 'And I'm hating being here, doing this without you. Everyone is ganging up on me, I need you here for the votes.'

'I know, babe,' he replies. 'But I have some good news for you on that one.'

I feel butterflies in my stomach and smile.

'You're coming tomorrow?' I reply. 'What time will you be here?'

'Well, I have a meeting tomorrow afternoon, which might run into the evening, but I know you have a lot going on and you're letting it get to you,' he says in a way that makes me think maybe he doesn't believe I should be letting it bother me like I am. 'But I know you need someone there, so Mother has agreed to come and help out.'

Oh, god, not Alicia. Honestly, no help would be more help than Alicia. She'll probably side with Eden more than she will with me.

'Teddy, I really need *you* here,' I remind him.

'I know you do,' he replies. 'But it's work.'

'I'm getting a call on the other line, am I okay to get it?' I lie.

'Yeah, of course,' he replies. 'Babe, look, I'm swamped, but I'll be in touch. You know work is important.'

'I know, gotta go, bye,' I say quickly.

I hang up.

I don't really have another call coming through, but I do have a message from Heidi asking me how it's going. It would be so good to tell her right now – although I'm sure her advice would be something I am not bold enough to go through with, that would undoubtedly scorch the earth – but I know how important her latest project is to her and I don't want to disturb her.

The thing is, though, with Heidi, I know that if I called her, if she knew I needed to talk, she would be on the other end of the phone. With Teddy, it's different. It's his wedding too, he should be here.

I know that his work is important to him – of course I do – but, right now, it seems like it's more important to him than our wedding. That, I didn't expect.

13

Walking out of the beach house and being almost immediately on the beach is certainly something I could get used to. Right now, as June edges closer to July, it's glorious. I wonder if the appeal might wear off slightly when the summer is over and the weather is awful. Ah, who am I kidding, I bet it's still amazing.

It's such a beautiful day. The sun is shining, a cool gentle breeze is blowing, and I'm walking across the beach, feeling the warm sand between my toes. The light wind gently blows my sundress and skims my bare shoulders. I love it when it's hot and sunny but it just feels so nice. If I were in London right now, I would be a frizzy, sweaty, bright red mess. Here the summer just suits me.

I didn't wake up with a cute morning message from Teddy but I know, I know, he's busy. I would rather he skipped the texts in favour of hurrying up, getting his work done, and coming here to plan our wedding. I don't suppose it helps that I feel like I have no idea what he actually does day to day. I ask him about it all the time and he always tells me it's too complicated, and ultimately too boring, to be worth explaining.

I did, however, wake up to a text from Hugo asking me to meet him on the beach. I don't have to walk far before I spot him chatting to a tall, blonde-haired man. He isn't wearing a shirt, just a bright red pair of shorts that say 'Lifeguard' on them.

'Good morning,' I say brightly.

The blonde spots me first.

'G'day,' he says, his Australian accent impossible to miss.

'Liv, hi,' Hugo says as he turns to greet me.

'She a friend of yours, is she?' the Aussie asks him.

'Chris, this is Liv,' he tells him. 'Liv, this is Chris. He's the beach lifeguard and a mistake many women have made on holiday here.'

I smile. It's cute, the way he teases his friend.

'Hi,' Chris says. I can't tell if he sounds flirtatious or just Australian and my brain is taking that extra leap.

'You're wasting your time,' Hugo says with a laugh. 'Liv is getting married in a week or so.'

'That doesn't always stop them,' Chris jokes with a wink. 'Anyway, I'd better get back to work.'

'Yeah, we don't want a repeat of 2014,' Hugo jokes.

'You weren't even here then, you don't know,' Chris says, giving him a shove. 'Catch you later.'

Okay, perhaps he wasn't joking.

'Well, he seems nice,' I say through a laugh.

'He's a great friend,' Hugo replies. 'But he's only an okay lifeguard and an even worse boyfriend, for lack of a better term.'

'Wow, thanks for the warning,' I reply, highly amused by his honest review.

'Anyway, enough about Chris, I had an email from the competition people,' he tells me. 'Shall we walk and talk? There's a gorgeous café just down the beach. We could grab a cuppa.'

'Sounds like a plan,' I reply. 'I arrived back at the house last night to find out that Eden had chosen the wedding flowers without me. And she still doesn't think I can sort a photographer.'

'Well, on the subject of the competition, I have found out that there are only three other couples taking part – presumably real ones – but it sounds like it's just three rounds of silly games that don't require any real skill. Totally winnable, even if we are faking it.'

I smile. I'm under no illusions, I know exactly why Hugo is helping me out. He's so worried about seeming like his reasons for talking to me, for offering to help, were not good ones. I suppose, with a friend like Chris (who is good-looking but sounds pretty amoral), he doesn't want to seem like he had bad intentions with me. Now he's working overtime to seem like he does this sort of thing all the time, like he would help anyone out in any situation, even if it's weird. Beggars can't be choosers, I'm more than happy to accept his help.

'The more people think I can't do this, the more determined I am to win,' I confess. 'And they'll never know what we did to try and win but I don't mind. They don't even think I could pay for a photographer.'

'What do you do for work?' he asks curiously. 'I suppose we should know some things about each another, if we're going to style out that we're a couple.'

'That's an excellent point,' I reply. 'I know that you're a bar manager. Prepare to be unimpressed. I'm a comedian.'

'Do people usually insist you tell them a joke when you say that?' he asks.

'Every time, without fail,' I reply.

'Do you ever tell one?'

'Sometimes, on the occasions where I don't roll my eyes,' I reply. 'Although, obviously, to me it seems so much funnier if I tell a joke that isn't very funny. And that's the joke. Either way, I usually lose my audience pretty quickly.'

'Go on then, I can't resist, tell me one of these terrible jokes,' Hugo insists as we stroll along the edge of the sea.

I'm carrying my sandals in my hand because half of the joy to be felt at the beach comes from everything it has to offer your senses. I love the smells, the foods that taste so much better at the beach, and the feelings – there is nothing like feeling the sand, then the sea, then the sand again. I love how it feels on my feet, and how soft my feet feel for weeks after.

'Knock knock,' I start.

'Who's there?' Hugo replies.

'Control freak.'

'Co—'

'Now you say, "Control freak who?"' I quickly, loudly and purposefully interrupt him.

'Very good,' he replies. I can tell he thinks it's cheesy from his smile.

'Or sometimes I'll ask: "Do you want to hear a time travel joke?" The other person will say yes, I'll wait for a beat and then tell them they didn't find it funny.'

'That's brilliant,' Hugo replies. 'Almost as though the person asking you to tell a joke to begin with is the joke.'

'Can you please just follow me around and laugh at all my jokes?' I ask. 'Because it's not going great. I mostly work as a ghostwriter, penning romcoms for people who are already established names. It's okay but I'm planning to try to write my own.'

'That's exciting,' Hugo replies.

'Yeah, it would be, if not for the fact that I usually write a story based on a rough idea someone gives me. I'm worried I won't be able to write one of my own.'

'Getting married, making plans last minute, having a joint wedding – that's all romcom-worthy, surely? You could write what you know.'

'You say that but, to be honest, everything you said is just, well, kind of tragic,' I reply. 'My co-bride is a nightmare, the planning isn't going well and Teddy, my fiancé, is too busy with work to even be here.'

'Presumably he'll show up for the ceremony,' Hugo jokes, lightening the mood.

'Presumably,' I reply. 'In the meantime, I'll have to find my romance somewhere else. So to speak.'

I am lightning-fast to add that on at the end.

'Well, I might be able to help you there too,' he says with a smile.

'Oh?' I reply, as casually as I can, but my brain is sending messages to my cheeks, telling them to blush.

'Yeah, this is the café I was telling you about,' he replies, nodding towards a small building sitting right in the heart of the busiest stretch of beach I've seen yet.

It's impossibly cute, painted pink (so it matches the wedding aesthetic, at least, that's a relief) with a big, sparkly sign outside that says 'Shell's'.

'Shell, the owner, is a romcom fanatic,' he tells me. 'She will tell you all about it herself, given half the chance.'

Shell's is quite busy inside. It isn't big but it's lovely. Everything is pink and floral, all the tableware is beautifully mismatched, and I would say at least 50 per cent of everything in here is covered in some kind of glitter – even the baked goods, which look out of this world.

As you queue for the counter, you stand beside a wall which is covered with framed photos and pictures. I only get a few seconds to take them in before Shell herself approaches us.

'Here he is, Porthian's most eligible bachelor,' she practically sings as she pulls Hugo in for a big hug. 'How's the week off treating you? Is the place falling apart without you? Or – I have my suspicions – are you struggling to stay away, hmm?'

'I'm sure all of the above is true,' he tells her with a smile. 'Shell, this is my friend Liv, she's staying in the beach house at the moment. We're here for two of your biggest cups of tea and enormous slices of cake. I thought you might like to meet Liv because she ghostwrites romcoms.'

'Oh, really?' Shell replies. 'Who do you write for? No, wait, don't tell me. You'll only ruin them forever for me. I should live in ignorance – it's the only real way to be happy. So, no, don't tell me, don't tell me. Unless you write for Mia Valentina? Have you heard of her?'

'She's romcom royalty,' I reply. 'I'm certain she writes all her own books – I'm pretty sure she used to write movies.'

'She did,' Shell replies. 'We're sort of old friends. She stayed in the beach house, years ago, before the remodel. She used to come in here – I basically swapped her a wedding cake for a scene in one of her movies to be shot here, in a roundabout way – lovely girl. I have photos on the walls, see.'

Now that I have a chance to look, I can tell what I'm looking at. Framed photos of set pictures, movie stills and even posters.

'Liv is actually just about to start writing her own romcom – her very first – so I said she should talk to you, sort of market research, from the industry's biggest fan.'

Seriously, can Hugo just follow me around, laugh at my jokes, and hype me up to people?

'Well, I'll grab your drinks, a selection of cakes, and be right over,' she insists. 'Grab that booth over there.'

We do as instructed, taking our seats while we can get them.

'She seems so nice,' I say.

'Everyone here is nice,' Hugo replies.

'Nice and just so normal,' I say. 'Normal people with normal jobs who are nice. I know that must sound so daft but, honestly, being around my family, Teddy's family, Eden's family... I just feel so... so cheap. It's nice to hang around with someone who appreciates the value of free cake.'

'Always,' he says with a smile. 'Have you sorted one for your wedding yet?'

'No,' I say with a sigh. 'I'm dreading Eden bringing it up. I already know we want completely different things as far as music goes. What are the chances we'll like the same kinds of cakes?'

'What does Teddy have to say about this?' he replies curiously.

'Nothing,' I say dramatically, as though I can hardly believe it myself. 'Not a thing. I guess he's just not that into weddings. I suppose guys often aren't.'

Shell places a platter covered with a series of small squares of cake all over it. She also unloads a large teapot, two cups, milk and sugar onto the table next to it. Then she takes a seat.

'I'm pretty sure I've watched or read – or both – any good romcom going,' Shell explains. 'A few bad ones too. I know all the tropes.'

'When I ghostwrite, I'm usually given a rough outline – characters, locations and I'm told what should happen from start to finish,' I explain. 'So, all I have to do really is turn those things into a book, fill in the blanks, write a bunch of jokes. It's an outlet for my observational comedy, and I feel like I have that bit down, but coming up with something from scratch intimidates me. I've been thinking about it and I just can't make my mind up on anything. Who is the main character? Where is the book set?'

'Oh, you should set it here,' Shell insists. 'And not just because I want another movie scene filmed here – should the book ever be made into the movie.'

I laugh.

'That's definitely getting ahead of ourselves,' I remind her. 'When I can't even name my main character.'

'I've heard it said Michelle is a very beautiful name,' she jokes. 'But seriously, Cornwall is a brilliant location for a romance, and Porthian Sands is simply divine. A lot happens here – you would be surprised.'

'Ooh, go on,' I insist. 'This sounds juicy. Perhaps you can inspire me.'

'Well, I'm usually a very discreet person,' she says, leaning in as she lowers her voice. 'But my café is a hotspot for runaway brides – and the occasional groom too. And let's see, a few years back we had a man who crashed his hot-air balloon into someone's house – parked the thing in some woman's roof – and at some point during the aftermath, they fell in love. It was here where Mia Valentina met the man she was destined to spend the rest of her life with. It's like I always say, come to Porthian if you want to find your true love, the person you're supposed to be with.'

'Shell thinks something magical goes on here,' Hugo teases. 'I think people just drink a lot when they're on holiday.'

'Now, now, Hugo, it's the locals too,' Shell insists. 'There's a story – practically an urban legend – that my granny used to tell me. At this point, who knows if it's all true, I'm sure the historical details get lost along the way. A couple were engaged to be married – we're talking back in the 1920s – a young woman and the heir to a tin mine. He was a very well-off young man, very handsome, a smart dresser in the finest clothes, soft hands from never working a day in his life.'

'A tale as old as time,' Hugo says with a playful sigh.

'Except the heart wants what the heart wants, and when his fiancée met one of the big, rugged, rough-around-the-edges miners by chance one day – and somehow he managed to convince her to go on a date with him – it was love at first sight. She gave up a life of comfort and money with a very rich man for a shot at true love with a poor, scruffy miner called Clarence. The heart wants what it wants. She called off her engagement and married Clarence a matter of months later. Maybe it's true or maybe it's just one of those stories grandmothers tell their grandchildren to try and encourage them to make good choices. Still, it's a lovely idea for a romance story.'

'My great-granddad was called Clarence,' I tell her, acknowledging the strange coincidence. 'He was a miner too. He lived here with my great-gran, they raised my gran here, she met my granddad here – they moved to Oxford just before my mum was born.'

'Your great-grandmother wasn't called Alma, was she?' Shell asks, expecting the answer to be no.

'Erm, yeah,' I say with a laugh.

'No!' Shell replies in disbelief. 'Do you think... surely not? I'm amazed. I think you need to have a word with your grandparents, see if they know anything.'

'My grandparents are no longer with us,' I tell her. 'I wonder if my mum knows anything about this.'

'It really would make a great idea for a story,' Hugo says.

'Oh, please say you'll write it,' Shell insists, flinging her arms out to show her excitement, only to smack the jug of milk. It tips over and floods the table in Hugo's direction. It reaches his T-shirt before anyone can do anything about it.

'Blooming heck, I'm sorry, see what happens when I get overexcited,' Shell mutters as she grabs serviettes from out of nowhere, like some sort of flustered magician.

'Don't worry about it,' Hugo reassures her with a smile. 'We've got places to be, I can pop home and get changed.'

'I'm sorry,' she says again. 'I'm not trying to get rid of you – although I should probably get back to work. Liv, let me know if you find anything out from your mum.'

'Of course,' I reply. 'It was so nice to meet you.'

'You too, my lovely,' she replies.

'Right, let's get out of here,' Hugo says. 'It's so warm today, this milk is already starting to make me stink.'

'Oh, boy,' I reply through a grimace. 'You're right, let's go.'

Back out on the beach, the breeze seems to have let up a little, whereas the sun has definitely turned the heat up.

'Well, now I get to go and ask my mum if her gran ditched her fiancé for someone else,' I say with a sigh. 'So that's...'

My sentence trails off as I glance over at Hugo a split second after he's whipped his milk-soaked T-shirt off. I don't know what I was expecting to see under his shirt – it was obvious he was a big, strong man from the moment we met – but I wasn't expecting him to be so built. He's like a rugby player. He must spend a lot of time outside with his shirt off because his skin has been kissed by the sun – lucky sun!

'I see you've clocked my scar,' Hugo says.

Yeah, okay, sure, we'll go with that.

Hugo rotates his forearm so I can get a good look at his scar – it's an old, faded one. You can only really see it because it interrupts his otherwise hairy arms.

'A buddy of mine slipped with a masonry bolster,' he explains – not that I know what he means. 'I guess I'm more like your *maybe* great-granddad. Rough workman's hands, see?'

Hugo stuffs his shirt into his waistband before holding out his hands for me to examine.

'You have nice hands,' I reassure him, reaching out to touch one lightly. I quickly take it back. 'Anyway, what was I saying? Erm... oh, yeah. Time to go and have an awkward conversation with my mum.'

'But maybe you'll get a book idea out of it,' he replies. 'So that's something.'

'That is something, that's true,' I reply. 'Although maybe I'll get some lunch first.'

'There's usually a place down the beach just a little further that sells wood-fired pizzas,' Hugo says. 'Fancy it? I can give you the competition dates, so you can slot them into your hectic pre-wedding calendar.'

'That would be great,' I reply. 'I could just eat a pizza. Will they mind that you don't have a shirt on?'

'They serve them out of a food truck,' he replies. 'They won't mind if you don't mind.'

'I don't mind,' I say, far more enthusiastically than I intended it to come out – my voice actually breaks in the middle of my sentence.

Hugo just laughs it off.

Maybe I'm avoiding being back at the house, maybe I'm enjoying spending time with someone who wants to talk to me about something other than the wedding, or maybe I just really want a pizza. I imagine the answer is a combination of all of the above.

Whatever the reason, I'm just going to go with it, because this is easily the most fun I've had since I arrived, and it can surely all be downhill from here.

Not something I ever thought I'd say in the run-up to my wedding, but here we are.

14

'Did you hear about the Italian chef who died?' Hugo asks me as we climb the steps from the beach to the beach house.

I forgot, this is his way home too. We're both clutching boxes with a few slices of leftover pizza in them.

'No?' I reply.

'He pasta-way,' Hugo says with a snort.

'Oh, my god, he's coming for my job,' I say with a cackle. 'Or maybe not, with terrible jokes like that.'

'It could be a good one for when people put you on the spot,' he replies. 'A good *bad* one.'

'I really like this bad one,' I start, before clearing my throat. 'What do you call an interrupting cow?'

'I don't know, what do you—'

'Moo!' I practically bellow at him but then my smile quickly drops when I spot my mum, sitting alone on a sunlounger in the garden.

'Hello,' she says, giving me what can only be described as an interesting smile.

She looks at Hugo, her eyes briefly scanning his body, then at the pizza box in my hand, then at me. She raises her eyebrows expectantly. She either wants an explanation or some pizza. Being able to read my mum's mind as well as I can, I strongly suspect she wants both.

'Oh, hi, Mum,' I say, playing it cool.

I don't know why I feel so weird, to be caught hanging out with Hugo. It's probably because of the competition, because I'm not telling anyone that that's how I'm planning on securing an amazing photographer, I feel like I'm being deceptive. Well, I'm going to see how the first round of the competition goes tomorrow – we might be knocked out and, even if we aren't, it might seem like it's going to be way too difficult to win as a fake couple, but if it is then, hey, I only wasted a day on shooting my shot. I'll just have to settle for the best I can get.

'Hello,' she says again.

'Mum, this is Hugo, he works at the hotel and he lives in the cottage next door,' I explain. 'He's been helping me with my romance.'

'I'll bet he has,' she teases.

Hugo laughs.

'With my romance *novel*,' I quickly add. 'I'm thinking of setting it here so he's been helping me learn more about the area. Would you like some pizza?'

'I never say no to pizza,' she replies. 'It's nice to meet you, Hugo, I'm Erica.'

'It's a pleasure to meet you, Erica,' he replies. 'If you burn through that box, you're welcome to some of mine too.'

I can tell my mum is biting her tongue. If it were just the two of us, she would probably make a dirty joke – yes, that's where I get it from. She just hides it better under her usual ladylike exterior.

'We were actually looking for you,' I tell her – which isn't strictly true, I was going to chat to her later, but it moves the conversation along, at least. 'We were just talking to the lady who runs the café on the beach. She was telling us all these real-life local love stories. Anyway, she went on about a miner called Clarence, and a woman called Alma.'

Mum freezes, a slice of pizza hovering in front of her lips. Still, she gives nothing away.

'Oh, yes?' she replies.

'Yes, she was saying there was a young woman called Alma who was engaged to some rich guy, but then she met a miner called Clarence and fell in love, so she called off her engagement to the first guy and married the second a few months later,' I say. 'And I couldn't believe the coincidence with the names, but then I wondered if the story might be about them.'

Mum laughs.

'My Granny Alma may or may not have told me stories suggesting that it might be about her,' Mum says.

'Really?' Hugo replies excitedly. 'Do you think?'

'Yes,' Mum replies. 'I mean, yes, well, she used to tell me stories about how she met my granddad, and that's pretty much it.'

'I can't believe you didn't tell me,' I say with a gasp. 'Mum, that's so juicy!'

'You need to get out more,' she teases me.

'It's 1920s juicy,' I insist. 'Why did Gran never tell me?'

'She was mortified by it,' Mum explains. 'It was quite the scandal when it happened and, even when your gran was growing up, it was still pretty unspeakable.'

'Grandma Edith, I am shocked,' I say to no one in particular. 'I can't believe she didn't tell me.'

'It sounded like Alma was quite the floozy,' Mum says with a smile. 'But she did love your great-granddad. They did get married quite quickly but then they stayed together forever. They died a matter of months apart, both in their eighties. You can't ask for much better than that, can you?'

'That's really nice,' Hugo says. 'Liv, you should definitely use that for your book.'

'Is that what you're thinking?' Mum asks curiously.

'Yes,' I reply. 'Well, a present-day romcom version, but the gist is the same: a young woman in Cornwall who is engaged to a rich guy she doesn't really love, who falls in love with a penniless hunk. What do you think?'

'I think that sounds like a great idea,' Mum replies with a smile.

We all fall silent for a second.

'Okay, well, I'd better go and get this shirt in the wash before the sun turns it into cheese,' Hugo tells me. 'But I'll see you tomorrow.'

'Tomorrow?' Mum says nosily.

'He's helping me with some wedding prep,' I tell her. 'Just between us, Hugo knows an amazing photographer. He thinks he can hook me up.'

'That's very good of you,' Mum tells him.

'Anyway, see you tomorrow,' Hugo says again.

'Yeah, see you later,' I reply. 'Thanks for the pizza.'

I watch Hugo head up the garden path to his cottage. Once he's out of sight, I sit down next to my mum.

'Oh, so you have told him you're getting married,' she teases.

'Shut up,' I reply with a smile, although I can feel myself blushing.

'Listen, if I was thirty years younger, and your dad was dead...'

I snort with laughter.

'I'm not sure why Dad would need to be dead,' I point out. 'But I take your point.'

'All jokes aside, though – so to speak – it's nice to see you so happy,' she tells me sincerely. 'It's been a while since I saw you laugh like that.'

'I was mostly laughing at my own jokes,' I tell her. 'Someone needs to.'

Mum just smiles but then her face drops ever so slightly – of course I notice it.

'It's very nice of Hugo to help you with a photographer,' she says. 'Maybe give Teddy a quick call, just make sure you're on the same page.'

'Oh, okay,' I reply, the strange feeling that perhaps Mum knows something I don't creeping in. 'I'll try him now.'

Unsure where everyone else is, I head for my bedroom – I would rather have guaranteed privacy and take my chances with the world's loudest toilet than risk Eden sitting down on the sofa next to me and taking over the phone call.

I try Teddy but he doesn't pick up. I send him a message, asking him to call me, and eventually he does.

'Babe, I can't talk for long,' he says right off the bat. 'Things are hectic here.'

'That's okay, I won't keep you,' I reply. 'I just wanted to let you know that I met a really nice guy who works at the hotel. He has a connection with a well-known photographer and he thinks he can hook us up, so I'm going to hopefully sort that tomorrow.'

'You don't need to worry about it,' he reassures me.

'I'm not worried about it,' I reply.

'I mean, you really don't need to worry about it,' he says again. 'Eden called me last night, she said you were having a bit of trouble making things happen, she was worried, so I promised I would sort it. So I did.'

'What do you mean you sorted it?' I reply. 'I told you all that I was going to sort it.'

'Liv, I took time out of my day – you know how busy I am – to book a photographer, so you didn't have to,' he says. 'I thought you'd be happy.'

'I'm not happy,' I reply. 'I was in the process of sorting it.'

'Look, it's not a big deal, if you get yours sorted, I'll just cancel mine, even if we have to pay for both, what does it matter? It's a contingency plan,' he explains.

'We don't have a contingency plan for anything else,' I point out.

Am I silly for feeling hurt? I know Eden didn't think I could do it, but Teddy is supposed to have my back.

'Liv, don't make this a thing,' he tells me, sounding ticked off. How is he the one who is annoyed? 'Who cares who takes the photos, so long as you get some?'

I don't really know what to say to that.

'Look, Mother will be there tomorrow, just give everything you don't want to do to her, she'll sort it,' he says quickly.

'It's not that I don't want to do things,' I reply, but there are more pressing matters at hand. 'Are you not coming tomorrow?'

'Liv, don't start, please,' he begs.

'It's just a question,' I reply.

'Honestly, probably not,' Teddy tells me. 'I've got a client dinner, it's the last piece of the puzzle, if I sign them up – look, you just need to trust me, that I'm doing the right thing for us. All you need to do is plan the wedding, okay?'

I don't say anything.

'Liv, is that okay?' he asks again.

'What choi—'

'Liv, my other line is ringing,' he interrupts me. 'I'll call you later.'

And just like that, the call ends.

Wow. I'm not shocked that Eden called him, to be honest, that feels really on-brand for her. What I can't believe is the fact that Teddy went over my head and booked a photographer just because she told him, what, that I wasn't capable? Was he even going to tell me that he did? Does he really have such little faith in me?

I tell you what, this has motivated me even more to win this Cutest Couple competition. Seriously, whatever it takes, whatever I need to do, I'll do it. I need to win. I need to show them that I'm not as useless – as worthless – as they seem to think I am.

That is, of course, if Teddy even cares about getting married. I'm sure I'll think differently tomorrow, when I've had a chance to calm down, but, right now, getting married on the eighth is the last thing I want.

15

Hugo gives me a gentle nudge with his elbow.

'What do you call a hippy's wife?' he asks me.

'I don't know, what?' I reply.

'Mississippi,' he says with a smile.

I can't help but laugh.

'I thought you might appreciate a bad joke,' he tells me. 'You look a little nervous.'

We're standing at the side of the stage, waiting for the competition to start, and to say I'm a little nervous is an understatement. I know what you're going to say: But Liv, weren't you just trying to get a job on TV where you would probably be watched by a lot more people than are currently standing in this room? Well, yes, but the difference is that on TV you have a script, when I'm doing my routines, they're all carefully planned in advance. But this, here, today, is a whole other thing. I'm nervous because this whole thing is a sham, a scheme to win a prize. Hugo and I are not only not a real couple – we're not even friends. Well, is it strange that I do feel like we're friends at this point? But no matter what we are to one another, the bottom line is we don't know each other all that well and I'm worried people are going to be able to tell.

The competition is being hosted by Mike King, a washed-up musician from a decade ago who has since found fame for a second time as a TV presenter. I remember him from his musician days, when he was the moody guitarist in a rock band, very much the quiet type. He doesn't resemble his former self these days, he has all the characteristics of a corny TV presenter – loud, excitable and full of life. He was even wearing a gold, sparkly jacket when we arrived, although he has since stripped down to a white short-sleeved shirt now that the midday sun has kicked in and the temperature has been turned up.

'So, we're going to bring you guys up one at a time,' a young woman with a headset and an iPad informs us. 'We'll introduce you as a couple, you'll take part in the first round, we'll call up the next couple and so on, and so on, and then at the end of the round, one couple will be out and the rest will be on to the next round in a few days – sound good?'

Sounds confusing, although that might just be because I'm feeling nervy.

'You guys are up first,' she tells the couple to my right. 'Mike will give you your cue.'

My stomach is really churning now. I need to relax, to push the potential sketchiness of the situation out of my mind – I just need to take a deep breath and try to focus on the moment. If I walk up onto that stage feeling like an edgy, guilty weirdo, then that's exactly what I'm going to look like. I'm genuinely astounded someone found me photogenetic enough to be here because I usually look like the dramatic chipmunk in photos.

'Okay, ladies and gentlemen, it's the moment you've all been waiting for,' Mike announces, his voice travelling instantly from his microphone to every speaker in the room.

It's busy today – busier than the last time I was here, that's for sure. We all had to agree to turn up on three dates, for three rounds, to be in with a chance of winning the photography session. It was made clear to us that any couple who didn't turn up for a round would be out, with no second chances. I imagine everyone here wants this just as much as I do. Surely Hugo and I don't stand a chance?

'Throughout the course of the fair, we're looking to crown Cornwall's Cutest Couple – and what better place to do it than here in Porthian Sands, one of the most romantic locations in the country?' Mike announces. 'To make it through the first round, all our couples have to do is answer a series of questions correctly – the catch, however, is that there are no right answers. It doesn't matter what our couples answer, their answers simply need to match and, yes, we have done this before and, yes, it has broken up stronger-looking couples than this motley crew standing in the wings, let me tell you.'

I'm sure that's just a joke – something he says about all the couples.

'First up, ladies and gents, we have... Thom and Sandi.'

Mike practically sings their names.

'Here we go,' Thom tells his partner as they head up onto the stage.

Thom is a tall, thin man with side-parted blonde hair. He towers over Sandi, who stands just above elbow height next to him. Sandi's long, curly brown hair hangs down the side of her face. As they take their positions at either side of Mike, Sandi uses her forearm to sweep her thick hair over to one side. She clearly means business. Everyone knows that's a long-haired person's version of rolling up their sleeves.

'Thom, Sandi, why don't you tell the audience a little bit about yourselves, what you're doing here, and why you would like to win?' Mike suggests, holding the mic out in front of them.

Sandi is right in there, taking the mic in her hand.

'Well, Mike, we're actually visiting from Plymouth, it's our first break away together since we had our baby, Tobias,' she explains. 'We actually want to win the prize for him – for a special family photo shoot.'

'That's lovely,' Mike replies, reaching out to take the mic, but Sandi pulls it back.

'Can I just say, I was a huge fan of The Burnouts, I had to have a day off uni when you guys broke up,' she tells him. 'Are you and your brother still not talking?'

'Okay,' Mike says through a just about disguised angry laugh. 'That's enough about me, I'm the one who asks the questions. Let's get you your iPads. Now, it's very simple, you will see two options pop up in front of you, for example: dogs or cats? And all you have to do is pick an answer. At the end of round one, we should have a good idea of which couples are the most compatible. Seeing as though all couples will be answering the same set of questions, and these questions will be shown on the screen behind me, the couples who haven't yet taken part will be given a pair of noise-cancelling headphones, and will be asked very nicely to turn away. So, let's do this...'

The lady with the headset thrusts a pair of headphones into our hands.

'We can only do our best,' Hugo tells me quickly and quietly before we temporarily switch off our senses.

Talk about being alone with your thoughts. All I can do right now is think. I try to think about the competition, about what I can possibly pull out of the bag to help us win this round. Of course, given that it's a compatibility quiz, and Hugo and I don't really know anything about each other, there's nothing I can do.

Instead, I think about Teddy. Would he appreciate what I'm doing right now? Definitely not. If he knew, he would be talking to a friend of a friend who – it would probably turn out – knew Cris Calimeris personally, who would ask him to shoot our wedding. He would agree, for a small fortune, and Teddy would happily pay it. But where is the fun in that? Where is *my* sense of achievement, how do I feel like *I've* contributed if it all comes down to what Teddy is willing to pay? He would think it was ridiculous that I was doing this. I'd imagine he would find it embarrassing – lord knows Alicia wouldn't approve. But I want to do this, if anything, for Dougie and Eden. They deserve it. Plus, to be honest, it's kind of exciting.

My palms feel sweaty, and it's not just because it's such a beautiful day, it's because it's just me and Hugo standing here now, which means we're next.

I glance at him. He gives me a smile, letting me know it's all going to be okay. I don't know about okay but, so long as we don't totally embarrass ourselves, I'll be happy.

I feel a tap on my shoulder and I jump out of my skin.

'Come on, you guys are next,' the woman with the headset says. 'You're on in three... two... one... go.'

'Just be honest,' Hugo says, taking my hand, giving it a squeeze. He doesn't let go of it, though, he keeps hold of it as we walk up the steps to the stage. It must feel so gross, given how wet my hands feel, it's a miracle he can keep hold of it.

'And now we have our final couple,' Mike says. 'What's your name and where do you come from?'

He puts on – what I'd imagine – is a Cilla Black accent for his question.

'I'm Hugo and this is my fiancée, Liv,' Hugo says, taking the lead, which I'm grateful for.

'Lugo,' Mike replies, giving us a couple's name. 'Wow, that doesn't sound great, does it? Anyway, tell us a little bit about yourselves.'

'Well, I work at Porthian Sands Resort,' Hugo says. 'So, if anyone is looking for somewhere to go for a drink...'

'Okay, okay,' Mike interrupts him. 'Hashtag ad. And what about you, Liv?'

'I'm a comedian,' I reply, with all the confidence of someone who does any other job.

'Go on then, tell us a joke, dazzle us,' Mike insists.

I think for a second.

'What's the best thing about going to Switzerland?' I ask him.

'I don't know, what's the best thing about going to Switzerland?' he replies, practically singing his response – well, everyone knows how to respond to a joke, don't they?

'I don't know either, but the flag is a big plus,' I reply.

Crickets. Nothing but crickets and then...

'Boo,' a man heckles from somewhere else in the room.

I look at Hugo, who is laughing, but I suppose, as my fake fiancé, of course he is. Although he does appreciate my love for telling a bad joke in situations like this.

'Yikes, okay, moving on,' Mike says. 'Oh, by the way, Jeffrey Dahmer called, he wants his glasses back. *That's* a joke.'

Mine was funnier – and mine was awful.

'You get an iPad each – not to keep,' Mike quickly continues, realising a serial killer joke probably isn't the way to go at an events fair in the middle of the day. 'You'll be presented with ten multiple-choice questions. Take your time, take your pick, and then we'll see how many matches you have at the end. Sound good?'

'Sounds great,' Hugo replies.

'Okay then,' Mike says. 'And... go.'

Summer or winter?

It could be easy to choose winter, on a day like today, but it has to be summer. I just love the sunshine, especially in a gorgeous county like Cornwall.

Burger or pizza?

Pizza. Every time. That one is easy.

Tea or coffee?

If I could only drink one, for the rest of my life, it would have to be tea.

Coast or city?

The coast, without a doubt. There's absolutely no contest for me.

Brunch or gym?

Brunch – of course. Would anyone really choose the gym?

Skiing or skinny-dipping?

Ha! Well, not that I think anyone wants to see me naked, it would be less embarrassing than them seeing me attempting to ski. I'd spend more time on my bum than I would on my feet. I would love to go on a skiing holiday, though, I'd just be the girl in the fluffy boots and big hat, sipping hot chocolates by a roaring fire all day.

Valentine's Day or Halloween?

Halloween. It's not that I don't *love* love, but you can't beat spooky season, can you? Romcom movies are a year-round thing for me but, when it comes to flicks like *Hocus Pocus*, watching is an annual thing, with a big bowl of sweets in front of me.

Sunrise or sunset?

Sunset. Not just because I'm never up early enough for a sunrise, but because I just find them so much more beautiful. Plus, there's something so gorgeous about watching the day being put to bed, especially if you've not had a great one.

Comedy or horror?

Oh, comedy, come on. At least this guarantees us one point.

Truth or dare?

Presuming they're not actually going to make us honour this answer, truth, every time. Well, a dare is a dare, you have to do it, and people can tell if you do. Whereas with truth, if it's a question you don't want to answer, you can always lie, and no one can prove that you have. Look at me, Little

Miss Deception, up here with my fake fiancé, acting like I'm Frank Abagnale Jr. from *Catch Me If You Can*, when in reality I keep having these single stress hiccups that I'm having to try to keep a lid on.

'Okay, that's them all,' Mike tells us. 'Go stand over there, with our other lovely couples, and we'll see which couples are the most compatible, and who is through to the next round.'

We take our places on our mark and await the results.

'Unfortunately, one couple has to go and that couple only managed to score – oof – three out of ten. That's not a good look,' Mike says, wincing.

I mean, it had to happen. We were never going to be compatible.

'Sam and Alex, I'm sorry, you're going home,' Mike tells them.

I feel a jolt in my chest. What? No! We're through?

'But Thom and Sandi, Ella and Paul, and Hugo and Liv – you guys are through to round two,' Mike announces excitedly. 'But do you want to know who got the most points? Two of our couples got an impressive six out of ten, with our round leaders scoring a perfect ten out of ten.'

We've got a little bit of a crowd around us now. We all get a few woos.

Look, I'm amazed we managed six, but who cares? We're through.

'Hugo and Liv, congratulations, you two must be perfect for one another, you scored ten out of ten,' Mike informs us. 'And that's not a joke.'

I whip my head to look at Hugo so fast it's a miracle I don't hurt myself. We got top marks? Unbelievable.

He picks me up in his arms and spins me around.

'That's all for today, folks, but be sure to come back for round two, which is much more, shall we say, physical,' Mike announces.

That sounds kind of ominous, but who cares, we won round one! We're a third of the way through. Perhaps we really can do this? God, I really hope we can do this.

16

Last night, inspired by the story of my great-gran and great-granddad, and on a high from not only getting through round one of the competition but scoring the most points too, I sat in my room and wrote a synopsis for a Olivia Knight romcom novel.

Sure, Hugo and I aren't a real couple, but competing with him in a competition for couples, pretending we were together, and just happening to have almost everything in common... I don't know, it's awakened something in me, a sense of excitement, a potentially different understanding of where romance can come from and what it means. I feel inspired in a whole new way, a way that I think is really going to benefit the story I'm going to tell. So many of the romcom novels I ghostwrite feature casts full of ultra-beautiful, super-rich babes who ultimately end up with ultra-beautiful, super-rich hunks, and it's not a necessity, just a tried-and-tested backdrop favoured by the reality stars I write for – who are ultra-beautiful and super-rich themselves. It's what people want. I think that's why I want to write my great-gran and great-granddad's story, because I want to explore a life where the girl doesn't go for the rich guy, she goes for the one who has less, but can give her so much more.

I stop in my tracks and think for a moment. Nah, it's not that deep, it's just a story.

I love the idea of a woman, betrothed to a man who may not be the man of her dreams, but someone she can comfortably settle down with – until, of course, a handsome, penniless dreamboat comes on the scene who is absolutely perfect for her. It reminds me of *Moulin Rouge* – just, you know, without my great-gran being a courtesan, and without the tragic ending. So I have a rough outline of the plot, set here in Porthian Sands – well, the place is known for being a romantic hotspot – and I've broken down each of my characters. Honestly, I'm in love with them already, and I can't wait to write their story. I'm going to send this by my agent first, to see what she thinks, but before I do that, I want to run it past Teddy. I excitedly sent it over to him last night, but I haven't heard anything back yet. I know he's busy, and I know that there's no reason he should have read it already given that it's only the morning after, but the problem is that I've already set the timer rolling, to see if he'll read it, to see how long it takes. We're supposed to be planning our wedding together and he isn't even here, doesn't seem to care on the phone – doesn't seem all that bothered how the day turns out. I swear, I could call him up and (if he answered, obviously) tell him that all the men will be wearing mankinis and the women will be standing on their heads for the ceremony and he would probably just ask where he needed to send the cheque.

Looking back, Teddy has always been like this, but it's never really mattered. I understood that he worked a lot, and I was happy to do my own things whenever he was busy, but this is different because this is our wedding, although, I swear, with the way he talks, he almost makes it sound as if the day is some kind of favour to me. I feel like he could take or leave it and that's just awful. But which Teddy is the real him? The one who makes these grand gestures, who sweeps me off my feet, or the guy who is always working? Because I'm not sure I can marry someone who works all the time. That said, if this is just while he secures his promotion, then I can live with that. Maybe he's just stressed at the moment, and working extra hard, and maybe I'm being harsh... What I do know is that we need to talk about it, but what I don't know is when the hell we're going to get to do that if he *doesn't turn up*, and it only feels like things are getting worse.

Take my future mother-in-law – please, take her – who is currently ticking off her driver for – just let me check my notes – taking a left turn, when she was anticipating a right.

Teddy not only not being here yet, but also thinking that sending his mum in his stead was going to be a good idea, that I would be happy to plan our wedding with her, is frankly one of the craziest things I've ever heard – and I'm the girl who is pretending that she's marrying another man to try to secure an amazing photographer for us, so I know a thing or two about wild ideas.

With a stern look on her face and her arms tightly crossed, Alicia marches to meet me outside the beach house.

Alicia is the kind of woman who knows what she doesn't like, and what she doesn't like is almost everything. She looks up and down, taking in the beach house, before quite literally turning her nose up at it. She looks like she's just caught a bad smell – perhaps it's her attitude.

'Another obnoxious modern monstrosity ruining an otherwise beautiful landscape,' she says by way of a hello.

'Hello, Alicia, how was the journey?' I ask as I lean in to kiss her on the cheek.

'Why don't you ask this ignoramus?' she suggests, nodding towards the sixty-something man who I've seen driving her before. 'One more bump in the road and I would've set fire to his pension fund.'

Oh, wow, she's in a great mood.

'Anyway, I'm here to save this wedding, I suppose,' she announces proudly, but not enthusiastically. 'Edward tells me you're not doing a very good job of planning it – no surprise really, given the, ahem, shotgun-esque urgency.'

Alicia isn't great at the best of times but, my god, without Teddy to keep her in check she's like a Bond villain.

'Alicia, hello,' Eden says brightly as she joins us. 'Lovely to see you. Teddy told me you were coming, and that I should get your room ready for you.'

'Yes, well, we'll see about that,' Alicia replies. 'I've looked into five-star hotels in the area, just in case.'

Oh, how I wish I could leave and go to a five-star hotel instead.

Eden tries to keep her smile firmly in place, despite Alicia's frosty reception. They've met only once before the dressing fitting, I think, at the New Year's Eve party we hosted, and when Alicia found out that Eden did influencing for a living, she laughed and pointed out that it wasn't a job.

We head into the hallway where Alicia's driver places her bags.

'Oh, leave them there,' she tells him. 'I'll have someone competent take them the rest of the way.'

Her driver does as he's told. I don't imagine this is an isolated incident, he seems quite used to it, not that he should be.

'Okay, well, let's go,' Eden says.

Alicia looks around the house with an air of disdain.

'We have a lovely room for you,' Eden tells her. 'I'm sure you'll love it. Teddy said it needed to be south facing, with a king-sized bed or bigger.'

'I suppose it will have to do,' Alicia replies, as though we just told her she was sleeping in one of the wheelie bins.

'Wait, I thought it was a single room we were saving for her?' I can't help but blurt.

'No, of course not,' Eden replies as we walk up the stairs. 'Teddy told me to keep this one for his mum.'

'This room has been up here all this time and I've been sleeping in the worst room downstairs?' I blurt.

'You begrudge me a nice room?' Alicia says. 'Of course you do. No respect. I'll never understand your generation, so entitled.'

'Oh, yeah, us millennials, walking around like we rent the place,' I joke – to absolute silence.

No, it's just that I've been falling asleep to the sound of the toilet next door aggressively chewing up human waste most nights, when I could've been sleeping upstairs. It says it all, that Teddy has insisted we keep this room for Alicia.

The bedroom is gorgeous, with the house's trademark floor-to-ceiling windows, a terrace, a large bed and an en suite that I'll bet delicately sends whatever you flush off to a better place, in silence, where it ultimately turns into rainbows.

'It's not to my taste,' Alicia announces. 'But it will do. A mother dreams about her only son's wedding day. I'm not about to let a powder blue, or anything else, ruin it.'

I love the blue walls. It's such a calming, beachy shade. Although I suppose it's going to take a lot more than a lick of paint to get through to Alicia. I think the beach-themed art and ornaments are fun and cute, but I just saw Alicia shoot a death stare at a decorative life preserver, so there's that.

Does a mother really dream of her only son's wedding? I suppose, for a control freak like Alicia, it doesn't sound out of character. What I need to ensure, at all costs, is that she doesn't take over the wedding planning. I know she's going to try, and that it will all most likely be against my wishes – against Teddy's wishes too, if she believes it is what is best. I'm worried that my big day is going to be a combination of the wedding of Eden's dreams, along with the wedding of Alicia's. Somehow that feels like the least of my problems at the moment.

'So, what are we doing today?' Alicia asks with a sour look on her face.

'Well—'

'Nothing today,' I insist. Eden shoots me a look. 'Alicia, you get settled in, I'll bring you up a cup of tea, enjoy the terrace, explore the area.'

'You're not doing any planning today?' she replies in disbelief. 'Thank goodness I'm here, I can take charge of things.'

'Right, well, we'll go grab you that tea,' I say.

'Only if it's Earl Grey, and only in a china cup,' she calls after us.

Once we're out of earshot, Eden puts her arm on mine, stopping me in my tracks.

'Don't tell me you've forgotten what we're doing today?' she says angrily.

'Of course I haven't,' I reply. 'Food and cake tasting first, checking out a band later. I just don't want Alicia there.'

'No, please, don't let her make any decisions,' Eden insists. 'I thought I was intense with the wedding stuff.'

I smile. It's nice to see her show a little self-awareness.

'Oh, I need your guest list, for the invitations,' she reminds me.

I think for a moment.

'Send yours,' I insist. 'I need to speak to Teddy, before we send ours.'

'Liv, you know we're already cutting it fine,' she reminds me, as though I could have possibly forgotten.

'I know,' I reply. 'But I can't do it until I speak to him – I don't know who he's inviting, don't worry, I'll sort ours.'

'Okay, on your head be it,' she says with a sigh.

Obviously I need to hear from Teddy, to find out who he wants to invite, but more than that, it feels like a way to put the brakes on, just a little, until the two of us have a chance to talk.

If we get a chance to talk. For that to happen, he'll need to pick up his phone or, god forbid, turn up to his own wedding.

17

When Hugo and I played the compatibility game, it was amazing just how much we had in common. Everything I chose, he chose too.

With Eden, today, choosing the food for the wedding – let's just say it's been the opposite of that.

Given how late in the day it is, our options for wedding food were limited. At Porthian Sands Resort, given how many weddings they do, they have two food packages that they offer – they can do more elaborate or specific things but just, you know, not when you only give them a few weeks' notice that you're having a wedding.

So, package A or B was what it came down to, and while package B was the one for me (a buffet with all kinds of delicious-sounding nibbles), Eden was more in favour (read: adamant) of us going with package A. It's not that I don't like what package A is, it's just that it's a large Sunday roast-style meal, and the thought of trying to eat a giant Yorkshire pudding filled with gravy while I'm wearing a white dress sounds like my own personal nightmare. Plus, I don't know about you, but whenever I eat a Sunday roast, all I want to do is put on my baggy trackies and have a nap. I don't want to head out onto the dance floor in a tight dress.

But while grazing on party food sounded like a pretty perfect plan to me, Eden insisted she didn't want something so informal, she wanted a sit-down dinner and, anyway, she doesn't eat much of 'that sort of thing' – one hell of a statement to make about a buffet, which is essentially a selection of all kinds of things. Knowing that I enjoyed a Sunday roast – she's seen me take down enough of them at my parents' house – backed me into a real corner. Package A was, ultimately, the only package we both liked, so my hands were tied.

Now we're at a bakery, luckily only about twenty minutes from Porthian Sands, who have managed to squeeze us in for a cake tasting, and can do us a cake in time for the big day. However, the detail to note in that statement is *a* cake. One cake. Meaning we're going to have to agree on that too.

I never would've given it too much thought, but I suppose when you're dealing with frosting and melted chocolate and all sorts of delicate ingredients, then being situated on the coast can be tricky in summer.

It was so lovely, on a sweltering day like today, to walk into a room with such glorious air conditioning. The cool air feels almost crisp, like it creates a protective shield that the heat couldn't possibly penetrate.

It's so nice to sit down at a table, with a cup of tea I can enjoy at the temperature it is intended to be, without breaking into a sweat. Having a table covered with cake samples isn't exactly a nightmare for me either. I could stay here all day.

Despite the cool air, the bakery is still so cosy and inviting. The room we're in has a pink-painted wooden table in the centre. Around us are shelves and counters covered with brightly coloured cupcakes and various other treats that all look seriously tempting. If I weren't about to take down a series of mini cakes, I would definitely be buying something. I'll have to come back before we go back to London.

The aroma of all the different cakes fills the air and, as the three of us start tasting cakes, each one is more delicious than the last. There's an orange and lemon one, a strawberry and vanilla one, and a triple chocolate one. They're all so light, fluffy and perfectly flavoured. Not too sweet, not too rich. Just right.

Julie is the genius behind these delicious creations and she's potentially even sweeter than her cakes, but in the best possible way. Obviously, anyone who offers me a cup of tea within a few minutes of meeting me is always going to waltz right into my good books. Julie has one of those warm, welcoming smiles, the kind that makes you feel like she gives everyone she meets the opportunity to be her new best friend.

'Finally, we have this one, which is a traditional fruit cake wrapped in white icing,' Julie explains. 'But they can all be decorated in whatever colours you choose.'

'I love a good fruit cake,' Dougie says excitedly.

I laugh.

'Honestly, when we were little, and all the other kids would be asking for a Twix or Penguin, Dougie would prefer one of those little red boxes of raisins,' I tell her.

'I just loved dried fruit,' he explains through a mouthful.

I pull a face.

'I don't really like it at all, even now, as an adult, my palate has just never really adapted to it,' I explain.

Dougie's eyes practically roll into the back of his head.

'Oh, my god, honestly, this is the best cake I've ever had in my life,' he groans. 'Not just the best fruit cake – the best cake hands down.'

Julie smiles proudly.

'I'll bet you say that to all the girls,' she jokes.

'For me it's the chocolate one,' I tell them. 'It's stunning.'

'Well, we're doing three tiers,' Julie says. 'So you could pick a flavour each, even.'

'Oh, no,' Eden says, horrified. 'Don't you know that you're supposed to save the top tier of your cake?'

Julie bats her hand.

'That's just a tradition, not a requirement,' she explains.

'Tradition is important to me,' Eden insists with a huff.

'No offence, babe,' Dougie starts, turning to face his fiancée. 'But if I care about one thing, if I can make one call, this would be it.'

'Let's put it to a vote then,' Eden says. 'It's the only way it's going to be fair.'

'Let me see if I can get Teddy on the phone,' I say, knowing full well I won't be able to.

'Liv, there's no time,' Eden insists. 'You know we've got our dance lesson in half an hour. Are you sure you don't want to join us?'

I hang up because Teddy isn't answering.

'How am I going to join you?' I remind her. 'I don't have anyone to dance with.'

'You could bring someone in his place,' she suggests helpfully. 'But we need to get moving, if we're going to check out the musicians later this afternoon.'

'My vote is for fruit cake,' Dougie says excitedly.

'Mine too,' Eden adds. 'It's traditional and tradition is something that really matters to me.'

What can I say when it's two to one? And when Dougie is clearly so in love with this cake. All of the decisions so far have been all Eden. I love my brother and if he wants a fruit cake then he's getting a fruit cake.

'Well, I was going to say chocolate, but if you two want fruit, then fruit it is,' I say, forcing a smile.

'Fab,' Eden replies, not at all appreciating the gesture I just made. 'Look, if we hurry off to our lesson, can you hang back here and finish making the arrangements, and then get a taxi back to the beach house?'

'Sure,' I reply blankly.

Eden jumps to her feet, grabbing her bag before heading to the door. Dougie isn't far but he pauses briefly to kiss me on the cheek before he goes.

'Thanks,' he tells me.

'You're welcome,' I reply.

Once they're both gone, I sigh.

'It must be tough, having a double wedding,' Julie says softly. 'I've certainly never made a cake for one.'

'I don't recommend it,' I tell her with a laugh, to let her know I'm okay. Is it sad that I'm actually used to it going like this now?

'Listen, I know you said all fruit cake,' Julie starts, lowering her voice. 'But what if I put a secret section of chocolate cake inside the bottom tier? That way, assuming you cut from a side each, theirs will be fruit and yours will be chocolate.'

'Could you really do that?' I reply, my heart fluttering at the thought of a few sneaky pieces of chocolate cake.

'It can be our little secret,' she tells me. 'I'll mark with decorations – I'll let you know. Even if she realises at some point, we'll just say we came up with a compromise after they rushed off.'

'Oh, my gosh, that would be so amazing, thank you,' I tell her sincerely.

Having something – even something as small as a section of the cake – go my way means so much to me.

I've also just realised something. It was when Eden mentioned a vote being the fairest way to decide things. It's not fair that they have two votes between them, whereas I only have one, so I need to level the playing field.

When I turn up to check out this band later, I need to take someone with me. Someone to vote with me. Alicia, obviously. Ha, no, I'm totally kidding. Not Alicia – never Alicia.

I do know someone who would be perfect, though.

18

'Thanks for coming with me,' I tell Hugo.

'Hey, what are fake fiancés for?' he replies.

We arrive at the rehearsal space just in time to watch Eden cooing over a string quartet, playing a song I'm far too lowbrow to recognise. Actually, at the risk of making myself sound even less cultured, I think I recognise this song from the movie *Black Swan*, so I'm guessing it's from *Swan Lake*.

'Is this for walking down the aisle?' Hugo asks me quietly.

'God, I hope so,' I reply.

I know this is going to seem strange but, without Teddy, or even Heidi, I have no one on my side when it comes to making wedding plans. Sure, my mum is doing her best, but she isn't impartial. She loves Dougie just as much as she loves me, so she can't exactly pick a child to vote with.

It's not fair, I'm getting consistently outvoted by Dougie and Eden at every turn. The only way to make this fair is if I have someone here to vote with me, and who has been a better friend to me since I arrived than Hugo?

'You can't go wrong with Tchaikovsky,' Eden announces to us once the song is over.

'Huh, is that what that's called?' Hugo replies. 'I thought it was from *Black Swan*.'

I give him a playful nudge with my elbow.

'Oh, my god, me too,' I say through a giggle.

Eden frowns at us.

'What is he doing here?' she asks us both. 'Are you the one helping her with her share of the wedding planning? Erica mentioned you.'

'That would be me,' Hugo replies with a smile and a slight wave.

'Well, we're making lots of decisions, and Teddy isn't here to vote with me, and you two always vote together, so I realised, okay, Hugo can be Teddy's proxy. He can stand in for him, for picking the band, the songs...'

'You might need him to stand in for Teddy at the altar,' Eden jokes – okay, now that is mean. 'I'm starting to think he's not going to show.'

She says it like it's a joke, but it obviously isn't.

'I think I draw my line at party planning,' Hugo insists. 'I love the music, these guys are great.'

'Yes, thank you,' she replies, finally feeling appreciated.

'That was gorgeous,' I agree. 'I think they'll be perfect for the ceremonies.'

'I'm thinking of the reception too,' Eden says. 'For ambience with a touch of class.'

'Do they do something you can dance to?' Dougie asks her quietly.

'A bit of Mozart always goes down a treat,' she replies.

'Yeah, in *Bridgerton*,' I say under my breath.

'I suppose you still want some tacky covers band?' Eden says. 'Something we can all get drunk to and then take turns at holding each other's hair back while a drunk dad bellows the words to "Livin' on a Prayer"?'

That's exactly what I want, yes, and I can tell by the look in Dougie's eyes that he wants it too, but there is no way he's going to side with me over Eden, his life wouldn't be worth living.

'We want something fun,' I say tactfully.

'No, you want something tacky,' Eden replies. 'You all keep harping on about a disco.'

'Eden's right, you want something classy,' Hugo says.

Wait, Hugo said that? He's supposed to be on my side.

Eden looks confused.

'Right,' she says. I don't think she was expecting him to agree with her.

'I think you're both right, these guys will be perfect for the ceremonies, but I know a band who will be even more perfect for the reception,' he continues. 'They do a lot of weddings at the hotel, they're really in demand. They're a folk band – seriously cool with a double bass, a box drum, the works – who do these great twists on contemporary tunes.'

'And you say lots of people who marry at the hotel use them?' she asks curiously.

'Oh, they're always booked up,' Hugo replies. 'Anyone who is anyone wants them.'

'Would we even be able to get them?' Eden asks. Suddenly, because she thinks she can't have something, she wants it. 'How do I know I'll even like them?'

'They're playing at the hotel tomorrow night,' Hugo says. 'They're doing a set in the bar. I could get you in, if you want? They're close friends of mine, I'm sure I could sweet-talk them into playing at your wedding.'

'We're willing to check them out,' Eden says. 'And we'll book these guys for the ceremony. Thank you, Hugo, you've been a big help.'

It takes everything I have to keep my smile under wraps.

Eden and Dougie head over to make the arrangements. I hang back with Hugo.

'You know that's exactly the kind of band I want, right?' I say quietly, barely moving my lips because I'm so worried that if Eden sees how happy I am, she will think she's making a mistake.

'I do,' he replies.

'You made it sound like something she wanted,' I point out. 'Are they really playing at the hotel tomorrow?'

'They are my friends, so they will be when I call to ask them,' he replies with a smile. 'Don't worry, I know a man with a bar. Sneaky high five?'

Hugo, so proud of himself, subtly extends his arm and briefly hook his index finger with mine. We squeeze each other subtly before letting go.

'So, we're going to a gig tomorrow night then,' I say.

'We are,' he replies. 'They're really great, I'm sure Eden and Dougie will love them. You will too. Trust me, they're exactly what you want.'

Why does it seem like Hugo is the only man on this planet who truly knows what that is?

19

Who was it who said absence makes the heart grow fonder? Because, oh, how wrong they are.

I know a few jokes have been made here and there about whether or not Teddy is going to show up for this wedding but, honestly, the longer he stays away, the more I have my doubts, and it's not just that I've been here on my own for days trying to plan our wedding – in all the worst possible circumstances – but the fact that his latest tactic is radio silence. Okay, okay, we all get it, you're busy. But he'd better have one hell of a good explanation for going so quiet on me.

Am I doing the right thing? Am I really? Teddy and I haven't been together that long. When he asked, I was over the moon – of course I said yes – but thinking about it now, it seemed like the only choices I had were yes (and we get married) or no (and our relationship ends). I suppose what we really needed was something in the middle, a yes (but not right now). I know Teddy was keen to tie the knot ASAP, and I really didn't want to miss my chance to get married here, but now I'm starting to worry that we're rushing into it.

I need to see him, to speak to him, to know that he does want to marry me, that this wedding is important to him, and not only that he loves me, but that he loves me more than he loves his job. It isn't that this promotion isn't allowed to be important to him, it's just that, if it feels like it's more important than me, and that's making me feel bad, then we have a big problem on our hands.

I find it difficult being in the house. Not just because Eden, Joanne and now Alicia have been driving me crazy, but because I'm starting to feel jealous. Imagine having a big house like this, all your family around you, everyone excitedly preparing for your wedding, and you and your partner being at the centre of all of it. I so, so wish Teddy and I were getting to enjoy this properly. I just feel like some saddo on the sidelines, watching other people get their happy ever after, and all the while I'm just riding their coattails, trying my best to scrounge a little happiness for myself.

I just feel so bad whenever I'm around the others, and whenever we're talking about the wedding. I shouldn't feel like this.

The times when I don't feel totally miserable about the whole thing are when I am with Hugo. He's just so great, he's being helpful, he's a good distraction because he's just so much fun, and truthfully, he is the only person who is making sure that this wedding – my wedding – is how I want it to be. He's helping me with the photographer, the band – and it's not just wedding stuff, oh no. It's my career too. He's so enthusiastic, so invested in what I'm doing already, and we haven't even known each other that long. We're new friends and he's doing all this for me – Teddy is going to be my husband in, what, a week! And he doesn't care about any of that stuff.

Of course, comparing Teddy and Hugo is a terrible idea, because Hugo might be a dream of a man on paper, but Teddy is the one I'm engaged to, who I'm supposed to be marrying. Now isn't the time to start measuring him against other people, not when I was so happy with him before all of this.

I was happy, wasn't I?

I shake off the thoughts I'm having and focus on the task at hand. In an attempt to escape everyone in the beach house, I slipped out the front door and now I'm at the hot tub, trying to make it work. Who knew these things had so many buttons?

Hugo isn't home, the cottage is in darkness apart from the lights outside. I did kind of hope I would bump into him, just for some company, because his friendly face is one of the few I'm enjoying being around at the moment.

'Don't tell me you're about to get in?' a familiar voice asks.

I turn around and see Dougie, standing there in his trunks, clutching a towel.

'I was going to, if I could get the damn thing to work,' I reply.

'It's been years since we had to take baths together,' he jokes. 'I'm not about to start again now.'

'Erm, I think you'll find I'm the one who is traumatised by our shared bath times when we were little,' I insist. 'You were the one who used to shi—'

'Hi,' Hugo says with a laugh. 'Are you guys trying to get the hot tub working?'

'I am trying and failing,' I reply.

Hugo walks over and pushes a few buttons to make the lights and the jets kick in.

'There we are,' he says.

'Well, I was here first,' I point out. 'So you could come back later.'

'There's room for at least six people,' Hugo points out.

'Yeah, I think we're both a bit traumatised from when our mum used to make us take baths together when we were toddlers,' Dougie explains. 'And who used to do what in the water.'

'Absolutely, without a doubt, that was all you,' I insist as we bicker like we used to when we were teenagers. 'And Mum will back me up on that.'

'Hugo, mate, do you want to join us?' Dougie asks him.

'Oh, I don't want to impose,' he replies.

'We're technically in your cottage garden,' I point out.

'Yeah, but the hot tub is for guests,' Hugo replies.

'Come on, you're a friend of the family now,' Dougie tells him with a laugh. 'I really appreciate you finding a possible solution to our wedding band problem, I had no idea how I was going to get through this decision without one of the brides killing me. You're definitely invited to the wedding and you can certainly hop in the hot tub with me and my sister to make it less awkward. I promise you, we're both toilet-trained now. You can tell us more about this band, arm us with info so we can persuade Eden it's a good idea. I do really, really want it to be a proper party, with everyone up singing and dancing.'

Hugo laughs.

'Go on then,' Hugo says. 'Why not? I'll grab my shorts.'

He disappears inside the cottage so I take this as my cue to slip off my T-shirt dress and hop in. I don't know why, but the thought of Hugo seeing me in my bikini freaks me out.

'Oof, it's warm,' I say. 'It might actually need turning down.'

'I've never been in one before,' Dougie says as he climbs in opposite me. 'Bloody hell, that is warm.'

A few minutes later, Hugo returns in his swimming shorts. He places a towel down on the table next to us and climbs in.

'I wish I could say this was the first time guests had asked me to join them in here,' Hugo tells us through a playful wince. 'We had a hen party slip through the net and, wow, they were a friendly bunch.'

'Oh, I can imagine you going down a storm with a hen party,' I reply. 'I can't say that I'm sad I'm not having one.'

'Are you not having a stag do?' Hugo asks Dougie. 'I'd be happy to organise you something in the bar.'

Dougie doesn't reply.

'Are you okay, Doug?' I ask him.

In an attempt to avoid accidentally staring at Hugo's body, I've made eye contact with my brother and he's looking a little green.

'Is it normal to feel so sick?' Dougie asks.

'It's a bit warm,' Hugo replies. 'I'll turn it down.'

'I think I'm going to throw up,' Dougie announces.

'Oh, so much for no bodily fluids in the water,' I tease him.

Wow, he really doesn't look well, though.

'Nope, this isn't for me, sorry, guys,' Dougie says as he clambers out. 'I need some water and a lie-down.'

I'm sure he's fine, just overheated. Dougie has never had much tolerance for heat. He's the kind of guy who spends more time outdoors in the winter than he does in the summer.

'I guess they're not for everyone,' I say. I adjust, making myself more comfortable. 'I think it's glorious.'

'Yeah, I love it,' Hugo adds. 'So relaxing – I will turn it down though, it is a bit warm. Sorry, can I just...'

Hugo reaches past me to reach the controls. As he does so, we are briefly face to face, his body pressed on mine. It takes one last stretch to hit the right button and now his abs are in front of my face, water cascading down them like a sexy waterfall.

'There we go,' he says, returning to his spot next to me. 'How's that?'

'Gorgeous,' I reply. 'This place is unreal, isn't it? I mean, the whole place is amazing, the beach house is stunning, but this spot right here... wow.'

We're both sitting on the side of the hot tub that backs on to the house, facing out to sea. We're essentially on the top of a cliff, so high up that you can't see the beach below, it's just the sea and then the sky. The water only looks like it's moving ever so slightly from all the way up here, but it pings light off it like a mirror. Above it, the night sky looks so smooth and full of stars.

'It's like looking at a painting,' I say.

'I love it,' Hugo replies. 'Honestly, the view never gets old. I visited here with my mum, the year before she died, and she fell in love with the place. We stayed in the beach house – this is before it was renovated – just the two of us. We knew we were, you know, making memories at this point. Now this place just makes me think of her. In a good way, though. Bad memories in the family home tried to push the good ones out but, here, the two of us just living it up... Here it's nothing but happy.'

'That's a really nice way to look at it,' I reply. 'There really is something special about this place – I'm so jealous you get to live here. My granddad actually built part of the hotel, and he and my gran got married here shortly after. We always joke that he built it for her. But that's why getting married here means so much to me, and to Dougie, it's a strange family tradition.'

'Something about this place just feels like home, doesn't it?' he replies. 'I'm glad you're getting married here. It sounds like that means a lot to you, I totally get it, so I'm happy for you that your wish is coming true.'

I purse my lips and nod in acknowledgement as I glance at Hugo. God, it's like he's looking straight through me, and he can't just see my secrets, he can see what I'm thinking in real time.

'So, it looks like I'm invited to your wedding,' he tells me, clearly making one last attempt at keeping things bright – which only goes to prove my point because that's exactly what I want him to do.

'Yes,' I say with an awkward laugh. 'I don't know why it hadn't yet occurred to me to invite you, given how hands-on you've been with the planning. You don't have to come though, don't worry about it.'

'Oh, no, I'd love to be there,' he replies.

'That makes one of us,' I say under my breath – I don't mean to say it at all, but the words leave my lips before I can hold them back.

'Liv, you can tell me to mind my own business, but is everything okay?' Hugo asks. 'You seem like there's something on your mind.'

'I'm not sure I want to get married,' I blurt. I say it so quietly, almost as though I'm too scared to let it out, but at the same time I can't keep it in any more.

'At all, or like this?' Hugo asks.

'I don't think I want to marry Teddy,' I confess. 'I don't think we want the same things. I've always known that his work was important to him – and that he's working for some big promotion that he tells me absolutely nothing about – but up until now, it's never been a case of him having to choose between work or me. This week, he's had to make that choice every day, and every single time, he's chosen work. I haven't even heard from him today. I sent him my synopsis and I doubt he's even read it.'

'Hey, it's okay,' Hugo reassures me.

I can feel myself getting more and more upset. This issue isn't only the problems that I'm having, it's the fact I've been bottling them up for so long, with no one to talk to, and now Hugo is here, and he's impartial and he's willing to listen.

'Try not to focus on what you don't want,' he tells me softly. 'Why don't you talk to me about what you do want? What do you want out of life? What do you see in your future?'

I sigh.

'I want to live in a place like this,' I confess. 'Here on the coast, I mean. In Porthian Sands. You're right, something about here does just feel like home. Obviously I would love to live in the beach house, or one like it, because who doesn't want to live in a big house? I want to live small, though. I want quiet days, walks on the beach, I want to cook – I'm not even that good at it, but I'd learn. I want to write books – my own books. I'm sick of sucking up to casting directors and I've had enough of trying to impress crowds. I've had enough of trying to impress *everyone*. I just want to feel happy and loved and like I'm enough. I want to be with someone who loves me more than they love their job. Someone who doesn't just want to be married to me, they want to marry me, to plan our wedding and make it something truly special.'

'That sounds like a pretty great life to me,' he agrees with a smile.

'Then why isn't it enough for Teddy?' I ask him, not that I expect him to answer. As my voice crackles, tears prick my eyes. Good lord, I'm crying in a hot tub with a handsome man.

I feel Hugo's hand find mine under the water. He holds it and rubs it lightly.

'We only get to do all of this once,' he tells me. 'Only you know who you want to do it with.'

My entire body stiffens.

'Teddy,' I say.

Hugo's eyes widen but then he realises I'm looking past him. He follows my gaze.

'Hello,' Teddy says flatly.

He's standing next to the hot tub, wearing a black suit, holding a bunch of roses by his side.

'Oh, my god, Teddy, you're here,' I say.

Hugo is still holding my hand under the water – thankfully hidden by the bubbles. I quickly whip it away from him and stand up.

It turns out there really is no graceful way to get out of a hot tub in a situation like this. Can anyone look good getting out of water? I know, Daniel Craig made it look so easy in *Casino Royale*, but my waterlogged bikini feels heavy, like it's going to fall off, and despite the floor of the hot tub being designed to not be slippery, I feel like I'm on ice.

I climb out and go to hug Teddy. He stops me and I just freeze on the spot.

Eventually he smiles.

'Dry yourself first,' he tells me. 'Come on, respect the Tom Ford.'

'Gosh, sorry,' I say with a smile.

I turn around and grab a towel.

'Who's this then?' Teddy asks.

'This is Hugo,' I reply. 'Hugo, this is Teddy. Hugo works at the hotel and lives here in the cottage. He's been a huge help with the wedding prep.'

'Yeah?' Teddy says.

'Oh, just small things,' Hugo insists, a little embarrassed but at the same time his usual friendly self.

'Dougie and I were just doing some last-minute prep with him,' I explain. 'He's sorted a band for us to go and see tomorrow. They might be perfect for the wedding – even Eden likes them. Now that you're here, you can check them out too.'

'A late-night wedding prep meeting, in swimwear, and no sign of Dougie,' Teddy says with a laugh. 'You're lucky I trust you. And you, Hugo, are you asking for trouble?'

'Wh-what?' Hugo replies, just about keeping his cool.

'You've left your front door open,' Teddy tells him, nodding towards the cottage.

'Oh, thanks, mate,' Hugo replies. 'I've hit my limit in here anyway, I'll head in. But I'll see you both at the gig tomorrow.'

'Actually, you won't,' Teddy tells him curtly. 'We've got plans.'

'We've got plans?' I reply.

'Yep, get yourself inside and get dressed – there's a helicopter waiting, to take us back to London,' he explains.

I stare at him.

'Don't worry, we'll be back for the wedding,' he says with a laugh. 'But it's a surprise, now come on.'

'See you later,' Hugo says, his back to us as he heads for his cottage.

'What's this surprise?' I ask Teddy, a big smile on my face, although it isn't coming easy.

'You'll just have to wait and see, won't you?' he tells me. 'I'm not telling you until you clean up and we're against the clock so come on, chop-chop.'

I tighten my towel around my body as we head back down towards the house.

I feel so guilty. I know, I wasn't doing anything wrong with Hugo, even if it might have looked a little bad to Teddy – I'd be freaked out too, if I'd found him alone in a hot tub with a girl, but once Dougie confirms that he was with us until he left because he felt sick, I'm sure that will be fine.

The real reason I feel so bad isn't because of what I was doing, it's because of what I was saying. I was sitting there talking about how I didn't want to marry him. And now here he is, in a suit, with flowers, with some kind of helicopter surprise which just sounds out of this world. Yes, he's been absent, and I've hardly heard a peep from him, but was that just temporary? Is it all over now?

I want to give him the benefit of the doubt – I *should* give him the benefit of the doubt – but now that the genie is out of the bottle, I don't know how to put it back in. With doubts like this, I don't think I should be marrying Teddy – not in a week, anyway.

I'll see how things go, now that we're in the same county again, and try and find the right time to talk to him. If he's different, if things feel better, then maybe I'll change my mind again, but I need to make sure we're on the same page.

It's like Hugo said: we only get to do all this once. I have to do what's right for me.

20

I've always wondered what it would be like to fly in a helicopter. I imagined it being cool, exciting, maybe even kind of scary.

When Teddy mentioned we were going to be flying in one, for some kind of surprise, I felt bad because suddenly he seemed like the Teddy I first met, the one who charmed me, who went out of his way to dazzle me. I got excited for the surprise, hopeful that this might be a turning point, that I would feel the way I used to again, and that Teddy would be putting me first from now on.

I had no idea what to expect from this surprise. I got dressed and I packed an overnight bag, just like he told me, my excitement growing, my imagination racing.

Of all the things I thought about, I tell you what didn't cross my mind: that Alicia would be joining us.

So, here we are, it's my first time in a helicopter, for my big surprise, with my husband-to-be, and I'm sandwiched between him and his mum. Obviously, the two of them, who have flown in helicopters multiple times, are both taking the window seats.

'Come on then, don't keep us in suspense,' Alicia says. 'What's this big surprise?'

Of course, it's a joint surprise. For me and his mother. Just... fantastic.

'My big surprise is... Grandmother has finally said it, she's stepping aside and yours truly is taking over,' he announces. 'She's throwing me a big party in London tomorrow night.'

I adjust my headset just to make sure I'm hearing that right. His big surprise is that he got his promotion. He's flying me away from my wedding – that he has done nothing real to organise – so that I can attend a party for him.

'And obviously I had to have my two favourite girls, my mother and my fiancée, there,' he adds.

A party where I'm practically reduced to being an accessory too.

'Oh, darling, that's fantastic news,' Alicia says. Her elbows hurt me as she leans over me to give Teddy a kiss. 'I did have my suspicions – your grandmother may have mentioned something.'

And I'm last to know, as always.

'Congratulations,' I tell him. 'That's amazing. It's everything you always wanted.'

'Yeah, I can die a happy man now,' he announces proudly. 'Not that I want to – keep flying safe, my man.'

Teddy cackles at his own joke to the pilot.

I don't know what else to say. Don't think I didn't notice that he's more than happy to die before he's married me. That's clearly not up there with this promotion.

'We're getting dropped at the hotel and I am knackered,' he tells us. 'I have meetings from pretty much first thing until the party starts, but I've arranged for you ladies to be pampered all day. Spa, hair, make-up – the works. Liv, if you're careful, some of it might last until the wedding.'

'Yeah, I'll sleep sitting up,' I joke – then I realise he isn't kidding and my face falls. Not just because he isn't joking but also because, if he's in meetings all day tomorrow, then that confirms my worst suspicions, that this promotion is going to mean more work, not less.

'Oh, I do have a surprise for just you, though,' he tells me. 'Just a small one.'

I smile as he reaches around in his pocket. Eventually he pulls out a ring box.

'Ah, my ring,' I say as brightly as I can.

'Here it is, the correct size...' Teddy takes it out of the box before he takes my hand and puts it on my finger. My face must say it all.

'Come on, why do you look so miserable?' he asks me. 'It's the right size now.'

'It's the right size but it's the wrong ring,' I tell him.

He frowns at me.

'What?'

'Teddy, that's not my ring,' I tell him. 'That's not the ring you gave me.'

'Are you sure?' he asks. 'It looks pretty similar.'

'It does look similar but, if it's all the same, I'd rather not wear *someone else's* ring,' I tell him, unable to hide my snippiness.

He examines it for a second before popping it back in its box, and the box back in his pocket.

'Well, we're going to be in London anyway,' he says. 'And you're right, we should get it swapped, even if it fits, this one might be worth less.'

'And the one you picked was so much nicer, darling,' Alicia somehow compliments him.

'Oh, yeah, big time,' he replies.

That's rich, coming from a man who didn't even realise he'd picked up the wrong ring.

I look down at my feet, unsure what to say.

Look, I'm here, I'm in the helicopter, I'm making the effort. I've been doing nothing but make an effort all this time, whereas Teddy just seems like he cares less and less each day. But it just doesn't make sense, if he's this unbothered by all of it, why is he so desperate to marry me? Right now, it doesn't feel like he's bothered about wanting to marry me, and I'm seriously doubting my feelings for him, so that only leaves one question: what the hell am I doing here in this helicopter?

21

Teddy's grandmother, Anne, has a house like a stately home – one that has been hidden away inside an eight-bed terrace. No, sorry, it's not a terrace, it's a semi, because Grandmother wanted it to be, so she bought out her neighbours and somehow (I'd guess: money) got permission to knock through. She'll buy out the last house when she can, I'm sure of it. She's probably just waiting for someone to die.

If having eight bedrooms and being situated in Mayfair doesn't give you enough of an idea of just how grand this house is, then allow me to point out, on our way into the Grade II-listed building, that it has a blue plaque on it. I swear, this must be the world's most expensive semi.

I've only been here once before and yet I have been told multiple times all about how the house boasts so many of its original features – of course, being me, I can't say that I know what any of them are.

The hallway is bigger than my flat, with ceilings twice the height. It's magnificent, truly, and yet it barely does anything to prepare you for the rooms beyond it.

Anne lives here alone – well, unless you count staff, which I'm sure she doesn't. Alicia doesn't live too far from here either, which begs the question, why are we staying in a hotel? It's also worth remembering that, even if my flat in Camden is too much of a trek, Teddy's apartment isn't exactly far from here. I would've much preferred a night in my own bed, or even Teddy's. It wasn't even like I noticed he was there, he fell asleep almost right away, too tired to talk wedding apparently, and he was gone before I woke up this morning.

I suppose when you have a house like this, in the city, why would you hire anywhere to throw a party? The last time I was here was for Anne's birthday, and I couldn't even begin to guess how many people were in attendance. A lot, obviously, and I know it was Anne's birthday, so she was understandably very busy, but I only got five minutes with the woman herself. You know me, it was just enough time to fail to impress her with my job, then for me to put the final nail in the coffin when the man next to her asked me to tell a joke, and my purposefully naff joke went down like a lead balloon. If you're interested... why do ants never get ill? Because they have anty-bodies. It really is amazing I don't get more work.

The reception rooms are only divided by large open arches, making downstairs (in this wing, or whatever you would call it) a massive space for parties. There are so many people here, it's hard to take in any real detail about the room, so I'm making all my assumptions on its grandeur exclusively on things I can see by looking up, like the ornate coving and the chandeliers.

Eventually I spot Teddy, who had to be here early for a pre-party meeting with *someone* (work details are always vague), which meant I had to take a taxi here alone. He and Anne are talking to a group of men, so I make my way over, shuffling carefully in the floor-length black silk gown Teddy had waiting at the hotel for me when I arrived. I wait for a pause in the conversation before I speak.

'Hello,' I say brightly.

Anne looks at me, raises her eyebrows, then looks at Teddy expectantly. My best guess is either that she's wondering 'What is *she* doing here?' or, potentially even more likely, 'Who is this?'

'Olivia, hello,' Teddy says as he steps forward to greet me with a kiss. 'Everyone, this is my fiancée, Olivia, the one who is finally going to make an honest man of me next week – well, in all ways apart from business.'

The men cackle and Teddy laughs a laugh I've never heard before.

'Oh, of course, the comedian,' Anne points out.

You've got to be impressed by anyone who can intend to offend you simply by repeating a fact back to you.

'The very same,' I say with a smile.

'Go on then, tell us a joke,' one of the men says.

Don't do it, don't do it...

'Did you hear about the Italian chef who died?' I ask, borrowing Hugo's hilariously terrible joke.

An especially camp man who just happens to be passing us, his arm linked with his wife, stops dead in his tracks, grinding them both to a halt.

'Not Arturo Bedacholli?' he practically cries. 'I wondered where he was.'

'Oh, no, sorry, it's just a joke,' I quickly tell him.

The man doesn't find it funny – I mean, it really needs the punchline for that.

'Anyway, when is this wedding?' Anne asks.

It's her only grandson's wedding, surely she must be counting down the days.

'The eighth,' Teddy tells her.

'I am so sorry I can't make it,' she replies. 'But you can expect a fat congratulations cheque, of course.'

'You can't make it?' I say, wounded on Teddy's behalf.

'Yes, well, now that I've relieved myself of many of my duties, I plan to take a little time off,' Anne explains. 'I'm going to the house in Malibu, I've earned the break.'

'You certainly have,' Teddy insists. 'Don't worry about it.'

It's hard to tell if he's just trying not to make her feel bad or if he's genuinely indifferent about whether or not his only living grandparent attends his wedding.

'Let's see this ring then,' Anne says. 'My grandson *usually* has excellent taste.'

I hold my bare hand to my body self-consciously.

'It's getting altered,' Teddy tells her.

'So close to the wedding, Edward,' she points out. 'I would say I hope I'm not working you too hard, but it's all downhill from here, excuse me.'

Anne doesn't even pause for breath before she excuses herself and walks off. That was actually quite impressive, I should work on how to do that, just float out of awkward situations before anyone even realises you've gone.

'Can you track us down some drinks?' Teddy says when it's just the two of us. 'I've got more schmoozing to do, but catch me up. I know Grandmother is keen for everyone to get to know us as a couple.'

Ha! Must be a different grandmother.

'You get to play the supportive missus now,' he teases. 'Bubbles has invited us on a hunting weekend with him and his wife, with some other big shots.'

'Hunting?' I squeak back.

'Don't worry,' he says with a laugh. 'The women don't hunt, they get facials and drink wine, or whatever it is women do when their husbands aren't around. We're in the big leagues now. Isn't that great?'

It's not great. It's not great at all. I don't want to go on hunting weekends instigated by grown men who go by the name Bubbles, banished indoors with all the other wives, drinking wine to make it all go faster.

Why does everything feel so, so awful all of a sudden? It's like I'm finally getting to see the real Teddy – a version of someone I once loved, who has realised his dream and changed so suddenly, although perhaps that's on me, perhaps the signs he wasn't right for me were there all along, and I was making excuses, laughing things off, thinking he would turn out different to the rest of his family.

I'm sure I should be upset that Anne doesn't seem to care about my existence, and that Alicia clearly isn't my biggest fan, but I'd never held that against Teddy. I'm sure we all dream of wonderful in-laws who give us these beautiful second families, but I suppose that's not realistic, is it? We love our own families, in spite of their flaws, because they're family. With in-laws, without that genetic obligation, how do you put aside those differences and just love one another?

I never would've held Teddy's family against him but, suddenly, he doesn't seem so different from them.

It takes me a while to get through the room, order us a couple of drinks, and make my way back through the crowd.

I've got an orange juice in one hand and a Scotch on the rocks in the other. Everyone here is in good spirits, so I clutch them carefully as I make my way back through the crowd.

I almost don't spot Teddy. I suppose it's because I'm not expecting him to be talking to a couple with Verity not only by his side, but he has his hand on the small of her back. Teddy is truly in his element, gesturing wildly with his free hand while he tells some kind of anecdote I'm sure he's probably never told me before. Verity bats the air and throws her head back while she laughs at his jokes. They look – and I don't say this as a compliment – great together. Verity very much looks and plays the part – a part I just can't see myself in.

Teddy spots me out of the corner of his eye.

'Here she is, my wife-to-be,' he announces, withdrawing his hand from Verity's back to welcome me in.

I smile at the two people I've never met before as I hand Teddy his drink.

'Hello,' I say, putting my game face on.

'Babe, this is Lucas, he works at Optecho, and his wife Anya, who is the creative director at ABO,' Teddy tells me. 'And this is Olivia, my wife-to-be.'

Optecho is a tech giant and ABO is one of the online fast fashion giants. These two people are clearly far, far more impressive than I am. I can't wait to dazzle them with a knock-knock joke.

'Congratulations,' Anya says. 'When is the big day? Let's see the ring!'

'It's being resized,' I explain.

'The eighth of July,' Teddy quickly adds, almost talking over me. 'So not long to go now.'

He wraps his arm around me and gives me a squeeze.

'We're tying the knot in Cornwall,' he says. 'Beautiful place on the beach.'

'How marvellous,' Anya replies. 'Do you have family there, Olivia?'

'Well, my grandparents were from there,' I reply. 'But my granddad helped to build part of the hotel where we're having the wedding, so the place means a lot to us.'

'Excuse me for one moment,' Verity says before leaving the four of us to it.

'Watch this one,' Lucas warns Teddy. 'She'll have you moving out there.'

Teddy laughs.

'I can't see that, somehow,' he replies. 'We're both definitely Londoners. Just between us, with Grandmother moving to Malibu for an extended break, we're going to be living here.'

'*We* are?' I can't help but blurt.

'Yes, isn't that amazing?' he replies. 'Just until we find our own Mayfair pad, of course, although I'm sure it will seem small after living here for a year or so. It's great, though, it means we can start a family, bring our kids up somewhere half-decent.'

Honestly, it's like I'm watching a stranger talk, not just because Teddy doesn't sound like himself, but because he doesn't sound like he knows me. None of that is what I want – and he's made the arrangements without even asking me.

'It was supposed to be a sort of wedding surprise,' Teddy tells me. 'But we're nearly married, so there you go, get excited.'

'Do you work?' Anya asks me as though she's expecting me to say no. I would be expecting me to say no too, after hearing that I'm about to be turned into a mass-producing Mayfair mummy.

'She does,' Teddy replies. 'Olivia writes books for the rich and famous.'

'Oh, how wonderful,' Anya replies.

'Well, I used to,' I add. 'I'm writing my own now.'

'Your first?' Lucas asks me.

'My first romcom novel under my name,' I reply.

'Ah, so they're fiction,' he replies. 'And you're writing a romance novel.'

'My first to be published under my *own* name,' I point out again.

Oh, the look on Lucas's face is priceless. It's as though I just confirmed to him that I am not a serious person, I'm just another unpublished novelist whimsically trying to churn out a book that will probably never get finished.

It's funny, they're more embarrassed than I am – I'm not embarrassed at all, but they clearly feel bad for me.

'Teddy, can I have a word with you?' I ask him.

'Sure,' he replies. 'Be right back, guys.'

I usher Teddy into the hallway but it's wall-to-wall people, each little cluster seemingly making more noise than the next.

'I'm not feeling great,' I tell him.

There's a very tall, very loud man standing next to us in absolute stitches over something. I dream of getting laughs like that.

'In here,' Teddy insists, ushering me into a room.

Once we're inside the bathroom together, he locks the door.

'It's crazy, isn't it?' he says proudly. 'Everyone here to celebrate me. It's been a whirlwind. Sorry, I feel like we've hardly spoken.'

'Yeah, it's been mad,' I reply. 'I'm really not feeling great. All I want to do is go somewhere quiet, get out of this dress, and just talk about everything with you.'

'Babe, I'm sorry you're not feeling well,' he says softly, placing his hand on the back of my head, rubbing it gently. 'Do you want to get out of here?'

'Yes,' I say happily. I release air from my lungs with a huge sigh of relief, not just because we need to talk, but because this is the Teddy I fell for. Perhaps all of that out there is an act and my Teddy is this sweet guy here, rubbing my head, willing to bail on his own party to make me feel better.

'I can sort you a taxi to the hotel,' he replies. 'I'll try to make sure I'm not too late in – or that I'm quiet, if I am.'

My relief lasts for about eight seconds.

'What, what's the matter?' he asks me. My silence must speak volumes. 'Do you expect me to leave too? Liv, this party is for me, this is my moment, please don't spoil it.'

'Oh, well, I wouldn't want to spoil it,' I reply.

'It's starting to feel like you do,' he says, sounding annoyed. He takes back his hand.

'What do you mean?' I ask.

'Why are you telling people you're a wannabe romance novelist?' he asks.

I raise my eyebrows.

'I mean, there's nothing wrong with that, but I'm telling people the truth,' I explain. 'That I'm going to write my own book.'

'It just sounds silly,' he replies. 'Not like a real job. Honestly, these people will respect you more if you tell them you're just a housewife.'

'Lucky I'm not trying to impress them then,' I point out.

'Well, perhaps you should,' he insists. 'You're not coming across well.

Here you are, wanting to leave, you're not seeming very supportive of me, you're not sounding like you're excited for this wedding at all.'

'You're one to talk,' I tell him.

I pause. Now isn't the time for this conversation. I'm not going to talk about our future on the night of his party. Emotions are running high, he's obviously had a few drinks, I just need to walk things back.

'I don't want to leave,' I insist. 'Let's just enjoy the party, this is all silly.'

'You're right, you're right,' he says. 'But do me one favour.'

Teddy takes the ring box from his pocket and pulls out the ring – the wrong ring – again.

'Can you just wear this please?' he asks. 'Everyone is asking to see the ring and it's starting to get a bit embarrassing.'

'I'm not wearing someone else's ring,' I say with a snort.

'Come on,' Teddy says, taking my hand.

'This is ridiculous,' I say, trying to snatch it back, but he manages to put the ring on my finger. 'Teddy, it doesn't even fit, look, it's too big.'

'Sorry,' he says, suddenly sounding so vulnerable. 'I've just missed you. I've been so busy, you've got to enjoy our engagement and the wedding planning but I've been stuck here when all I've wanted is to be with you. I'm sorry.'

'I've already told you a bunch of times that all I wanted was for you to be at the beach house too, celebrating with me, planning our wedding together,' I reply.

'I'm sorry,' he says again. 'I've just missed you. I've missed you so much.'

Teddy leans in to kiss me. His pecks quickly turn into something more passionate. Next thing I know, he's pushing me up against the wall.

'Oi, come on,' I insist with an awkward laugh as Teddy moves to kiss my neck.

'I want you so bad,' he whispers into my ear.

'We're not doing this in your grandmother's bathroom,' I say, trying to laugh off his advances.

'It'll be fun,' he insists. 'Naughty too. Anyone could hear us.'

Teddy presses his body up against me. He doesn't even feel that into it, as far as I can tell, and maybe it's because I'm questioning my feelings for him, but his hands and his kisses just feel irritating. I almost feel a little panicky.

'Teddy, I said no,' I insist, pushing him back a little.

As he stumbles backwards, he grabs me to steady himself. I grab the sink next to me so that I don't fall with him. As I do, the loosely fitting engagement ring that doesn't belong to me slips off my finger. It almost happens in slow motion, as I watch it slide down the sink and fall straight into the plughole. Now, this is an original feature in the house, with its large open plughole, and a pipe that leads to god knows where.

'Oh, shit,' Teddy says. 'Shit, how are we going to get it back out? Oh, god, they're probably going to need a specialist to retrieve it.'

I know I said earlier that this house might be the world's most expensive semi but, after what's just happened, I think Teddy's might be a close second.

Losing some poor stranger's ring in Anne's bathroom that is practically a piece of history, I bet Teddy is probably regretting putting the moves on me now, don't you?

22

I know I was complaining about Alicia being in the helicopter on the way to London but, on the way back, I'm kind of glad she's there, not because she's being any nicer to be around, but because things are so awkward between me and Teddy today.

We haven't had a chance to talk yet. Well, it was all hands on deck last night, trying to make the arrangements to get the ring out of the pipe (which thankfully is sorted now), without anyone else at the party realising there was drama. In the end, I did leave early, and I was fast asleep before Teddy joined me, I didn't even hear him come in and, thankfully, he didn't try put the moves on me again.

He was already out when I woke up, although I knew he had been back because his stuff was all packed up by the door. By the time he arrived back again, he had his mum with him – and my ring.

I keep looking down at it, on my finger. It really is a beautiful ring, and it does fit me now, but we had to make it fit. Is that what I'm doing with Teddy, or what he's trying to do with me? Just making it fit.

I need to work out what I want and, while I do need to be fast (the wedding is in a week), I don't want to make any hasty decisions. I know, things aren't feeling right, but falling at the first hurdle doesn't sit well with me either. Am I being too quick to give up on this? Am I being unfair?

It's lunchtime when we arrive back at the beach house. Walking through the living room, it sounds like everyone is out on the patio and, judging by the volume coming from them, it sounds like they're all having a great time.

'I'm going to my room,' Alicia says, the sound of fun clearly putting her off even saying hello.

Everyone is at or around the outdoor dining table, as though they just recently finished eating. My mum is standing there with Hugo next to her. He has his arm draped around her shoulder and she's rubbing his tummy with her other hand.

'Honestly, where does he put it?' she asks no one in particular.

'Erm, hi,' I interrupt.

'Sweetheart, you're back,' Mum says, cheering.

She lets go of Hugo to come and give me a hug.

'And Teddy, hello,' she says as she hugs him next.

'We thought you weren't coming,' Eden jokes.

'And miss marrying this stunner?' Teddy replies, pulling me close, pecking me on the lips.

A few people 'woo'.

'You guys sound like you're having fun,' I say, changing the subject.

'Dad and Mick just had a competition to see who could make the best omelette,' Dougie explains. 'They both looked pretty disgusting...'

'Mine looked egg-cellent,' Dad chimes in.

'They *both* looked pretty disgusting,' Dougie says again. 'And Hugo ate them both. *Hugo!*'

'*Hugo!*' Dad and Mick sing too, like it's some kind of in-joke.

'They tasted good,' he says with a cute smile and a casual shrug.

'Bless you for lying,' Mum tells him.

I smile at Hugo, as if to ask, what are you doing here?

He sits down at the table, in a place that was clearly his because he picks up his drink and takes a sip. He very much seems like part of the family all of a sudden.

'Staying out of the hot tub?' I tease Dougie as I sit down next to him.

'It's pool or sea for me,' he replies firmly.

'No one wants a repeat of 1992,' Mum chimes in.

'See, I told you it was you,' I whisper to my brother.

'Anyway, you guys missed an amazing night last night,' Dougie tells us.

'We did?' I reply.

'Hugo took us all to the gig,' Mum tells us.

'*Hugo!*' the boys shout again.

'And you'll be pleased to hear that the band is amazing and we've booked them,' Eden replies. 'I actually think you'll love them. I think we both will.'

She says that as though she's known all along that I've hated everything else.

'It was such a fun night,' Dougie says. 'We all had too much to drink, we danced – Joanne's got peas on her feet.'

I glance over at Joanne, who does indeed have a bag of frozen peas held on one of her feet.

'Hugo dipped your mum,' she tells me.

'*Hugo!*'

'So Mick tried to dip me but he dropped me and I rolled my ankle.'

'What can I say? All the ladies fall for me,' Mick chimes in.

Something has changed, while I've been away, it's the atmosphere. Everyone seems so happy, so relaxed.

'All the wedding plans are in place now,' Eden tells us. 'Everything is sorted – I think we're good to go. Now all we have to do is wait.'

'And I can't wait to marry you,' Dougie tells her.

'I can't wait to marry you too,' she says.

The two of them kiss. It's actually quite sweet.

'But, despite having a whale of a time, we have missed you both,' Mum tells us. 'And, Teddy, congratulations on your new job. To show you how proud of you we are, we're throwing you a barbecue tonight.'

'We have a barbecue?' I ask.

'I do,' Hugo replies. 'Up by the cottage.'

'You don't have to do that,' Teddy insists. 'I could pay for us all to go out.'

'Oh, no, we want to spoil you here,' Mum insists. 'Plus, I've heard all about Hugo's sausage, I can't wait to see it.'

If Mum knows what she's saying there then the woman is a hero, because she doesn't let her face slip.

'Okay then,' Teddy replies, not sounding all that impressed. 'Thanks.'

'Sweetheart, come help me with the cups of tea, will you?' Mum says.

'Of course,' I reply.

In the kitchen, when it's just me and Mum, she pulls me to one side and lowers her voice.

'Is everything okay?' she asks me. 'You don't seem yourself. Did you not have a nice time in London?'

'Not really,' I reply. 'Mum, did you know you loved Dad before you got married?'

'Is that the kettle on?' Alicia asks.

I jump out of my skin.

'Tea for me,' she says. 'Just milk.'

She heads out to the patio as fast as she appeared.

'Do you think she heard that?' I ask.

'I don't think so,' Mum replies. 'But to answer your question, yes, I knew without a doubt that I was head over heels in love with your dad – bad jokes and all.'

Suddenly it feels like things are clicking into place for me. It would be to seriously oversimplify things to say that real love is laughing at the bad jokes too, but that's what it is, taking the rough with the smooth. Does Teddy feel like someone who is going to be there for me when times are tough? I don't think so.

And if he can't even laugh at my jokes, what chance do we have?

23

The sun is setting, the fancy lights are on inside and out, the music is pumping and Dad and Mick are grilling up a storm.

The party is in full swing and everyone is having a great time. Everyone but me, that is, because I'm pretty sure my relationship with Teddy is over.

I've been going back and forth with it all day. One minute, he's calling me a stunner and saying he can't wait to marry me, the next he can't even be bothered to see what the wedding colours are or going down to see the wedding barn. But then he's walking up behind me, massaging my shoulders. *But then* I try to talk to him about my book and he fobs me off, saying he'll talk about it later.

For every pro there is a con, but for every con, there's another pro. Is balance normal? Or are the deal-breakers simply that: deal-breakers? How many red flags are enough to call time on our relationship?

We need to talk, just the two of us, away from everyone about all the problems we're having, but we just haven't had a chance yet. Alicia has been parked next to him pretty much all day and I really, really can't have this conversation in front of her because you know she would join in.

I haven't had a chance to catch up with Hugo yet either. As wild as it sounds, I think my family might have fallen head over heels in love with him, and they've been hogging him all day.

Gosh, I just don't know what to do. I wish I could get some sort of sign.

'Do you fancy Hugo?' Dougie asks me.

'What?' I reply, whipping around to look at him.

He's holding a plate of sausages out in front of him.

'Do you fancy Hugo's?' he asks me again.

Oh, that's what he said.

'Yes, thank you,' I reply, stabbing a sausage with my fork.

'I'm just not a fan of sausages when they're like that,' Teddy says. 'I prefer Mick's. Are there any of those left?'

'Erm, yeah, we left a couple on the barbecue,' Dougie tells him. 'Mick said to leave them there, because these looked much nicer.'

'Yeah, I'd still prefer one of Mick's,' Teddy insists. 'Babe, will you grab me one?'

'Erm, okay,' I reply.

We're sitting on the sofa in the living room. I've been sticking close by him all day, waiting for a moment alone to talk, and it was starting to seem like I was going to have to wait until we go to bed, but this could be our chance.

'Do you want to come with me?' I ask him.

'What?' he replies. 'Why?'

'Just, you know...'

'Ohh,' he says, finally getting the message. 'You want to sneak off somewhere outside, have a bit of fun?'

Okay, maybe he isn't getting the message.

'Actually, don't worry, I'll go grab it for you,' I insist. 'Everyone is up and down there anyway and I think the parents are talking about getting in the hot tub.'

'Yeah, fair enough,' he replies.

He reaches forward and grabs his beer along with the TV remote.

I sigh. Has he always been like this, or is it just since his promotion that he's expecting me to run around after him?

I head out into the garden and up the pathway to the cottage, where the barbecue is. Now that the last of the food has been put out, everyone is inside or on the patio furniture tucking in.

But Teddy needs one of the discarded sausages because apparently Hugo's are not barbecued the way he likes them, so here I am.

It's amazing how just being a little bit further away from the house really turns the volume down on the party.

I stand by the hot tub and look out to sea for a moment. How have I got myself into such a mess? Look at that sea, reaching out as far and wide as it can go, leading to other countries, other continents, connecting us to billions of people. And here I am, so small, so insignificant in the grand scheme things, and all of a sudden it feels like I'm fucking it all up.

I let my memories take me back to different moments in time, moments where I had choices to make, choices that could have led me to different opportunities. Even when I thought I was making the right calls, hello, here I am, with a stalling career, a difficult extended family, and a fiancé who I'm just not sure I love.

This moment, right now, is one of those moments. What do I do? Ending my relationship with Teddy might feel right, but am I just overre-acting to a bad week? Has Teddy been worse? Has he always been like this? Has a certain someone come along and just been so amazing that it's warped my view – or has it given me a glimpse at how I could be treated if I just found the right person for me?

Overwhelmed, and alone for a moment, I can't hold back the tears any longer. At first, it's just a tear, just the one, running down my cheek. Then it's both eyes. Then the sniffling starts and soon enough I'm sobbing. This place is like the UK's answer to paradise and here I am, crying.

'Liv?' I hear Hugo ask. 'Liv, are you okay?'

I quickly wipe the tears from my face.

'Oh, yeah, I'm fine,' I insist, playing it down. 'I'm just embarrassing myself.'

He smiles.

'Do you want to talk?' he asks.

Laughter roars up from the garden below us. I feel self-conscious that people will be able to hear us. It's amazing how the noise carries in the night air here.

'Come with me,' Hugo says softly. 'I'll show you my secret spot. It's not as dodgy as it sounds.'

I laugh.

'Okay,' I reply.

Just behind the cottage there is a small, hidden pathway that leads down the face of the cliff and into a sort of mini-cave that looks out over the beach and out to sea. The only thing there is an absolutely stunning two-seater bench.

I lean closer to take a look at it.

'There's a guy in Yorkshire who makes these memorial benches,' Hugo explains. 'I knew I wanted one here somewhere, for Mum. He hand-makes them and carves the names and dates of your loved ones into the wood, but see down here.'

I glance down at the seat to see a vivid flash of green sandwiched between the wood.

'You send him a picture of the person you've lost,' Hugo explains. 'And he puts this channel of resin between the wood with their exact eye colour. I suppose it's to make you feel closer to them, or like they're watching over you.'

'That's incredible,' I say as I lightly stroke the wood.

'Yeah, it means a lot to me,' he replies. Then he smiles. 'You are allowed to sit on it, though.'

'Thanks,' I laugh as I sit down.

'Is it your wedding?' he asks.

'Yes,' I reply. 'Well, no, it's hardly my wedding, and that's the point. Teddy hasn't done a thing to help me plan it, and even now that he's here, he doesn't seem that bothered. And as for everything else, it just feels like it's Dougie and Eden's wedding. I didn't even really get to choose my own wedding dress. I haven't even tried it on again since I was fitted for it because I really, really don't like it. I can't believe I let myself get carried away and talked into buying it.'

'That's a shame,' he replies. 'I'm sure you'll look amazing in it, but you want to feel good on your wedding day too.'

'It's not even that it's a bad dress,' I reply. 'It's this very grand, very expensive, big thing. All I really wanted was something subtle and simple. I wanted to go to a small boutique, not one where royalty goes, where all the dresses are so famous people can tell where you bought them. What's so special about that? Oh, amazing, and now my mum is calling and messaging me to see where I am, and I'm a crying mess.'

'Listen, don't worry, you take all the time you need,' Hugo insists. 'I'll go and distract your mum. I'll tell her you're sorting something – something for the wedding – and then I'll ask her to dance and she'll be away.'

I laugh.

'She does seem to really, really like you,' I say with a smile.

'Hey, I'm a likeable guy,' he jokes. 'I'll head back down. You sit here until you feel like you can come back, but just know that everything is fixable. It isn't too late to make this wedding the wedding of your dreams.'

I smile and nod, but I'm not sure he's right.

Alone with my thoughts, looking out over the sea, I try to relax myself and clear my mind for a moment. I'm almost certain that I'm trying to decide between two things: do I go with my gut, that Teddy just isn't the one for me, or do I stick with him and see if we can make things work, because perhaps I'm giving up too soon? But going back and forth over both options isn't helping me at all, that's why I need to try to clear my mind, and think about what I want. Not what I can do, what I should do, or what I said I would do.

Of course, it isn't easy, when I can practically hear Teddy's voice in my head. No, hang on a minute, I can hear Teddy's voice. Scooting to the edge of the bench, I can see him standing on the beach below me. Alicia is with him too.

'Mother, you can't just drag me away from the party to have a secret conversation on the beach,' he tells her with a laugh. 'Is this about a present?'

'It's a gift, of sorts,' she replies.

I don't know if it's the quiet of night, the fact I'm sitting in a cave – it could be bloody mermaids screeching everything Teddy and Alicia are saying, for all I know – but I can hear them perfectly, as though I were standing next to them.

'She doesn't want to marry you,' Alicia tells him.

My jaw drops.

'What?' he replies. 'Liv? Of course she does.'

'*No*, she doesn't,' Alicia replies. 'I heard her talking to her mother, asking questions – questions that made it sound like she was having doubts.'

'Everyone has doubts before they get married,' he replies. 'I've had doubts too.'

'All the more reason to call it off,' Alicia insists. 'You and I both know that, if the image of the company wasn't so important to your grandmother, and you didn't think you needed to be a married man to get this promotion, then you never would have asked Olivia to marry you so soon. And look, you have your promotion now, so you don't need to go through with it.'

What? He proposed to me to help him with his promotion? That's why it was so early, and so out of the blue?

'Mother, look, just don't worry about it,' Teddy insists. 'Yes, that might have been the reason I asked her when I did, but that doesn't mean I don't love her.'

'She's just not right for you,' Alicia continues. 'Now, Verity, on the other hand...'

Oh, my god, give it a rest, woman. They had a fling, a long time ago, but it's over. You might want her to be your daughter-in-law but it's never going to happen.

'Mother, you have to let that go,' he insists. 'Verity has.'

'I know but I thought that when the two of you, you know, rekindled things in Amsterdam, that you might finally be realising she was a much better fit for you than Olivia is,' she continues.

I cock my head curiously. Amsterdam – I remember him taking that trip a little while after we started dating. He was so pleased to see me when he got back, it felt like a real turning point in our relationship.

'Mother, that was one night, ages ago, and it was a mistake,' he replies. 'Bloody hell, Verity shouldn't have even told you about it, that is beyond messed up, and anyway, it was that night that confirmed things for me. Liv was the one I wanted. No one else.'

It's hard to focus on the positives of being Teddy's chosen one, despite what his mother wants him to do, when it turns out that I only came out on top after he slept with us both in the same week.

'What am I going to do with you, Edward?' she asks with a sigh.

I peer down and see Teddy giving her a big hug.

'Mother, I appreciate your concern, but I know what I want and it's Liv,' he tells her. 'Now, come on, let's head back inside before they realise we're gone.'

It's interesting to hear just how certain Teddy is that he wants to marry me, because I had been having my doubts, with him seeming like he wasn't all that interested in the planning of it, and if I had only heard that part of the conversation, it might have been all I needed to let my heart know what I should do. Why wouldn't I want to marry someone who was so sure he wanted to be with me that he would defy the advice of a mother he adores?

Unluckily for Teddy though, I heard all that other stuff too, and while he might be sure that he wants to marry me, well, my mind has been made up too. As if it isn't bad enough that he probably only proposed to me to try to get ahead at work, but to find out he had one last fling with Verity – the woman who stood there and helped me pick my wedding dress, who is coming to the damn wedding – nah, I'm sorry. My mind has been made up.

This wedding – or my half of it, at least – is officially off. Now I just need to let the groom know.

24

I am very much a person who likes to see people get what they deserve –
for better or worse. People who do good things should be rewarded. People
who do terrible things shouldn't get away with it and they should have to
face the consequences of their actions.

That said, I am a grown, considerate woman, and even though Teddy
has made me so angry, and left me feeling so hurt, I would never make a
big, ugly scene in front of my entire family, upsetting everyone and ruining
the party.

So I've had to wait and, my gosh, it has felt like the longest night. I tried
to get back into the party mood. Hearing Teddy and Alicia talking might
have been horrible, and obviously I'm hurt, but I am so grateful that I did
overhear them because with their words came a clarity I had been begging
the universe for, for days. It was the sign that I needed to know for sure that
this wedding, and Teddy, are not what I want. Now that I'm so certain about
it, that I'm no longer in turmoil, I don't even feel like crying. I have this
calm, almost creepy level of acceptance of the whole situation. My only
motivation now is to call the whole thing off, so I've just been biding my
time, watching my family have fun, Hugo charming them, Alicia looking
down her nose at everyone, Mick somehow twisting Joanne's other ankle
on the dance floor – luckily, we still had the peas.

But now the party is over and it's time to face the music.

The macerator grumbles angrily, tipping me off that Teddy is on his way out of the bathroom, and that he will soon be here with me.

'Wow, that thing is loud,' he announces as he enters the bedroom. 'I'll be happy when we swap rooms with Dougie and Eden tomorrow. If I had been here when we moved in, there's no way I would've agreed to stay a single night in this room.'

'Well, it turns out there was another double room upstairs,' I say. 'But I only learned about it when Eden told me you had reserved it for your mum.'

'Yes, well, Mother would not have stayed in this room,' he says with a laugh. 'She would've been on the first chopper back to London.'

I really, truly wish I had taken the same approach.

'It might not be the best room, or the most romantic, but it's not so bad with you here,' he tells me with a smile. Then he waggles his eyebrows. 'And a bed is a bed.'

'Wait, stop there,' I tell him as he approaches the bed. He freezes on the spot. 'I know.'

'You know what?' he replies.

'Come on, Teddy, cut the shit,' I insist. 'I know.'

He tries to laugh it off.

'You're going to have to tell me what you know,' he replies. 'So that I can know what you know.'

'*Or* that's what you have to say, because you need to work out for sure which secret I'm referring to: you only proposing to me because you thought it would help your promotion, or you sleeping with Verity after we started seeing each other. Well, it turns out I know both.'

A car must be driving down the road to the hotel because the lights shine in through the window, illuminating Teddy. He raises his hand to shield his eyes. I snigger to myself. He looks like a rabbit caught in the headlights.

'Liv, let me explain,' he insists as he approaches me cautiously.

'There is nothing you can say to me,' I insist.

I'm sitting on my pillow at the top of the bed. Teddy decides not to get too close. He sits at the foot of the bed before he continues.

'What happened with Verity was just a silly mistake during a work trip,' he insists. 'It was a long time ago, when you and I first started seeing each other. We had too much to drink, it wasn't even worth it, and I regretted it right away. But you know what, in a weird way I am glad that I did it, because that's what it took for me to realise I had something special with you, and that I wanted to take our relationship to the next level.'

'Yeah, you came back and asked me to be your girlfriend,' I remind him. 'And I said yes but, funnily enough, I didn't need to shag my dad's bestie to be sure that I wanted to.'

'It wasn't like that,' he insists. 'But I promise you, from that moment on, I haven't even looked at another girl. I'm marrying you.'

To be totally honest, yes, I was always going to be upset when I found out about him and Verity, but it's mostly just because I feel so silly. If he had told me, early on, then I wouldn't have had to spend time around her, her knowing what they had done, me looking like a fool. But he's right, it was before we were properly together, I probably would have forgiven him. But that doesn't matter now.

'Teddy, that's the least of our worries,' I tell him. 'You only proposed to me to get your promotion.'

'Now, that is not true,' he replies firmly. 'Yes, okay, I knew that Grandmother would prefer me to be married before giving me the promotion, but I wouldn't have asked you if I didn't love you. For me it was like a two-birds-one-stone kind of deal. And look, I got my promotion already, I don't need to marry you, but here I am.'

'But you never would have asked me so soon, if it weren't for the job,' I point out.

'Liv, come on, you're overreacting,' he insists. 'Look, it's not a big deal. I asked you to marry me because I love you. Am I certain we'll be together forever? No, but who is? People get married and divorced and married again all the time. It's not a big deal like it used to be. That's why we should still get married, give me a chance to show you that I love you, let me prove it to you, and if it doesn't work out, then just divorce me.'

More than Teddy's words, it's his attitude that speaks volumes. He really, genuinely believes that getting married isn't a big deal. That if things don't work out, hey, we tried, we can get divorced and go try again with someone else.

I know, I shouldn't be thinking about Hugo right now, but I can't stop thinking about what he said to me: we only get to do all this once. And, while I'm sure he was probably talking about life in general, to be honest with you, call me old-fashioned, but that's how I feel about getting married. To me, it's a big deal, and it's something I want to enter into for life, until death do us part. I don't want to go into it thinking about how I can get out of it if I change my mind.

'We just have totally different beliefs,' I tell him. 'And we want totally different things, and that's fine, but I don't think we should get married.'

'Oh, come on,' he says. 'You're just being silly. Don't throw all this away for nothing. Is it him?' he asks me, his tone shifting to something edging towards angry.

'Who?' I reply.

'*Him*,' he says again, unhelpfully. 'Hugo.'

'What?' I reply in disbelief. 'No, of course not. He's been helping me plan the wedding, for crying out loud.'

'I read your synopsis,' he tells me. 'When I arrived here and found you with him, I knew right away, I recognised him, he's the guy in your book. The hunky love interest you describe.'

'Okay, now you're just being ridiculous,' I tell him. 'That's not what that was.'

'Some way to break up with someone,' he points out, annoyed.

I need to nip this in the bud. This isn't getting us anywhere and it doesn't alter the facts.

'Teddy, look me in the eyes,' I demand. 'And tell me that you want to marry me because you want to spend the rest of your life with me, and that you're confident we'll spend the rest of our lives together.'

'Liv, it's 2023, no one is making promises like that any more,' he replies. He says this in what I'd imagine is supposed to be a reassuring tone, like, silly little Liv, you don't know how the world works.

'Do you want to be with me forever?' I ask him simply.

He puffs air from his cheeks.

'How do I know how I'm going to feel in five years, fifteen years, fifty years?' he asks, frustrated.

'Okay, but whether I'm going to spend five, fifteen or fifty years with someone, that's five, fifteen or fifty years out of my one precious life,' I reply. 'You want to live in the city with a housewife who is going to raise your kids.'

'Right,' he replies. 'Commitment. It sounds great.'

'But it's not what I want,' I reply. 'I don't want to live in the city forever, and I'm not ready for kids, I want to write books, I want to make a home first, to relax in it before I move on to that phase of my life – if I even want to.'

'Not having kids is a real deal-breaker for me,' he replies, almost angrily. 'I thought you said you were thinking about it.'

'Yeah, *thinking* about it,' I say. 'Teddy, we haven't even been together for a year, I didn't think we would be getting married so soon, I thought I had more time to figure out what I wanted.'

Do I want to have kids? I think I probably do, although not any time soon, but the one thing I do know for certain is that I don't want to have kids with Teddy. What kind of life would our children have, with him working all the time, me trapped in a Mayfair mansion bored out of my mind – and that's if he doesn't decide we should get divorced because he gave our marriage a go and it wasn't for him.

'Teddy, I don't want to marry you,' I tell him plainly. 'I'm so sorry. I've been thinking about it all week, and I've wanted to talk to you about it, but you've just been so busy. But truthfully, I don't think you want to marry me either. I think you were going to give it your best shot – to secure your job – but that's not enough for me, and it shouldn't be for you either.'

'Liv, we can just give it a go,' he says again. 'Yes, okay, I did it with the job in mind, but we all have to marry someone at some point, right? The best person to start a family with.'

'And for us, that person isn't each other,' I tell him softly.

He sighs.

'I do love you, you know,' he insists. 'But you're right, I'm not that bothered about getting married. But I would have done it, to make you happy.'

'It won't make me happy,' I reply. 'And it won't make you happy either. You've got your dream job, go enjoy it.'

He hesitates for a second.

'I can't believe this is it,' he says. 'Are you sure?'

I have never been so sure, but to tell him how positive I am that this is the right decision for me feels harsh. I just nod my head.

'Okay, well, I guess I'll go then,' he says. 'I'm sure Mother will still be awake, we can fly back to London tonight.'

'I'm not kicking you out,' I quickly insist. 'You don't have to leave. You could stay for the wedding.'

'I think I'd rather just, you know, cut ties,' he says. He stands up and starts gathering his things. 'But you never know, maybe we'll bump into each other in a few months' time and things will be different.'

I smile.

I feel bad, watching him gather his things, getting ready to head home a single man again. I know it's for the best, though, and I know that he does too, because he didn't exactly put up much of a fight. We both know that we want different things.

In some ways, I feel lighter already. This is the right thing to do, and I know I'm going to be much happier in the long run. But for now, in the short term, I'm going to have to face the music and tell everyone the wedding is off – further proof that I'm doing the right thing is the fact that I'm more worried about telling everyone else than I was about telling Teddy.

Unluckily for me, though, even though I am no longer getting married, I am still actually going to have to attend my own wedding. That's going to be fun.

25

Standing on the edge of a cliff, looking out to sea, my entire life flashes before my eyes. After royally stuffing it up, today, we go again.

'Are you okay?' Hugo asks me.

'Oh, yeah, I'm fine,' I reply. 'Just thinking.'

'Don't stand too close to the edge,' he replies. 'Not with all that cake in your hair. The seagulls might carry you off.'

I snort with laughter.

'I had cake in places I didn't know you could even get cake,' I confess.

'Well, covered in cake or not, you look great in that wedding dress,' he replies.

'Oh, thanks,' I reply. 'Hilariously, I like it more than the one I actually chose for my wedding, even if this is just a cheap joke dress they gave me to wear for the competition.'

We've just stepped to one side, away from the grass, just outside the Maelstrom Hotel, where we've just participated in round two: the wedding day obstacle course.

Nowhere near as fancy as it sounds, the obstacle course involved little more than jumping into wedding outfits, running down a sort of aisle while people in the pews pelted us with wedding cake, before finally reaching the altar where a blindfolded Hugo had to piece together a vicar mannequin while I gave him directions. Utterly, totally bizarre. Truly a case of just embarrassing ourselves to win a prize but, again, I had a lot of fun doing it, and it's really taken my mind off things today.

I woke up this morning alone in my bed, Teddy and Alicia already back in London, given that they set off the night before. Under the cloak of darkness, and with my ring in his pocket, Teddy walked out of my life, and my wedding was officially cancelled – and compared to that, being covered in cake doesn't even come close, in terms of embarrassment. How tragic, to pull the plug on my own wedding, days before, but needing to still attend it anyway.

And there, in that fact, is the bottom line for me. My wedding day might be off but it's full steam ahead for Dougie and Eden. This wedding has been planned by them, they have everything they want, the only thing they didn't really want was me and Teddy, cramping their style, and now they're going to have their wish. Everything is sorted, all the plans are in place – Teddy and I never even got to send out invitations. So, other than a sneaky conversation with the caterers earlier today, before I came here, no one needs to know just yet. I think I'll wait until the rehearsal, the day before the wedding, to let them know that they don't need to make space for me, or perhaps I'll tell them later today, I just can't face it right now.

That's why I'm here, though, covered in cake, because even though my wedding might be off, Dougie and Eden still need a photographer, and I want them to have the best, I want to win this slot with Cris Calimeris – it can be my gift to them. Yes, I'm gutted that I'm not going to be able to get married in Granddad's barn, but what would be the point getting married there, but to the wrong person? I want nothing but good memories to come from here, and not throwing it all away on the wrong person can only be a good memory.

Oh, and we totally smashed it just now, completing the obstacle course in the fastest time, putting us through to the final round. I have no idea what the final round involves, but hopefully, whatever it is, we beat Thom and Sandi.

'You really don't like your wedding dress?' Hugo replies, still horrified at the thought.

'Not really,' I confess. 'I still think it's beautiful, it really is, it's just not what I wanted. I fancied something subtle and floaty. What I got was pure glamour. I let myself get swayed by what everyone else in the room thought I should get.'

'That's such a shame,' he replies. 'But, hey, we won today, and we've got just one round to go. Let's focus on the positives.'

That's exactly what I need to do right now.

'You're right,' I reply.

'We've got a couple of days, I'm not sure there's anything we can do to prepare, so just take it easy, finish your plans, show Teddy the sights – I can recommend some places to check out, if you like?'

'The wedding is planned – photographer pending – and Teddy has had to go back to London, unfortunately, more work,' I lie.

'Oh, no, that's such a shame,' Hugo says sincerely.

'It's fine,' I insist. 'I'm going to throw myself into writing my book. I'm going to set it here, for sure, so I have plenty to be getting on with.'

Throwing myself into my work will definitely help to distract me. You would think I wouldn't be feeling romantic right now but, honestly, I am so sure I'm doing the right thing, it's almost romantic that I've called my wedding off. No, I'm not deluding myself, it's true.

Another happy coincidence of participating in the competition is that it has been a welcome distraction for me today, right when I need one. Getting up, dressed and heading out to do something useful – and something so much fun – has been the perfect antidote. I haven't had the chance to dwell, yet, but the day is young.

Hugo reaches forward and uses his thumb to wipe a little cake away from the side of my mouth.

'You had a bit of cake on you,' he says with a smile.

'Did you get it?' I ask.

'Not all of it,' he replies, both of us knowing full well that I am absolutely coated in the stuff. 'Do you want to do something with me tomorrow?'

I wasn't expecting him to say that.

'Me?' I reply.

'No, the cake-covered girl behind you,' he playfully corrects me. 'Yes, you. I have some ideas about how I can help you.'

'Very intriguing,' I reply, ever so slowly. Then I smile again. 'Okay, sure. Whatever it is, count me in. it can't be any weirder than today.'

'I love a challenge,' he replies. 'Right, let's get you out of that dress.'

'Yes, and then home for a shower,' I reply. Then I realise what I've said. 'Separate showers, obviously.'

Hugo just laughs.

'Obviously,' he replies. 'Ten a.m. tomorrow sound good?'

'Sounds great,' I reply. 'Looking forward to it.'

I really, really am. I know I should be devastated – and I am sad, don't get me wrong – but this feeling that I've dodged one hell of a bullet, that I've stopped myself from making a huge mistake with almost no time to spare, truly, it is such a huge relief.

We only get to do this once – those words won't stop echoing in my head.

I've managed to change course, now all I need to do is steer myself through the storm. It will all be plain sailing after that.

Here's hoping.

26

I have visited Porthian Sands god knows how many times but, today, Hugo has shown me sights I didn't even know existed.

I suppose, as a family, we've always been drawn to the tourist side of things. The cute cafés, the piers, the amusement arcade – and I must have clocked days on the beach over the years.

But I've never walked through the hidden park – a place tourists haven't been able to find yet – with its perfect lawns, bright colourful flower beds, and a large fountain at its heart. I'd never seen the old abandoned boat wreck (although it is supposedly haunted, so I'll happily never see it again). And, despite seeing Porthian Castle many times from different points in Porthian Sands, I've never actually taken the tour. It's a beautiful old building that you just know is full of secrets, most of which will never be uncovered, sitting in the most stunning subtropical gardens. All absolutely perfect settings for my novel.

'You're quite the tour guide,' I tell Hugo as we make our way back into the heart of town, sipping delicious cooling iced drinks as we stroll. 'You really know your stuff about the local area. I suppose you have to, working in a hotel.'

'It definitely helps,' he replies. 'But, not to put too much of a downer on the day, when Mum and I came here for our break she wanted to do everything, to see everything, to pack in as much as possible. So I did a deep dive into everything the place had to offer, I chatted with locals – and then, when I moved here, I learned even more about the hidden gems.'

'The amount of love you have for your mum really shines every time you talk about her,' I tell him. 'She was so lucky to have a son who cared about her so much.'

'We were really close,' he tells me. 'My dad left us when I was five, so all I really remember is it being just the two of us. Mum was amazing, though, she worked hard, she started her own estate agency, opened other branches, and then retired early to enjoy her success. She was diagnosed not long after that. Life is horrible sometimes, isn't it?'

'It really is,' I reply. 'I'm so sorry.'

'I'm not saying it's a good thing, I wish she was still here, but knowing that her time was running out gave us a gift, it meant that we could make the most of the time we had left,' he says. 'If you knew you only had so much time, would you do things differently?'

I open my mouth, to say *something*, but the words don't come out.

'You don't have to reply,' he insists. 'It's just something to think about.'

'It really is,' I say. 'I know it's not good, to dwell on the fact that everyone's number will be up sooner or later, but people would do well to remember that – well, as a wise man once said to me – we only get to do this once.'

'My motto too,' he says through a smile. 'He must be smart.'

'Oh, he's so smart,' I reply. 'And I'm hoping he knows where we're going now because I am just wandering aimlessly down this street.'

'We are exactly where we're supposed to be,' he insists. 'Seeing as though you've humoured me all day, visiting all the locations I've been pitching for your book, even though I'm sure some of them have been totally useless – unless you think kisses on a shipwreck are hot – I have a surprise for you.'

'Really?' I reply in disbelief. 'What is it?'

'It's here,' he says, nodding towards a dress shop. 'Follow me.'

Curious, I follow Hugo into Hearts & Hems, a small shop with rails and rails of clothes – so many, it's hard to know where to begin to look.

'Hugo, my lover, how are you?' a tall fifty-something brunette says as she hurries out from behind the counter.

'Hello, Lisa, I'm great, how are you?' he asks, kissing her on the cheek.

'Can't complain, can't complain,' she replies. 'Is this her?'

'This is her,' he replies. 'Lisa, this is Liv. Liv, this is Lisa.'

'Lovely to meet you,' Lisa says. 'Come this way, everything is ready.'

We're shown into a second room with even more clothes than the last. So many tall, overstuffed rails, it's actually a little dark in here. The place smells lovely, like lavender, and ginger biscuits for some reason.

A bell rings.

'Oh, a customer,' Lisa says excitedly. 'I'll leave you to it, you know what you're doing.'

'No worries,' Hugo replies. Then he turns to me. 'Right, are you ready for your surprise?'

'More than ever,' I insist, unable to control my grin.

'Step into that changing room,' he tells me. 'Now, I'm no expert, but Lisa is, and hopefully my description of the brief was enough.'

'I've never been so confused and so intrigued,' I reply.

'Go on in,' he says simply.

As I head into the fitting rooms, two wooden venetian doors snap closed behind me. Alone in the room, I shift my gaze from the full-length mirror to the hooks on the wall. Hanging on there are three bridal gowns. Subtle, floaty, long-sleeved gowns with high backs and absolutely zero glitter.

'Oh, my god,' I blurt.

'That's the reaction I was hoping for,' Hugo replies – I can hear his smile. He clearly gets a big kick out of helping people.

I feel silly, standing here looking at dresses, when my wedding is off. I should probably tell the truth – or tell another lie, at least. Say that I've come around to my dress, or something.

I'm about to head back out when curiosity gets the better of me. There's one, in the middle, that looks exactly like the dress that I thought only existed in my head. It has a round neck, long lace sleeves, very subtle, delicate beading on the top, and a nice floaty – but not poofy – skirt at the bottom. It's perfect. So perfect that I can't resist trying it on. Would it be weird, to buy a wedding dress, without a groom on the scene? What are the chances I'll be able to find this dress again if/when I do tie the knot?

Unbelievably, it fits me to perfection. A fluttering in my stomach moves to my chest, then forces its way out of my mouth in the form of a small, squeaky gasp. This is how I expected to feel, when I tried on my dream dress, and this is without a doubt my dream dress. A tear rolls down one of my cheeks – this is what happened with Eden when she found her dress. It must be what happens. This is how you know. Except tears are coming from both my eyes now, big, uncontrollable ones, and now my chest is bouncing as I try to stifle my cry but no, it's no use, it's coming out. It's all coming out.

There's a knock on the door.

'Liv?' Hugo says in a loud whisper. 'Liv, can I come in?'

'Oh, I'm fine, honestly,' I sob, sounding nothing at all like a person who is fine.

'Are you decent?' he asks. 'I just want to make sure you're okay.'

At this stage, what choice do I have but to tell the truth? It isn't a pretty truth, but it's got to be better than... whatever this looks like.

'Come in,' I tell him.

Hugo walks through the door and stops in his tracks. He smiles for a second but then it quickly falls.

'Liv, you look incredible,' he tells me. 'Incredible in the dress, at least. But you look so heartbroken. What's wrong? Should I not have brought you here? I knew it was weird but, when I heard you still didn't like your dress, I knew Lisa stocked them here, I thought she might be able to help.'

'No, no, it's not you,' I insist, quickly wiping away my tears, careful not to get any make-up on this dress that I absolutely cannot buy. 'I, erm, I haven't told anyone else this yet but... my wedding is off.'

'What?' he replies. 'Oh, no, what happened?'

'Don't feel sorry for me,' I insist. 'I'm doing that for myself right now. But I'm fine, honestly, it's all for the best. Teddy was not the right person for me and I knew it. We were both getting married for the wrong reasons. Honestly, I'm happy, because I know I've made the right call, but what an unfortunate time to meet my dream dress.'

Hugo grabs me and gives me a hug. It's a warm, friendly, reassuring hug packed with this inexplicable comforting vibe. I suppose it's just nice to finally tell someone.

'I know your mum will be looking after you, but I feel like you needed that,' he says, then he raises an eyebrow. 'You have told your mum, haven't you?'

'Not yet,' I confess. 'I will tell them all, as soon as possible, but I just needed a bit of time to get my head around it all. And I do still want to win the competition, to get the photographer for Dougie and Eden.'

'That's so, so sweet of you,' Hugo tells me. 'Oh, my god, I'm so sorry, I've got you standing here in a wedding dress. I'm going to go back out there, let you get your clothes back on.'

With Hugo on the other side of the door, I start changing back into my clothes.

'Listen, don't feel bad,' I insist. 'I'm okay, really, I am. And, hey, you introduced me to my dream dress.'

'That makes me feel worse,' he calls back.

'Well, don't,' I reply. 'I've been flirting with the idea of fate, and things happening for a reason recently. So, you never know, if it's meant to be, if I do ever get engaged, maybe I'll come back here and it will be here.'

'My mum believed in fate,' he says eventually. 'She would always say that, if she hadn't met my dad, then she wouldn't have had me, she wouldn't have started her business. If we hadn't come here to stay, I never would have moved here – we never would have met. You wouldn't be taking part in the competition, you wouldn't get your photographer... I know, it all seems silly, and there's probably nothing in it. It's a nice way to think, though. Reassuring.'

I pop out from the changing room, leaving my dream dress behind me. It is a nice way to look at things. To think that even the bad stuff is leading me to something good.

It's certainly going to make leaving the wedding dress of my dreams behind me a lot easier to take. Well, here's hoping.

27

I feel so much lighter for telling Hugo that the wedding is off. I know it sounds daft, but it feels more real, for telling someone else, and all that stuff about fate has given me a boost, reassuring me that some good could come from this eventually.

Hugo and I walk up the path, into the back garden of the beach house.

'Hi, sweetheart,' Mum says brightly.

'Hello,' I reply.

Dad is snoozing on a sunlounger next to her. Heidi is sitting on the other side of the table, casually sipping a cocktail.

Wait, oh my god!

'Heidi, what?' I scream. 'No, oh my gosh, you came!'

'Of course I came, you silly cow,' she teases me. 'Do you think I'm going to miss the joint wedding of the century?'

'You shouldn't have left work, not for this,' I say, the guilt creeping in.

'Don't worry, all finished, everything went amazingly,' she replies. 'Everyone else stayed on for a few days to enjoy the facilities but I was like, nope, not me, who wants to hang out in Abu Dhabi, all expenses paid, when I could be in Cornwall with my girl?'

Her sarcasm fills my heart with so much joy I feel like it could burst.

'There's a bedroom for me, right?' she asks. 'Your mum wasn't sure.'

'There's Alicia's room,' I say.

'Yes, but we're not sure when she'll be back, sweetheart,' Mum says.

We are – never.

'Right,' I reply. 'Well, listen, just come in with me for now. We'll figure it all out later.'

Heidi looks fantastic in a short summer dress, topped off with the biggest straw hat I've ever seen. The large bow on the top is the icing on the cake.

'What's in the bag?' she asks curiously. 'And why aren't you introducing me to your handsome friend?'

'Oh, it's just a dress,' I reply – it's actually my dress for the wedding. Well, when in a dress shop, and you suddenly realise that because you're not wearing your wedding dress, you don't have anything suitable to wear for the wedding you're suddenly a guest at, you have to act fast.

'I'm Hugo,' he says, stepping forward to shake her hand.

'I'm single,' she replies playfully.

'It's nice to meet you, single,' he jokes.

'Heidi is my best friend,' I tell him. 'And, Heidi, Hugo has been helping me with the wedding plans. He's been amazing, honestly.'

'We all love Hugo,' Mum chimes in.

'*Hugo!*' Dad shouts – who knew he was awake? His eyes are still closed.

'I'm her best Cornwall friend,' Hugo tells her with a smile.

'Oh, I'll have to keep an extra close eye on you then,' she replies flirtatiously.

I lightly shake myself. If anyone was looking when I did that, it probably looked like some kind of half-hearted shimmy. It's strange, though, to see Heidi flirting with Hugo. I'm not sure how I feel about it.

'Liv, can I see this room?' Heidi asks. 'Check it's up to my high standards.'

I laugh.

'Of course,' I say.

'Well, I'll head home,' Hugo announces.

'You live up there?' Heidi confirms.

'Yep,' he replies, with the most adorable awkward laugh.

'Good to know,' she says. 'Right, Liv, this room...'

'Yeah, follow me,' I tell her.

As we walk through the house, Heidi hands me her cocktail. I take a big sip.

'So, Hugo,' she sings. 'If I were the bitchy kind, which I absolutely am not, I might point out that it is seriously weird that you're spending the week before your wedding with that hunk, and not with your absent fiancé. Your mum told me you've hardly seen or heard from him. He should be here now.'

'Well, what my mum doesn't know is that the wedding is off,' I tell her in hushed tones.

'What?' she yells.

I push her through my room's door and close it behind me.

'Shh,' I insist. 'No one knows.'

'I can think of a thousand reasons why your wedding is off, and if I'm honest, I am very pleased to hear it, but what was it for you?' she asks.

'Looking back, there were so many red flags,' I confess. 'But his general attitude towards this wedding told me everything I needed to know. I'm pretty sure he was only doing it to get a promotion, then, when he got it, he seemed to care even less.'

'You should've told me, Liv,' she says softly. 'Are you okay?'

'Honestly, I'm fine,' I reply. 'Like, really, really, oddly fine. I know it's the right thing to do.'

'So Hugo is, what, the one you're getting under to get over Teddy?' she teases.

'Stop,' I insist with a laugh. 'You're awful. He's been helping me to sort a photographer, and with all sorts of other wedding plans – Dougie and Eden are still getting married, obviously – and he's also been helping me with the book I'm planning to write. He took me out today, to visit some amazing settings for chapters. And then, well, he did take me to a wedding dress shop, because I told him that I hated my wedding dress and he remembered, which was kind of amazing, but then I told him it was off, so I just bought a dress to wear to the wedding instead.'

'Wow,' she blurts. 'That's... wow.'

'Yeah, he's really nice,' I continue. 'He helped us find a band and, just between me and you, he's been pretending to be my fiancé, so I can win a decent wedding photographer.'

'That's really cool,' she says casually. 'And when did the two of you realise you were in love?'

I snort.

'You definitely like each other,' she persists. 'No one does stuff like that, spends all that time together, if they aren't into each other. What's his mum like? Better than Alicia?'

'His mum passed away,' I reply.

'Well, that's the best kind of mother-in-law,' she jokes. 'But, seriously, come on, I've been here a matter of minutes and I can already tell there's something between you.'

'Yeah, well, it's too soon to be thinking about any of that,' I tell her. 'So, if you fancy him, you have my blessing.'

'Hoes before bros,' she replies. 'I am here to spend time with you – and now I know Teddy isn't going to be around, well, that's even better.'

I knew she never liked him but, wow, she really is over the moon for me. I guess she could just tell that he wasn't the person for me. Best friends just have a sixth sense for these things, don't they?

'Do you fancy lunch tomorrow?' she asks. 'If I find us somewhere fancy?'

'Lunch would be amazing,' I reply.

Well, with a day to go until the final round of the competition, and nothing else to do, the distraction would be more than welcome.

'I would say dinner tonight, but your mum says she's going to cook,' she says. 'Perhaps we can invite Hugo?'

'Given how taken my mum is with him, I would hazard a guess she already has,' I say with a smile.

'Hey, come here,' Heidi insists.

She wraps her arms around me, holding me close, squeezing me tightly.

'Just because I didn't think Teddy was right for you doesn't mean that I don't feel sad for you,' she says. 'You don't deserve this. All you did was love someone with an open mind and an open heart. Sometimes that's all we can do.'

'Thanks,' I reply. 'But I know I'm doing the right thing.'

'Plus, you have me, your fairy godmother, here now,' she replies.

'You're more like a fairy godfather,' I say through a chuckle. 'But it's great to have you here.'

It really is so, so amazing to have my best friend here with me. I feel like now I can just enjoy myself, with thoughts of the wedding out of my mind. Obviously I'll have to still be at the thing but I'm hoping that, with Heidi and Hugo there to have fun with, it might not be so bad.

This may not be my wedding but it's my holiday and I intend to make the most of it. All I can do from this moment on is look forwards. Nothing good ever came from dwelling on the past, did it?

28

I was excited to hear that Heidi had booked us a table in the hotel restaurant. I'm not actually sure I've ever eaten here, even when I was a kid, but I've heard wonderful things about the view.

I'm less excited that Heidi appears to have stood me up, which is incredible, even by her standards, given that the beach house is next door to the hotel.

I take my phone from my bag to give her a call but, before I get a chance to press her name, Hugo appears.

'Sorry I'm late,' he says, brushing creases out of his white shirt.

I raise my eyebrows.

'In my defence, I didn't know I was coming until about ten minutes ago,' he explains, although I'm none the wiser.

'That's, er, that's okay,' I reply. 'The competition is tomorrow, right?'

'Yeah, tomorrow lunchtime,' he says. 'But I'm here because Heidi said you wanted to have lunch... and I've just realised from the look on your face that you know nothing about this.'

I smile.

'I think I know what's going on here,' I start. It's a little embarrassing, I wish I could come up with a believable alternative, but I've got nothing. 'She's, erm, set us up. She told me to meet her here for lunch.'

'She told me the same,' he says through an amused smile. 'She seems fun.'

'Oh, she is,' I reply. 'A real laugh a minute.'

'Well, we're here, there's a table booked in someone's name, we would be crazy not to take it, right?' Hugo suggests. 'I eat here often. It's really, really good.'

'I never turn down lunch,' I reply happily. 'Plus, I came here thinking I was about to eat, I dread to think what would happen to my body if I denied it the food it was expecting.'

'That sounds scientific,' Hugo says with a nod. 'Let's do it.'

We make our way through the large old wooden door into the dining room where we are greeted by a hostess.

'Oh, hello,' she says as Hugo approaches.

'I know, you weren't expecting me,' he replies. 'But do you think you could set up table six for us, please?'

'Of course,' the woman replies. 'Go take a seat at the bar, order your drinks, I'll get on that right away.'

'Thanks, Jess,' he replies.

'Ooh, table six,' I reply playfully. 'Is that the best one?'

'It really is,' he confirms. 'Let's grab some drinks.'

'It's great, having insider information,' I say. 'Heidi better watch her back, there might be a new bestie in town.'

'I would *never* set you up on a lunch date with someone,' Hugo jokes.

'I still can't believe she's done this,' I say, smiling, because I'm not exactly mad at her. 'But I'll get my revenge.'

'What doesn't she like?' Hugo asks playfully. 'Or what is she scared of?'

'She doesn't like people saying Hi-de-Hi to her,' I tell him. 'And as far as what she is scared of goes, I don't think that girl is scared of anything – intimacy, maybe? Not second-hand intimacy, clearly, setting the two of us up for a one-on-one lunch, but this is the last thing she would want for herself.'

'So, we set *her* up on a date,' Hugo jokes. 'Maybe at the wedding.'

'She is sitting on the singles table,' I reply thoughtfully. 'I could ask Eden about who else is sitting there, and sandwich her between two people who will drive her absolutely bananas.'

'I like it,' he replies. 'I think that's a way better kind of revenge. Forget big, dramatic shows of anger and upset. Petty revenge is where it's at.'

'I might do it, you know,' I tell him. 'Even if I'm not that mad at her.'

'Yeah, I can't say I mind too much either,' he says with a smile.

'Your table is ready,' Jess says, interrupting us grinning at one another like idiots.

The restaurant boasts enormous floor-to-ceiling windows, facing out on to the beach, a view I never grow tired of. But Jess leads us away from the tables and around a corner to a table for two in a small space, almost entirely surrounded by windows, with panoramic views. It's a private space with smooth music playing from hidden speakers and, being so high up, not a single other person's eyes on you. Now this really is intimate.

'I'll go get your menus,' Jess says.

'Okay, wow,' I blurt. 'This is just... incredible. I can't believe it. No way Heidi could score us a table so beautiful, so you have her beat there. I can't believe you just called this "table six".'

'Someone told me it was something to do with astrology,' he replies. 'Something about six being the most romantic number. So it's only fitting it's the table number for the most romantic spot in the restaurant. I just thought you might appreciate the space, and the privacy.'

'And you would be right,' I say. 'Wow, this is just... wow! Oh, my gosh, look over there, you can see... is that an island?'

I realise I'm sounding like an excitable child and try to dial it back a notch.

'Sorry, you must have seen this view a thousand times,' I say. 'This isn't having any effect on you at all, is it?'

'You would be surprised,' he replies. 'Today... it's never looked so beautiful.'

'Right, menus,' Jess says, interrupting a moment.

We take our seats and browse pages of delicious food – I don't even know what to choose. I love Heidi to pieces, but this is really, seriously special.

I really appreciate the company too but I suspect she knew that already, that's why she did it.

I'm not going to overthink it, I'm just going to enjoy my lunch. But this might be the happiest I've felt since I arrived. And to all those involved in helping me feel this way, I can't thank them enough.

29

'We've had tears, tantrums, torn ligaments and ten-year relationships coming to an end,' Mike says, in the most sinister of voices, into the microphone. 'And it's all come down to this, the final round, to find... the Cutest Couple in Cornwall. Come on!'

Everyone cheers, as though they're in the audience at the Colosseum, and everyone on stage is about to be brutally murdered.

I'm not sure any of Mike's claims about the competition so far are true – unless of course you count Sandi's eyes watering when she got caught off guard by a fistful of buttercream. Still, I suppose it drums up an audience of people who are in no way invested in what is going on here on the stage today.

'Two couples...' Mike continues. 'We have Thom and Sandi, parents, partners, long-time fans of yours truly. Then we have Hugo and Liv, peddlers of local ales and some of the worst jokes I've ever heard. Both are young, happy, loved up. They're compatible, they can survive a crudely put together, vaguely wedding-themed obstacle course. But who will come out victorious, take the crown, and win the much-coveted Cris Calimeris photo shoot? Ladies and gentlemen, it's time to find out.'

I glance out into the audience, where I eventually spot Heidi. When I told her what we were doing today, she said there was no way she wasn't coming to watch.

She flashes me a reassuring thumbs up, which catches Mike's eye.

'Oh, hey, hello, who is this?' he asks no one in particular.

'That's Heidi, my best friend,' I tell him. 'She's here to cheer us on.'

'And what a fantastic cheerleader she is,' he adds, but then he composes himself. 'Anyway, the final round, and it's the simplest round yet, but potentially still the toughest. To be crowned the Cutest Couple in Cornwall, you need to possess more than just compatibility and the physical skills needed to survive, oh yes. You need that certain something, that *je ne sais quoi*. What we want to see from our couples is chemistry, the kind that once you unleash, it's plain for everyone to see why you're together. We'll be measuring this chemistry with a good old-fashioned clapometer so, audience, it's your job to make some noise for your favourite couple.'

The problem with not knowing what the rounds are going to involve is that we can't plan for anything. We can't rehearse, we can't practise – we turn up to these things and have to figure out a plan on the spot, without even being able to confer. We got lucky with the compatibility round, and somehow we managed to complete the ridiculous obstacle course in the fastest time which, again, does feel like a stroke of luck. Chemistry, though – this is going to be a tough one. Depending on how they measure it, surely you can't fake chemistry, not when you're up against a married couple with a baby?

'Ladies and gentlemen, this round is the simplest, the ultimate test of true love,' Mike continues. 'The only thing standing between our couples and the photographer of their dreams – the only thing left for them to do is... kiss.'

What?

'Our couples will take it in turns, one after the other, to lock lips,' he explains. 'Then it's your job, as an audience, to make some noise for the couple who you think shares the best kiss. Now, it's worth noting, this is a family competition. No heavy petting, nothing too handsy, let's keep this PG. But what we're looking for is passion, genuine love, fireworks shooting up from between you, crackling overhead – is that so much to ask?'

I notice the crowd growing denser by the second. Everyone wants to see how this plays out.

'Thom, Sandi, you guys are up first,' Mike tells them. 'And... go.'

It's a relief to see that, even for a real couple, this is weird. Thom and Sandi approach each other. He's much taller than she is, so he has to stoop down to get her in an embrace. She stands up on her toes. It's quite cute, really. He places his hands on her back, almost pulling her up into his kiss.

With the audience captivated, and not a microphone in sight, Hugo takes this as his opportunity to whisper to me.

'Listen, we can just bow out,' he tells me. 'We'll just tell them that we're a very private couple who doesn't believe in kissing in public.'

I sigh. How infuriating, to fall at the last hurdle, and for something so simple too. I really, really wanted to win this, and I'm not going to – all because of a silly kiss. Then again, it is just a kiss, will I kick myself if I don't try?

'It's fine with me,' I say quietly. 'If it's fine with you, obviously.'

'Erm, no, yeah, I mean,' he babbles. 'It's fine.'

Thom and Sandi finally separate.

'Wow, there we go, now we know where the baby came from,' Mike jokes. God, I hate his jokes. At least my bad jokes are supposed to be bad, his are just awful.

'Lugo, you guys are up,' he tells us. 'We're all ready when you are.'

Hugo and I turn to face one another. Then we take a step forward. Then we just freeze for a second, staring into each other's eyes.

'Oh, intense eye contact, I like it,' Mike says. 'Ladies and gents, I think they're teasing us.'

I take a deep breath, psyching myself up, because suddenly it's almost as though I've forgotten how to kiss. How do you kiss? You just sort of do it on autopilot, right? Is that right? When was the last time I passionately kissed Teddy? Before we came to Cornwall. My god, that's so, so sad. No wonder I'm not getting married any more – thank goodness I came to my senses. This is further proof that I have made the right decision, but nothing to do with the task at hand. Okay, here we go.

I reach up and hook my arms around Hugo's neck. He rests his hands gently on the small of my back. Hugo somehow gestures at me with his eyebrows, a move that I somehow just know is a sign that he's asking me if I'm sure about this. I give him a subtle nod before going for it.

I reach up to kiss him. He's taller than me, but the height difference isn't as drastic as that between Thom and Sandi, so it doesn't look awkward for us. Our lips touch – wow, his lips are soft. So unbelievably, deliciously soft. Addictively so, even. At first, we're both nervous, gently easing into it, trying to find a rhythm. It's such a sweet, nice, gentle kiss. Eventually, we naturally part, but it leaves me certain of two things. First of all, a kiss like that isn't going to win a competition like this. Secondly, all I can think about is kissing him again. Our lips are only parted for a second before I place my hands on Hugo's face and pull him back in. We're in our rhythm now, both full of confidence, both so into it. It's like someone just turned the volume up from 40 per cent to full blast. As Hugo's tongue touches mine, it feels like my entire body turns to jelly, then ice, then fire. I feel like I'm going to burst into flames, it's just so... so...

'Wow, okay, I think we've seen enough of that,' Mike says.

Suddenly I remember where I am, and what we're doing. I genuinely got so lost in that kiss, my mind went blank.

We quickly part, taking a step away from each other, neither of us expecting that to go... like that.

'Mamma mia,' Mike exclaims. 'Right then, time to get the clapometer out.'

The clapometer is actually an iPad app, rather than the crazy gadget I was imagining in my head.

'First of all, give it up for Thom and Sandi,' he says.

As the audience clap, Hugo and I exchange looks. I don't think either of us can quite believe we just did that.

'Okay, now, give it up if you think Hugo and Liv should be named the winners,' he continues.

As the audience erupt into roaring applause and cheers and whoops, it is clear, without the clapometer, that Hugo and I are the winners.

I can't believe it, I'm stunned into motionless silence. The only thing that shocks me more than the two of us winning – when we competed against a real couple – is the sight of my parents, Dougie, Eden and Eden's parents all standing in the audience, staring right back at me.

'Ladies and gentlemen, our winners, officially the Cutest Couple in Cornwall 2023... Hugo and Liv,' Mike screams, ring-announcer style.

I notice Eden shake her head before swapping a few words with Dougie, then they all walk away.

Shit. Shit, shit, shit. I need to run after them, to tell them all it's not what it looks like.

'How does it feel to win, guys?' Mike asks, shoving the mic in front of us.

'Amazing,' Hugo tells him. 'I can't believe it.'

He sounds so modest, but I know his disbelief is coming from the same place as mine. How on earth did we pull this off?

'Well, if the two of you follow Erin over there, she'll get some photos taken, and arrange the details of your prize with you,' Mike informs us. 'And now I'm going to judge the Cornwall's Bonniest Baby competition – I can't imagine how they are going to tackle the obstacle course...'

I take Hugo's arm as we walk offstage, pulling him in close so I can whisper to him as quietly as possible.

'Are you okay?' he asks before I get a chance to say anything. 'You don't look very happy. Sorry, was that too awkward? At least we won...'

'No, it's not that,' I reply. 'My family were in the audience, and I haven't actually told them that my half of the wedding is off.'

'Ah,' is all he can say.

'The rehearsal is in a couple of hours, I was going to tell them then,' I confess. 'I thought, potentially, Eden would be so pleased that she wouldn't have to share the day with me, that she would do a lot of the work for me, convincing everyone else that it's ultimately a good thing. Plus, no one would make a scene at the rehearsal, would they?'

'Have you done this before?' Hugo jokes. 'Come on, let's get these photos over with, and then when you do turn up to the rehearsal, you can tell everyone about the amazing photographer you've scored, and everyone will just be so pleased about that... hopefully.'

'Okay, Cornwall's Cutest Couple, time to take some romantic photos,' a woman who I'm assuming is Erin tells us.

I exhale deeply. It's all going to be fine – we won, hurray, that's a good thing, an amazing gift to give to Dougie and Eden. They should be pleased that I took one for the team like that, kissing Hugo just to win them a prize.

Although, if I'm being honest, that's not the only reason I did it. Obviously, without the competition, I wouldn't have kissed him at all, but it was certainly a good way to do something that I hadn't even dared to acknowledge has been on my mind. It really, really has, though.

And now all I can think about is how I get to do it again.

30

I hover outside the wedding barn for a second. I've been avoiding visiting it, pretending that it isn't here, I think because deep down I knew that my wedding was never going to happen. I can't believe they aren't going to be holding weddings here any more. Whatever they end up doing with it, I hope it brings people as much joy as it did those who were able to get married here.

'It's a beautiful thing, isn't it?' a twenty-something man in chef's whites says.

He's leaning against it, smoking a cigarette. I hate to see people with particular jobs out of context because it reminds me that they are human. The people who make your food do smoke, they itch, they use the bathroom. Isn't it funny how I'll think about anything but the matter at hand right now? I'm hiding from myself, in my own head, that's quite the feat.

'It really is,' I reply. 'My granddad built it.'

I feel so proud, that someone I knew had a hand in something so beautiful, so admired by so many people.

'Oh, man, you must be gutted they're tearing it down,' he says with a sympathetic smile.

'They're tearing it down?' I reply. 'What? When?'

He winces.

'Sorry, I assumed you knew, although I suppose the final meeting to get the sign-off is tomorrow lunchtime, so I'm not sure if it's public knowledge yet,' he explains. 'But, yeah, they're going to knock it down. Such a shame.'

He puts his cigarette out on the floor before flicking the end away. Then he heads back inside.

Time for me to face the music.

I walk inside the barn and everyone falls silent.

'Hello,' I say brightly.

'We've got five minutes before the rehearsal starts,' Eden says, cutting to the chase. 'You've got some serious explaining to do. Give me one good reason why I shouldn't get Teddy on the phone and tell him to call off the wedding?'

'Erm, because I already called it off,' I confess. 'Days ago, actually. That's why he and Alicia left.'

'Oh, sweetheart,' my mum says, rushing over to me. 'What happened? Come on, sit down.'

The room is already set up for a wedding ceremony, with rows of chairs separated down the centre, forming an aisle. The wooden rafters are wrapped with lights and flower garlands in bright, summery colours. As the sun pools in through the windows, it gently warms the wood, creating the most delicious smell. I cannot believe I'm not going to be able to get married here.

'I don't think I need to tell you that Teddy has been pretty MIA throughout this entire process,' I tell them. 'It turns out we want totally different things, we were going into this way too quickly, and... and I just know he isn't the right person for me.'

I don't think it's worth telling the room all about the reasons why I know Teddy isn't the man for me. The red flags, the different ideas about our future, our differing views on marriage generally – none of it matters now, not when I'm so sure I've made the right decision.

'So, what, you're just kissing men in front of crowds now?' Eden chimes in. 'Are you okay? Do you need, like, therapy or something?'

She seems only lightly annoyed. I think there's a little concern in there at the end.

'Honestly, I know it seems like a shock for you guys, but I've had more time to come to terms with it, and deep down, I think I always knew, I was just trying to live with hope and optimism and give a good thing a chance,' I explain.

'There's no shame in that, sweetheart,' my mum says supportively. 'I think we all felt that way about Teddy, just a little.'

'He wasn't quite one of us,' my dad adds in a rare moment of serious-ness. 'I always wondered if he thought he was better than us.'

'Yeah, he was a posh tosser,' Mick, Eden's dad, says, just wanting to join in.

'Wait, so Eden gets the entire wedding?' Joanne says, unable to hide her excitement.

Even though I know it's for the best, it does still hurt, just a little, espe-cially standing here in the barn, knowing it's going to be demolished.

'Yes,' I say softly. 'I never sent any invitations out – because I suppose I knew there was no point – all the arrangements are, well... I know Eden is happy with everything, so that's all good. And the reason you guys saw me kissing Hugo, as weird as it sounds, is because he has been helping me compete in a competition, to win a photographer for the wedding. And we did win, so Cris Calimeris will be doing the photos tomorrow – all the plans are in place.'

'Cris Calimeris?' Eden says back to me. '*The* Cris Calimeris? The one I've heard of? He's doing my wedding photos?'

'That's the one,' I reply with a slight smile.

'And you kept going with this, even after you knew it wasn't going to benefit you in any way?' she continues.

It's almost funny that Eden finds the concept of doing something purely for the benefit of someone else so unbelievable.

'I want you guys to have a great photographer,' I tell them, shrugging my shoulders.

'Oh, my gosh, Liv, thank you,' Eden says. 'You don't know how much this means to me. Oh, my gosh. I'm so sorry I ever doubted you.'

'Ah, that's okay,' I reply. 'Anyway, I think I'll wait outside, while you guys do what you need to do in here, if that's all right?'

'Oh, no, of course,' Eden says. 'Go ahead. I can't even imagine how hard it must be, being in here.'

'I'll walk you out,' my mum says, hooking her arm with mine.

Eventually, when we're out of earshot, she gives my arm a squeeze.

'You're a wonderful, thoughtful, kind young woman,' she tells me. 'I can tell, I can see it in your eyes, that you know you've done the right thing, and I'm proud of you. I'm sure some people in your position would have gone ahead with it anyway, despite their doubts. But you were brave – and you still went on to bag that photographer for Eden. I haven't heard of him, but she seems excited.'

I laugh.

'Yeah, she seems really happy,' I reply with a sigh. 'I think all I can do now is make the best of what's left of the holiday.'

'It certainly seems like you are,' Mum replies, a grin spreading across her face. 'That kiss you shared with Hugo, wow. I never saw Teddy kiss you like that.'

'It was all for show,' I insist. 'Now, go on, go do your mother-of-the-groom duties, I'll be out here waiting for you.'

Mum kisses me on the cheek before heading back inside.

The response from my family has only made me feel even more certain that I have made all the right decisions, from calling off my wedding to pushing on with the competition with Hugo. I know that he knows now that I am no longer getting married, but even when he did think it was still going ahead, he was really there for me – he's been there for me this whole time, exactly where Teddy should have been – so it's only natural I've developed some... sort of feelings for him. He's just so kind and caring and down to earth – everything I had hoped to find in Teddy, and I thought I had seen fleeting bursts of some of these qualities, I guess I was just seeing what I wanted to see. I can't believe it took me deciding that he was the right person for me to see how he was really so, so wrong for me.

I look out to sea, leaning on the old wooden fence that surrounds the wedding barn, and think about what my life is going to look like moving forwards. I should leave London, move somewhere quieter, somewhere more me. I would love to live here, but I don't imagine I can rent the beach house indefinitely (mostly because I don't think I could afford more than a night on my own), but maybe I can take my time, push on with my work, and see if I can find somewhere in a location like this, at least.

'Hey, sis,' Dougie says as he takes up the spot next to me. 'Ever the drama queen, eh?'

'Oh, you know me, always happy to steal the show,' I joke. 'But now it's all done and dusted, you can have a wedding day to yourself – a major event that you don't have to share with me. Make the most of it.'

'I've got to admit, you've freaked me out a little,' he says quietly. 'Pulling out at the last minute like this. I suppose you do just kind of get swept along with it, you don't stop and wonder if you're making a mistake... but you have.'

'Okay, stop right there,' I insist. 'You're not making a mistake. You and Eden are solid, you're so happy. There were so many red flags with Teddy, the decision came so easily in the end. For starters, he pretty much told me that the main reason he proposed was so that he could secure his promotion at work – his grandma likes the company to uphold this safe family image – I suppose that's how you get people to trust you with their millions – so he was kind of using me for that. But there were other things too. Like I found out he slept with someone else, when we first started seeing each other, and it was someone we knew but he kept it from me, which made it feel like this whole thing, like a little glimpse at... even if it wasn't a lie, just a lack of truth. That's not a good start for a relationship. Well, not for me, at least.'

'Wow, Liv, I'm so sorry,' Dougie says, wrapping an arm around me. 'That's awful. If it's any consolation, I think you've done the right thing. Any dishonesty, even at the start, would be a deal-breaker for me too, 100 per cent.'

All of a sudden, I feel my entire body involuntarily stiffen up, which Dougie notices, because he knows me so well.

'What was that?' he asks.

'What? Nothing,' I insist. 'Nothing.'

'It wasn't nothing,' he replies. 'You just went all weird – and you're still being weird.'

I don't know how exactly I'm being weird, so I can't stop whatever it is I'm doing, but he's not wrong. I feel so uncomfortable.

'Do you know something?' he asks, narrowing his eyes at me.

'Okay, look, it doesn't need to be awkward, but Teddy told me about

Eden seeing someone else when you guys were first together, but I promise you, there's no judgement here, I wasn't being funny, our situations are completely different,' I reassure him.

'Teddy told you that?' he says angrily.

'No, no, not really,' I reply. 'He isn't going around telling people or anything like that. I overheard the two of them talking about it, and you know I'll never tell anyone either. It's none of my business. If you're happy, I'm happy.'

I pause for breath.

'I didn't know about it,' he says eventually, his jaw muscles tightening. 'I, er, I need to go.'

Dougie runs off, down the beach, before I can stop him.

'Dougie, wait, come back,' I call, but it's no use. He gets smaller and smaller until he's eventually out of my sight.

'Where's Dougie?' Eden asks me.

I jump out of my skin.

'Oh, erm, he just went to get something, I'm not sure what, I don't know if it's a surprise... or... or something,' I tell her, which is a terrible excuse to make, if no surprise materialises. Although the surprise could be that her wedding is off too, so I might not be too far off the mark.

'Listen, while it's just the two of us, thank you so much for sorting us an amazing photographer, even in spite of everything that you're going through,' she tells me sincerely. 'I can't even imagine what you're going through.'

Oh, god, you might have to try...

'But, for what it's worth, selfish reasons for wanting the day to myself aside, I know you're doing the right thing,' she reassures me. 'I don't know if Teddy told you that I knew, but I overheard him and Verity talking at that New Year's Eve party you guys threw. She was begging him for another chance, so I quickly worked out what was going on. I know that you had forgiven him but... I don't know, it's nothing to do with me, but I never could've forgiven someone for keeping secrets like that.'

I stare at her for a moment.

'Right, yeah,' I reply. 'There's no real coming back from that, is there?'

'Exactly,' she replies. 'So, yeah, know that you've done the right thing.'

'Sorry, I've just remembered that I told Heidi I would meet her, I didn't realise the time,' I say, without so much as glancing at my watch. 'But thank you so much. I appreciate your kind words.'

'That's what family is for,' she replies with a smile.

I walk slowly at first, trying not to raise suspicion, but then once I'm around the corner I quickly pick up the pace, until I'm practically running, rushing to the beach house to see if Dougie is there.

I mean, the good news is that, it turns out, Teddy is an even bigger liar than I first thought, so I have definitely, without a shadow of a doubt, done the right thing by calling off the wedding – good riddance. The bad news, however, is that in falling for Teddy's lies, I have inadvertently passed them on to Dougie, who has taken me at my word and done a runner. But Dougie and Eden's wedding is one that should absolutely go ahead. I may have put doubt in his mind but, if I can just find him, I can take it away again, before any damage is done.

I just hope I can find him before he says or does something he can't take back.

31

'Hey, Liv,' I hear a familiar voice call out.

I whip around to see Hugo walking down the beach house path. He eventually joins me on the beach.

'How was the rehearsal?' he asks when he catches up with me. His face falls. 'Oh, no, did they not take the news well?'

'It's not that,' I reply, unable to hide the fact that I'm out of breath. 'Everyone took it well – like, *really* well, which, you know, great for me, further proof I'm doing the right thing, etcetera. But, to make a long story short, I accidentally told Dougie that Eden had cheated on him – which she hadn't, I'd got the wrong end of the stick – and he's run away. So now I'm trying to find him, before anyone realises, but I'm having no luck. His phone is going straight to voicemail too, so I can't even call him.'

'So just your classic pre-wedding hiccups,' he jokes, lightening the mood, but then he's straight back to business. 'Don't worry, okay, I'll help you find him.'

'Thank you so much,' I reply. 'His car is still in the car park. I've checked the house from top to bottom but there's no sign of him. He seemed like he ran off down the beach. The thing is, I know my brother, and before he settled down with Eden, he was your typical guy-who-works-in-finance kind of party animal. I'm worried that, if this has rattled him enough, he'll already be somewhere knocking back shots, trying to revive the good old days.'

'I've only known your brother a week or so, but he and Eden seem so in love, I don't think there is anything he wouldn't do for her,' Hugo points out. 'We'll find him, okay? We can head down the beach, take a look around, most of the bars are that way anyway, in the town centre. It's going to be fine.'

God, I hope he's right.

A little way down the beach, a shifty-looking man at the end of a jetty flags us down.

'Oi, are you one of those cool couples who likes to get wild?' he asks.

'We're not a couple,' Hugo replies, dismissing him.

'Even better,' the man replies, in the strongest local accent I've heard so far. 'How would the two of you like tickets to the hottest, wildest party boat this side of Ibiza?'

'No, thanks,' I reply.

'Speak for yourself,' the man says. 'What about you, fella, you want to meet some nice girls looking to have a good time? You can forget all your troubles on the party boat.'

I stop in my tracks. No... surely not?

I take my phone from my pocket and pull up the most recent photo of Dougie from Eden's Instagram page. She posts so many photos of him, we'll never have a problem if we ever need to show anyone what he looks like.

'Have you seen this man?' I ask. 'Did he get on the boat?'

'Oh, yeah, I sold a ticket to that fella,' he confirms. 'He couldn't wait to get on board. So, you want one ticket or two?'

'If we buy tickets, can we go get him?' I ask.

'No, sorry, you can only buy tickets for the next party voyage, see, the boat is already way out there,' he informs us, gesturing to the large boat that is far out to sea. 'I can recommend a pub while you wait, though – great place if you love to sing Elvis on the karaoke machine.'

'Thanks for your help,' I say in a normal tone, although I know in my head I meant it sarcastically. Now isn't the time to piss off a man who probably knows a great place to hide bodies.

'You don't think he's gone to even the score, do you?' I ask Hugo, not that he'll know the answer. 'Oh, my god, we need to get to him. How can we get to him?'

'Follow me,' Hugo insists as he picks up the pace, heading back toward the hotel. 'I've got a boat. Well, it's the hotel boat. I'm not exactly an expert but I've taken it out before, I know how to operate it.'

'Like a real boat, with a motor and stuff? And you can definitely drive it?' I ask, checking the credentials of the boat/sailor all while knowing absolutely nothing about boats generally.

'Yeah, absolutely,' he replies. 'It's nothing fancy. It's certainly seen better days.'

'No, that would be wonderful,' I reply. 'I'm not exactly in a position to be demanding a superyacht.'

There is, however, a whole spectrum of boats that exist, and while a superyacht might be up there with the best of them, the hotel boat must be all the way at the bottom, just above a rubber dinghy, and maybe above a pedal boat. This isn't a superyacht, it's a super mess.

'Best I can do,' Hugo says with a wince, seeing the look on my face. 'But, if we can get close to it, we can flag someone down maybe, try get through to them on the radio, or something. We'll figure it out. What do you say?'

'I say you definitely don't know what you're doing,' I reply with a laugh. 'But I say... let's do it.'

I've always thought it would be nice to hire a boat here, to go exploring beyond the shore, to enjoy the sea air and look back at Porthian Sands and enjoy the view from a whole new perspective. Not on this bad boy, though.

I'm hoping it's just superficial. The paint is all chipped and faded, and the cabin is way past its prime, but it floats and presumably it moves. That's all I can ask for right now.

Hugo starts up the engine. It coughs and splutters but then it settles.

'There we go,' he says proudly. 'Let's go!'

Under any other circumstances, even on board this heap of junk, this would probably be fun and exciting. But not when there's a wedding hanging in the balance – the only wedding we have left.

At first, it's fine, not exactly plain sailing, but we're on our way. But then, as the boat starts to bob up and down on the waves, I get this horrible feeling in the pit of my stomach.

'Are you okay?' Hugo asks. 'Sorry, I should have mentioned it would be a bit of a rough ride.'

'I bet you say that to all the girls,' I joke, despite feeling like I'm about to throw up. I suppose it's a good sign, I haven't felt my usual jokey self lately, perhaps the old me is starting to come back out. God, I hope that's the only thing that comes out.

'Is that your phone?' Hugo calls out over the noise.

I pull it from my pocket to see Dougie's name on the screen.

'Hello?' I call out when I answer.

'Liv, listen, I need to talk to you,' he says seriously.

'No, I need to talk to you,' I reply, shouting a little.

'Let me go first, please,' he replies. 'Listen, I've been for a run to clear my head, I've had a think, and I think I can forgive Eden. If, like you said, it was early on, it was before we were exclusive or whatever then, yeah, okay, I can forget about it. But I need you to promise not to mention it to anyone else, not even Eden, and definitely don't tell her that I know. I don't want anything to ruin tomorrow and I don't want her worrying that this might change the way I feel, or the way I look at her, because it hasn't and it won't.'

I smile to myself. Wow, she's got herself a good one there.

'Dougie, listen, I made a mistake,' I tell him. 'Eden hasn't done anything. I got the wrong end of the stick. When I caught her talking to Teddy, it was about Teddy, not her, he just told me it was her to take the heat off him. But I promise you, that's the truth, and no one else knows a thing.'

'Oh,' he says simply. 'Well, that makes all that easier. Maybe check your facts before you tell people potentially relationship-ending tales the day before their wedding.'

He's joking – or at least half joking.

'Where are you?' he asks. 'It sounds like you're on the wing of a plane.'

'That might be safer,' I joke. 'Listen, I'll tell you later, but right now I need to go sort something out.'

'No worries,' he says with a laugh.

Perhaps I won't tell him that I thought he was on a party boat, trying to forget about his fiancée by drinking, dancing and god knows what else with a bunch of out-of-control drunk people. In my defence, the guy trying to sell us tickets did tell us he was on there, although the clue is in the statement, he was trying to sell us tickets, he would've told us anything.

'Phew, false alarm,' I tell Hugo. 'He's not on the boat, he's not upset, and he has the facts now, so crisis averted, you can turn the boat around.'

'That's a huge relief,' Hugo says, but as he begins to turn the boat around, the engine seems to be struggling. The boat makes these horrible noises, like nothing I've ever heard before, as it starts to shake.

'Oh, no. No, no, no,' I say. 'Come on, don't do this.'

Fantastic, I'm talking to the boat.

Suddenly the engine cuts out and the cabin falls into eerie silence.

'Ah,' Hugo says simply. 'I guess it doesn't like turning any more.'

I take a deep breath in, then push it out. In, then out again.

'I don't suppose you can really know that you're claustrophobic until you're, you know, *stranded in a small, knackered old boat in the middle of the sea.*'

My sentence starts out so calm before quickly shifting to something more unhinged.

Hugo hurries over to me and rubs my shoulders.

'It's okay, listen, breathe, breathe,' he says soothingly. 'It's all going to be absolutely fine. Step out of the cabin, get some air, and I'll call for help on the radio.'

'Okay. Okay, yeah,' I reply, doing my worst impression of a calm person.

Out on the – what? Deck? – I take deep breaths, filling my lungs with the fresh sea air that only minutes ago seemed so appealing to me. But now, looking out, seeing nothing but water on three sides, and the Porthian Sands shore so far away in the other direction, with the dead boat I'm standing on still bouncing on the water below me, I'm a wreck.

'Okay, nothing to worry about,' Hugo says. 'Either the coastguard or some other nearby boat will come and get us as soon as they can. We're perfectly safe in the meantime. Do you want to wait out here, in the fresh air, or in the cabin?'

'The cabin,' I quickly insist. 'I think I stand the best chance of pretending I'm not on a boat in there.'

Hugo leads the way back into the small cabin. We sit down together on a little sofa that I'm guessing pulls out into a bed. It's impossible to ignore the feeling of bobbing up and down but I do feel slightly more shielded in here. Basically, it's fine unless we sink – why would I say that?

'Sorry, Liv, I was just trying to help,' he says softly. 'But I'm glad that Dougie is okay, and happy, and I'm impressed at the lengths you would go to, to save his wedding.'

'Eden will be *livid* if I drown,' I point out, relaxing a little. 'She'll probably say I did it on purpose, to ruin her wedding, like, *if I can't get married, no one can.*'

I say this in a quiet, faux-angry voice. Then I smile.

'Actually, she's been a little better today,' I tell him. 'I'm really happy for them.'

'Maybe you can use this in your next book,' he suggests. 'If the retelling of your great-grandparents goes well.'

'Here's hoping,' I reply. 'There's always a worry, when you write fiction, that people will see what they want to see in it, and make wild assumptions. I remember ghostwriting a book for someone who was on *Just Married UK*.'

'What's that?' he replies.

'Oh, it's just another reality show, one where people marry a stranger, and then a camera crew follows them around to see if they can make it work,' I explain. 'Anyway, the woman I wrote the book for won the series, and she was a gorgeous, middle-class, privately educated trainee doctor – although she's turned her back on her profession to live her best influencer life. Anyway, I wrote a Christmas romance for her, and obviously with it being fiction, I invented this gorgeous little village in the Scottish Highlands, I came up with the personality for the main character, her family – the works. All me, all from my brain.'

'Is it hard to see someone else take credit for your work?' he asks.

'I think, as a ghostwriter, you understand it's part of the job,' I reply. 'But the problem was that a reviewer, who devoured the book in a few days, said she was disappointed that the author – assuming it was the reality star – had just written about her own childhood, and her own parents, and that it wasn't very original to describe herself.'

'But she didn't write it,' Hugo says.

'Nope, and I didn't know anything about her, her childhood or her family – I didn't even have an especially detailed brief, just that it should be a romance between a young local woman and a mysterious businessman, set in the Scottish Highlands, at Christmas. That's the worry with writing fiction. You can write anything you can imagine, the possibilities are endless, but then people can read into it however they want, and make whatever assumptions they want.'

'Yeah, I don't think I could do that,' he replies. 'That must be a nightmare.'

'I love writing, I love making jokes, and I do like to be inspired by real life but, yes, it's problematic,' I continue. 'I sent Teddy the synopsis for my new book. He didn't mention it, so I assumed he hadn't read it, but eventually he brought it up in an argument, saying that my description of the love interest was, well, a description of you.'

Hugo wasn't expecting me to say that. His eyes widen.

'He thinks I'm in your book?' he replies. 'The one we've been talking about?'

'Not exactly,' I say. 'I suppose he thinks that the love interest is like you, as though I'd sat down to write the perfect man and describing you was where I landed.'

'I am pretty perfect,' he jokes, making short work of a potentially awkward moment.

'Oh, you really are,' I say playfully. 'It's the eyes, the hair, the teeth, *the muscles.*'

'And don't forget my dazzling personality,' he adds. 'Are you the leading lady in the book?'

'Oh, no, she's far nicer, cooler, more stylish, better hair, and she has her shit way more together,' I reply.

'Oh, no, I think you'd make a great leading lady,' Hugo insists. 'You're kind, funny –absolutely hilarious, in fact. You're beautiful too, although you don't seem to realise it, which is seriously cute. You're smart, you know what you want in life. I think that's exactly the kind of main character you should have.'

I'm a little taken aback by his compliments. I don't know what to do other than carry on the joke.

'Says you,' I reply. 'A leading lady based on me would be no match for a leading man based on you. Those big, sexy shoulders. The dimples when you smile. And that kiss earlier, that was... a romance-worthy kiss, that's for sure.'

'It was something else, wasn't it?' he says through a smile. 'I don't think I've ever felt a kiss like that.'

'Me either,' I confess. 'Do you think it was just the moment? The audience, the stakes, the craziness of it all?'

'Perhaps,' he replies. 'But if you ever want to give it another go and find out, I can't think of a worse time, place or atmosphere to test the theory.'

I laugh as I lean closer to him on the sofa. Would it be so bad to kiss him again?

Hugo leans in too, stopping just short of my face, almost as though he isn't going to move another inch, not unless he knows I want him to. He waits for a second, to see if I bring my lips to meet his again.

Screw it.

This time, there is no warm-up required. Our kiss goes from nought to me climbing onto his lap, running my hands through his hair in a matter of seconds. Hugo places his hands on my body, running them up and down my back as we kiss. As he stands up, I wrap my legs around his body and my arms around his neck. We kiss until he eventually lays me down on the sofa. Then he takes a step back.

I suppose we could call that a successful experiment – and a completed one too. The buzz of the competition earlier wasn't the reason why our kiss was so electric, in fact, the audience only held us back. But now, here, there's no one watching, nowhere to go, it's as though the rest of the world doesn't exist.

Hugo puffs air from his cheeks.

'Sorry, sorry,' he says as he runs a hand through his hair. 'That was... wow. I don't know what came over me. Sorry.'

'Don't apologise,' I insist, holding out my hands, beckoning him down on top of me. 'This is exactly how I would write it. Although, if this were a romcom, I would probably write it so that the coastguard turned up while we were in the middle of... something, but I'm willing to risk it if you are.'

Hugo shrugs.

'I'm sure they've seen stranger things happen at sea,' he says with a laugh.

I'm not even going to think about whether or not this is a terrible idea. My life is a bit of a mess, I'm stranded at sea, and I'm no longer getting married so, if something is going to make me happy, then fuck it. Why not?

Plus, I refuse to see how anything could be wrong when it feels this right. And this really does feel right.

32

'Champagne,' I sing brightly, brandishing a silver tray with a bottle and four glasses on it.

'Wow, you're awfully chipper considering this is supposed to be the morning of your wedding, but you're not actually getting married any more,' Heidi replies.

Cindy, Eden's best friend, who arrived from LA in the early hours of the morning, gasps dramatically.

'It's okay,' I reassure her. 'Not everyone is blessed with a lovely best friend like you. Mine has a horrible sense of humour.'

'Says the girl who, when we bumped into Harry Styles in a bar in London, told him a knock-knock joke,' Heidi teases.

'Don't worry, this is their thing,' Eden tells Cindy.

'And, honestly, I am chipper,' I admit. 'I've made the right decision for me, I'm sticking with it, and yes, this is weird, but it's not like I spent months planning this wedding, dreaming of it, counting down the days. It's been a few weeks, I'd barely adjusted to it, I've adjusted back.'

I say all of this like it's a joke and, yes, I am playing down how I feel, but I don't want anyone feeling sorry for me today, or even thinking about me at all. This is Dougie and Eden's day, all of the attention should be on them, and I'm sure I'll have my own wedding to hog the limelight at – just not today.

We're all dressed up, all ready to make the short journey from the house to the wedding barn. The ceremony takes place on the patio area outside, which leads out on to the beach. Then everyone heads into the wedding barn for the reception. I can't believe it's getting knocked down. It's such a shame, and such a loss to the hotel. They don't realise what they have.

Eden drops a straw into her champagne, to avoid ruining her lipstick, and of course this makes her drink fizz uncontrollably.

Cindy is on her feet in a flash, snatching the glass from Eden's hand, getting it as far away from her dress as possible, like it's a live grenade or something.

'See, that's what real friends do,' I tell Heidi with a nudge as I follow her out onto the master bedroom balcony.

'You're right, I'm awful, I don't know why you're friends with me,' she replies.

'I know I've said this already but thank you so, *so* much for coming,' I say sincerely.

'Well, there was no way I was going to miss your wedding,' she replies. 'But there was definitely no way I wasn't going to be here for you in your hour of need. I feel like I just knew you needed me.'

'Because we have this telepathic bestie connection?' I say.

'Yes, well, that or because I knew Teddy wasn't right for you,' she replies. 'Plus, your mum sent me a photo of Hugo days ago, and oof. I came here just to see him.'

I laugh.

'Yeah, he has that effect on everyone,' I reply.

'You can tell he really likes you,' she points out. 'I wouldn't stand a chance.'

'I know that we haven't known each other long, we live in different counties, and I am very fresh out of a mistake of an engagement, but it's just so nice to be spending time with someone nice and honest and normal,' I reply. 'For a change.'

'Don't worry about silly things like time and distance,' Heidi insists. 'If you like him, be with him. Life is too short to be worried about grace periods. Lord knows Teddy won't be sweating it.'

She's probably right. All I care about is focusing on being happy, and all the good in the world, instead of dwelling on the bad.

'And after reading the synopsis you emailed me, and all the stuff about your great-grandparents, who knows? Perhaps Hugo is your scruffy, skint leading man?'

I snort.

'I wouldn't have put it like that, but I take your point,' I reply. 'Now hug me. I love you, Heids.'

'Love you too, Liv.'

So, the coastguard didn't quite catch Hugo and me getting up to no good on the boat, but it was a bit of a close one. We didn't exactly get a chance to debrief afterwards, and by the time we got back on dry land, and headed to the beach house, the dinner party Mum was throwing was already in full swing. Until we talk, until we figure out what it is we're doing, I don't want to tell anyone else that anything happened.

But I do like him. My gosh, I really do.

'Okay, ladies, let's go get married,' Eden announces as we head back inside. Ordinarily, that would be a fine thing to say, but I see her beat herself up for her choice of words. 'I mean, let's go get me married!'

She says it with just as much enthusiasm the second time. I can't help but laugh.

As we make the short journey from the house to the wedding barn, I do my best to keep my cool but, as soon as the barn is in sight, I feel my heart start pounding. One tear manages to escape my eye. I quickly wipe it away, confident I've gotten away with it, until Eden links her arm with mine.

'Are you okay?' she asks me.

'Oh, I'm fine,' I insist.

'I'm sorry things didn't work out between you and Teddy,' she says. 'And that you're not getting married today.'

'Don't be,' I insist. 'Honestly, it was all for the best, and I know I'll marry someone I truly love one day. This little wobble is just because I'm not going to get to do it here, in Granddad's barn, that's all. I'm fine.'

'I'm sorry about that too,' she says. 'But thank you for being here for me.

I don't want to upset you, and I know we said we weren't having brides-maids, but I would love it if you would walk down the aisle before me, and stand with me at the altar, as my sister. But only if you don't think that would be too painful or weird.'

'I would love to,' I tell her honestly.

Yes, okay, it's pretty weird to still be walking down the aisle, and still standing at the altar, but Eden calling me her sister and wanting me by her side is something I never thought would happen. So I'm going to forget about my problems, about my wedding being cancelled, about the wedding barn being destroyed for good. I'm just going to focus on being there for my new sister. Because that's what families do.

33

For the first three or four steps down the aisle, I wondered what people might think of me. I'm sure everyone was feeling sorry for me, how could you not? But I worried about whether or not they pitied me. If they looked at me, treading the path I was supposed to walk under much different circumstances, and thought to themselves: oh, how tragic is this? Her, still walking down the aisle, with no one waiting for her at the other end.

But I hadn't even made it halfway before I let go of notions like that. Because even if people did think it was tragic (which I doubt they do), I can think of something so much worse: marrying a man you don't really love, only to live unhappily until your inevitable divorce.

I can honestly say that I was so proud, and so happy, to stand up there with Dougie and Eden as they made things official. Even though it might not have happened for me today, the two of them are absolute goals. They look so gorgeous, and most importantly so happy, that you can't even feel envious, just inspired to find someone who loves you so much that they want to spend the rest of their life with you.

The ceremony is over, the confetti has been thrown, and now it's time for the photos.

Everyone is being ushered around, baking under the midday sun, as the photography team sets up.

I can't resist running a hand up and down the wall of the wedding barn, stroking the wood, making a memory of how it feels, how it smells – things that won't show up in the photos.

'Give me your phone,' Eden demands, snapping me from my thoughts.

I should probably ask why, but I don't. I take my phone from my clutch, unlock it and hand it over.

'Right, there you go,' she says, handing it back to me. 'The town hall is a seven-minute walk from here. Go to the meeting, see if there's something you can do.'

'Don't be daft,' I insist. 'It's photo time – I'm not skipping your photos.'

'We'll do the couple photos first,' she replies. 'Everyone else can go inside and have a drink. It's too hot out here anyway. We'll do the family and group photos when you get back.'

'Eden, are you sure?' I reply.

'If there is even a chance that you can get married here too then you have to take it,' she insists. 'So, go, give it your all, and get back here so we can celebrate.'

I lean forward and kiss her on the cheek.

'I never realised how much I needed a sister until today,' I tell her. 'Thank you.'

I glance at the map on my phone. If you go up past the hotel, up the drive and out onto the road, then you don't have to follow it for long before you're in the main part of the town, where the town hall is. But, looking at what is around it on the map, I notice Shell's Café right across the road. I'll get there potentially even faster if I go via the beach.

I kick off my heels, grab them in my hand and make my way down to the beach. Once my feet hit that sand, that's it, I'm off. At first, I start with a fast walk but, before I know what I'm doing, the hot sun of the day be damned, I am running as fast as my feet (and the sand) will allow. I'm not just running to make the meeting, I'm running to save the barn. Maybe Eden is right, maybe I can still get married there one day. I feel like my fate is in my own hands and I like it. Right now, I feel like I can do anything.

I'm a little sweaty, and a lot warm, as I huff and puff my way through the town hall doors.

'I'm here for the meeting,' I practically pant at the woman behind the desk. 'About... about the hotel.'

She pulls a face at me as she looks me up and down. Ultimately, she deems me harmless.

'The public viewing gallery is up the stairs, second door on the left,' she replies. 'The meeting is already in session, but you can watch from up there.'

'Thanks,' I reply.

I don't quite have it in me to Rocky my way up the stairs but I'm proud of my fast walk, given the circumstances.

I follow the lady on reception's instructions until I find myself on a balcony that looks down over the meeting below.

'...and obviously in circumstances like these, the council believes that demolishing the building is the only option,' says a man who seems to be chairing the panel.

'And you know you have the whole community's support,' a woman sitting next to him adds. 'Not one resident has turned up to object.'

I feel stupid. Of course you have to live here to make an objection. Even if I did say something, look how pally they are, they're not going to listen to me. They have all clearly made up their minds.

I think about what to do for a moment. Okay, I've definitely seen enough movies to know how this goes, sometimes all it takes is an emotional speech from someone who opposes what is about to happen, who can charm their way into the hearts and minds of everyone involved. If I can just find the right words.

'Well, if that's everything covered, we'll let you go, we know you're a busy man,' the chair says.

I just need to say something, anything, and hopefully the rest will follow. If I don't, the hotel owner is going to leave and I won't get a chance to say anything.

Speak now, or forever hold your peace.

'Thanks very much,' the owner replies. He stands up, walks over to the table and shakes hands with each of them. 'I've got a wedding to get to.'

He turns around and my worst suspicions are confirmed. It's him. It's Hugo.

I step out of the way quicky, pressing my back against the wall so that he can't see me. Incredible that I'm the one who feels embarrassed, I'm the one hiding from him. I can't believe he made himself out to be just some bar manager who happened to live in the little cottage next to the hotel. He owns the hotel. He's the one stopping the weddings and he's the one tearing down my granddad's barn.

I pick up my shoes from the floor and leave the room, hovering at the top of the stairs for a moment until I see Hugo leave first. Once I'm confident he's out of the way, I head down the stairs.

I can't believe it, I honestly can't. Hugo seems so normal, so down to earth. He can't be another well-off, selfish, out-of-touch idiot, and yet here we are, he doesn't only own the hotel but he's the one demolishing the wedding barn my granddad built and, with it, my chance to get married there.

And if all of that isn't bad enough, I can't even melt down over it. I can't throw myself to the sand and cry and punch the ground because, of fucking course, I have a wedding to go to – a wedding that Hugo will also be attending.

My chances of my dream wedding may be over, but Dougie and Eden can still have theirs. And I'll be damned if I'm going to let Lord Hugo ruin it.

34

Remember that thing I said about how grown, considerate adults don't make scenes and ruin people's parties? My god, that's going to be hard today.

Still, whatever I'm going through, however I'm feeling, dearly beloved, we are gathered here today to join together this man and this woman in holy matrimony, and it's my job to keep a lid on things.

So, as much as I want to shout at Hugo, to call him out, to embarrass him in front of everyone, to stick him on his broken-down boat – *that he owns* – and push him out to sea, I can't do any of that. The temptation is there, though, and I am only human after all, so since I arrived, I have taken the necessary steps to keep Hugo well out of my way.

The first thing I did, when I arrived back here, was sneak inside and change the seating plan. Luckily, the board is magnetic, so it's easy to edit. Eden sat me with Hugo – because of course she did, why wouldn't she? How was she to know that in a matter of minutes I was going to go from loving him to hating him? Well, you know what I mean, I don't *love him* love him. I've gone from *liking* him to hating him. That's better. So I crept up to the seating chart and started making slight adjustments. At first, I moved things so that Hugo and I would be at opposite sides of the same table – a subtle way to ensure that I didn't have to sit next to him. Then I realised that would mean I was looking at him, though, and I didn't want that. He would be smiling across the table and I would be scowling back at him. No, no, that's not how you avoid a scene.

In the end, I decided that I would move Heidi from the singles table, to sit next to me, and I would banish Hugo to the singles table where he deserves to be, but someone almost caught me in the act so I had to hurry and, in doing so, I later found out I'd made a slight error, sitting Hugo and Heidi together, and sitting myself at the singles table.

I've got to say, as much as I wasn't sure about the idea of wedding colours and so on, Eden has done a fantastic job. The colours do look amazing, so soft and summery, and most people have happily obliged with the dress code – myself included – which may be super extra, but I can appreciate the effect. I'll bet the photos are going to look amazing.

The wedding barn is decorated so beautifully. I love all the twinkling lights that hang from the rafters, the giant illuminated letters – an E and a D – in honour of the happy couple. From the table settings to the flowers to genuinely just about everything, this wedding is a dream and I would have loved it to have been mine… but not with the wrong person. *Never* with the wrong person.

'You're on the singles table, that can't be right?' Mum said to me when we arrived and looked at the seating chart – which is a work of art in its own right. 'Let me double-check with Eden what's going on.'

'No, no, honestly, don't bother her with it,' I insisted. 'I would actually quite like to sit at the singles table.'

Mum pulled a face at me, as though she was unsure what my game was. I think everyone with eyes has realised that there is something between me and Hugo, and everyone is so happy for us. But my mum knows that I am a grown woman, so she let it be.

So, yes, here I am, at the singles table, sandwiched between one of Eden's influencer friends and a man called Andy who I already know because he and Dougie were best friends all the way through school.

I haven't really spoken to Andy since I was a teenager. He seems nice enough. He's a PE teacher now but I'm not holding it against him.

Hugo has tried to approach me a few times, and it's been quite easy to dodge him, given that we've just had a sit-down meal, but now the food is finished and I'm starting to wonder how I'm going to keep him away from me.

I know the plan for the day – it was once my wedding too, after all – so I know that the first dance is coming up, and then the band are going to play for a while. When everyone is allowed to move freely, there's going to be no stopping him coming up to me and talking to me.

I fast worked out that this is only the singles table in a very literal sense. It isn't for people who aren't in relationships, it's simply for people who came without a guest. Andy isn't single, he has a wife and three kids. Most of the other people at the table are single, though, and many of them have been flirting up a storm. Andy and I have sort of stuck together. It's been nice talking to him, though, seeing pictures of his kids and his dog and the rear extension on his house, and I genuinely mean it. Just a nice, normal person showing me their nice, normal life.

It turns out – for the best, funnily enough – that Eden was slightly embarrassed about the two of us having a joint wedding, so she neglected to mention it on her wedding invitations. I suppose it could have been quite awkward if it had gone ahead, or if she had mentioned it, but the fact that she didn't means I don't have any explaining to do to anyone. Andy doesn't know a thing other than what I've told him. He didn't roll his eyes at my job, he's been laughing at my jokes – my self-confidence is at an all-time high.

'To be honest, I don't think Eden wanted kids at the wedding,' Andy tells me.

Ah, that sounds like Eden. I doubt kids are on-brand.

'But it was fine because, now that we've got three, anywhere we don't have to cart them along, it's much easier. Plus, it's nice to get a break from them, every now and then,' he explains. 'I love them all, so much, but sometimes it's just nice to enjoy some adult company.'

'Hello,' Hugo says, squatting down next to us.

Shit, I take my eye off the ball for a second. He does genuinely make me jump but me accidentally pouring my drink all over his trousers is no accident.

'Oh, my goodness, I am so sorry,' I insist.

'No worries,' he says with a laugh, although I think he can tell something is up. 'I'll just go... see what I can do about this.'

So much for Andy enjoying some adult company. Thankfully, he laughs.

'Wow, what did he do to piss you off?' he asks me.

'Nothing,' I insist with a smile.

'Oh, yeah, then why are the two of you acting like an old married couple?' he asks. 'Oldest trick in the book, that. You would be amazed how many cups of tea or plates of baby food my wife "mishandles" to avoid me.'

He thinks for a moment.

'I don't mean that as bad as it sounds,' he quickly adds.

'Can you do me a favour?' I ask him. 'How would you feel about slipping off that wedding ring and hiding it in your pocket?'

Andy's face drops.

'Look, Liv, I'm flattered...'

'Oh, no, god, no,' I babble. 'Nothing like that. It's just that guy, he won't take the hint. Maybe if he sees us talking, and he doesn't realise you're married, he'll back off a bit.'

'Well, I'm sure if it's in the interest of chivalry, my Donna won't mind,' he says, taking his ring off, popping it into his inside jacket pocket.

'Ladies and gentlemen, the bride and groom will be taking to the floor for their first dance,' a voice says through the speakers.

Dougie and Eden make their way to the floor before the song they chose – Elton John's 'Can You Feel the Love Tonight' – starts playing.

Ahh, they look so happy.

Teddy and I never got around to choosing a song for our first dance. I wonder what we would've chosen. I mean, he probably wouldn't have cared what it was, or been all that bothered to choose one to begin with but, if we both had to write a song down, you can guarantee our choices would be polar opposites. He would probably choose something slow but ultimately sad – like a Lewis Capaldi break-up ballad, without ever realising that was what it was. I would probably make a case for something fast and kind of silly. Something tongue in cheek like Silk Sonic's 'Leave the Door Open' or something fun like 'You're My Best Friend' by Queen. I've never really been one for slow dancing.

'Ladies and gentlemen, the bride and groom would like to request that you all join them on the dance floor.'

'Will you dance with me, please?' I ask. 'Just so that guy doesn't ask me.'

'Go on then, why not, but I'll warn you I have two left feet.'

'I have two right feet,' I reply. 'We'll be perfect together.'

'You never know with men, do you?' Andy says as we dance. 'That guy seems like a nice bloke. It must be a nightmare, being a single woman.'

'Thanks for reminding me,' I say with a smile. 'He's not like a major creep or anything. But he's not as great as he seems.'

'Is there history there?' he asks curiously.

'Only about a fortnight's worth,' I admit with a laugh.

'Hey, mate, do you mind if I cut in?' Hugo asks.

How has he crept up on us again? Once again, I jump out of my skin. As I pull away from Andy a little, his wedding ring falls to the floor – it must not have been all the way into his pocket. He bends down and quickly picks it up.

'Sorry,' he mouths to me as he backs away.

I bat my hand, to show him that it's not a big deal.

'So, can we dance?' Hugo asks.

'Sure,' I reply, still eager to do what I can to avoid making a scene.

Hugo places his hands on my waist. I hook my arms around his neck, although I try not to get too close.

He looks good, really handsome with his hair neatly styled, in his cool navy suit. He's really made an effort – although it's the same suit he had on earlier, for his big meeting, so it's impossible to know whether he wore his wedding suit to the meeting, or if he's wearing his meeting suit to the wedding. Either way, it reminds me of who he is and what he's doing and it gets my back up.

'Is everything okay?' he asks me.

'Yes, of course,' I reply. 'Why?'

Why did I ask why?

'You've hardly said a word to me all day,' he replies. 'In fact, what you just said to me a second ago might be the most words you've said to me all day. And I'd kind of hoped we would be sitting together...'

'Yeah, I wanted to be at the singles table,' I reply. 'Now I'm back on the market, you know, no time like the present to get back on the horse.'

'Well, I'm pretty sure that guy is married,' Hugo points out, smiling, but clearly concerned something is up – the man really can read me like a book. 'And I don't want to sound like a teenage girl, but I kind of thought, after last night...'

'You're right, you do sound like a teenage girl,' I tell him.

'Sorry, am I getting the wrong end of the stick here?' he asks. 'If you want rid of me, just say. I'm a big boy.'

If I was going to make a scene, then now would be the perfect time. I could call him out in front of everyone – I could get creative, grab the mic from the lead singer of the band and warble aggressively (as well as completely out of key) a version of a not all that thoughtfully selected song, like 'Shout Out to My Ex' by Little Mix, in Hugo's direction, because that would show him. I suppose now might also be the time to sit down with him and have an honest conversation, to ask him what he was thinking, to calmly tell him that I'm mad at him and that he's just like all the rest – no, see, I'm getting upset already. There is no calmly talking about this.

So I only have one option, really, to take a bit of the truth, forget what is upsetting me, and make it all about something else.

'I don't want it to be a whole thing,' I start, my faux confidence growing with each word. 'But that... whatever it was, on the boat... it was, I don't know, a moment of madness. What do they call it? Cabin fever or something like that.'

'Cabin fever?' Hugo repeats back to me. 'We weren't even out there an hour.'

He isn't making this easy for me, is he? But why would he? The last time he spoke to me, things were great, and what I'm saying now doesn't really make a lot of sense.

It's probably best for everyone – me, him, everyone at the wedding – that I nip this in the bud ASAP. Cruel to be kind, it's all I can do.

'Hugo, you're not really taking the hint,' I say, which should hopefully do the trick. 'I'm going home tomorrow and we're not exactly going to keep in touch, are we?'

'So, you're saying...'

'You're reading too much into what was essentially a misjudged rebound kiss taken too far,' I say, even though it's not true. 'Let's not make a thing of it, yeah?'

He looks at me for a second before letting go of me. As he pulls his hands away from my body, I feel like he takes a bit of my heart with him.

'Sorry, yeah, I don't know what I was thinking,' he tells me, his face and his words completely void of any sort of feeling. 'I'll go home, give you some space.'

I just nod.

As Hugo walks away, leaving me alone on the dance floor, the only comfort I have is that having it out with him would have made everything so much worse.

'Fancy a dance?' I hear a man ask as he taps me on the shoulder.

'I would love to,' I say with a smile.

It's not a man at all, it's Heidi, putting on a deep voice.

'You looked like you needed someone,' she says. 'Want to talk about it?'

'Not now,' I tell her with a smile. 'Maybe later.'

'Got you,' she says. 'Come on then, let's dance. I've put in a request for something fun next.'

'Sounds perfect,' I reply.

No matter how messy things get, so long as you have your friends, you're always going to be okay. I just thought that, at the very least, I would have left here with Hugo as a friend.

But you know what they say: with friends like that...

35

At the end of the day – especially one that is hectic, tiring or stressful – you really can't beat kicking off your heels, stepping out of your dress, wiping off the layers of make-up and curling up on the sofa with a nice cup of tea.

One of the things that I love about the beach house is the fact that, despite it being this large, open-plan, ultra-modern space, it's still so cosy when you want it to be. Everyone else has gone to bed so that just leaves me, Mum and Heidi sitting on the sofas.

Aside from being a bit tired, and a few achy feet, there is no sign of the party on any of us. We're in our nightwear, cradling cups of tea, and passing around packets of biscuits as we chat about what a fantastic wedding it has been.

At night-time, all of the floor-to-ceiling windows and large patio doors turn black with the night sky. I actually find them quite cosy, and prefer not to close the blinds. I do like that if you look out into the garden, you can see all the pretty lights, and I love the look of the sea at night.

I'm trying not to think about Hugo, even though I can't get him out of my mind, but even if he is still in there, I'm trying not to let it show. If I keep trying to push him out, then hopefully he'll stay out.

'What about Hugo?' Heidi asks.

So much for trying to keep him out of my head. I look to my mummy, like a little girl, hoping she'll jump to my defence.

'We have all been wondering what's going on with the two of you,' Mum chimes in.

And so much for my mummy defending me.

'Nothing is going on,' I insist.

'The two of you have been inseparable,' Mum points out. 'In fact, I would go as far as to say that he is the only thing that has made you smile the entire time we've been here.'

'You know we're here on holiday, don't you?' I remind her with a laugh. 'We'll never see him again.'

'You speak for yourself,' Mum replies. 'Your dad and I have been having a chat about maybe moving out here. Don't get me wrong, we love the house in Oxford, but retiring by the sea would be a dream come true, wouldn't it?'

'I would love to live out here,' I say with a sigh. 'It's nice to think you'll be somewhere beautiful, when I have to move back in with you.'

Sadly, I'm only half joking.

'And, well, to be honest, I suspect we will see Hugo again,' Mum continues almost cautiously. 'If we move here, if we come back to stay at the hotel – whatever we decide to do. I know it's only been a couple of weeks, but he's sort of felt like part of the family. Instantly, really, unlike...'

Mum stops in her tracks.

'Unlike anything I've ever seen before,' she says, instead of what she was going to say, which was 'unlike Teddy'.

'Well, you might not want to say his name, but I will,' Heidi says, passing me my emotional-support chocolate digestives. 'I think it's clear to see, for everyone who has eyes, that you and Hugo clearly really like each other. Similarly, I think we all know that you and Teddy weren't right for each other – even you knew, and you know you did.'

I laugh at her clunky choice of words.

'I got caught up in the romance of the proposal,' I confess. 'I thought my options were to get married or break up, so obviously I went for the former, it felt like things were going so well.'

'There's no shame in being an optimist,' Mum tells me. 'Hoping for the best and giving things a go with an open heart is not a crime.'

'Exactly,' I reply.

'Yes, exactly,' Heidi continues.

I frown at her, puzzled, because I wasn't expecting her to say that.

'You were willing to give things a go with Teddy but he showed you his true colours,' she reminds me. 'You knew, before you called things off, that you didn't want to marry him, and that he wasn't right for you. You didn't mean to fall for Hugo, you just found the right person for you at the wrong time.'

'Hugo and I are just friends,' I stress.

'Just friends who want to rip each other's clothes off,' she points out.

I glance at my mum.

'Sweetheart, we've all seen the chemistry between the two of you,' Mum points out. 'It won a competition, didn't it?'

I sigh.

'I appreciate what you're both saying, I really do, and I would be lying if I said I didn't have feelings for him, but the fact is that it's too soon after Teddy to even be thinking about anyone else,' I tell them.

'You and Teddy weren't even together a year,' Heidi says with a flippant bat of her hand. 'But really, how long are you supposed to wait?'

'More than a week,' I say with a laugh.

'Who says?' Mum asks. 'Who says you have to wait? What amount of time will make people happy? A month? A year? And why do you care?'

'People will say it's too fast,' I point out.

'Not people who care,' Mum says with a smile. 'Sweetheart, life is far too short to worry about what people think, and to waste precious time with the wrong person – or with no one at all.'

I really do appreciate what they're both saying. My feelings for Hugo may have started as purely a friendship thing but I would be lying if I said they hadn't developed into something deeper this past week. It's the way he's brightened up my days, the way he was all for helping me make my wedding amazing before turning his attention to making me feel better when I finally told him that the wedding was off. He's kept me smiling, he's helped me stay positive about Dougie and Eden's wedding when all I've wanted to do is mourn my own, and as the week has gone on, it's become crystal clear to me that I felt the saddest about not getting married at my dream venue, and not things with Teddy not working out.

Surely a healthy relationship can't start in the shadow of another, though? And anyway, that's the least of my worries.

'To be honest, none of it matters,' I tell them. 'I was happy just taking things a day at a time, seeing how they went and, to be honest, we did kiss.'

Mum and Heidi smile the biggest, giddiest smiles I think I've ever seen.

'*But*,' I say, putting extra emphasis on the word so that they stop getting their hopes up. 'But the idea of moving on quickly, and whether or not it is too soon, is irrelevant because I found something else out about our friend Hugo.'

'Oh?' Mum says, her heart clearly in her mouth as she wonders what could be wrong with him.

'He's been lying about who he said he was,' I tell them. 'He owns the hotel – he owns this house.'

'What?' Heidi squeaks and I take back what I said before. Now she is smiling the biggest, brightest, happiest smile I have ever seen on a person in real life. 'You mean he's fit *and* rich?'

I can't help but laugh for a moment.

'Heidi, he's been lying to us all about it,' I tell her.

'No, he hasn't, sweetheart,' Mum tells me softly, correcting me, but with a smile as always. 'We knew that he owned the place, he told us all about it that night you were in London. He's actually planning on moving into this house, when all the bookings are completed – I know because your dad was trying to buy it off him.'

Mum laughs and rolls her eyes.

'He told me he was the bar manager,' I point out.

'Did he?' she replies. 'Well, that's strange, but I've heard of men doing worse things recently.'

'Liv, what are you doing?' Heidi asks. 'Why aren't you banging on his door, apologising for giving him the cold shoulder all day? You can salvage this.'

'He's the reason I'm not going to be able to get married here,' I tell them. 'Not Teddy. Teddy might not have been right for me, and I would've realised that in advance if we hadn't had to rush the wedding planning, and all because Hugo doesn't want to host weddings any more.'

Mum pulls a face, as if to suggest that doesn't really matter.

'Mum, he's knocking the barn down,' I tell her. 'The barn that Granddad built. It's a piece of history, and everyone else has been able to get married there, everyone but me.'

'Have you asked him why he's knocking down the barn?' Mum asks. 'Perhaps he has his reasons. And would you rather marry the wrong man in the "right" place or the right man in the "wrong" place? Beautiful wedding venues are ten a penny. Good men are hard to find.'

'Good, fit, rich men who like you back, no less,' Heidi adds with a smile.

I want to be with him – of course I do – but it's too soon, and it's not a good way to start something new and... and...

'I'm being ridiculous, aren't I?' I eventually say. 'I should talk to him, at least. Scorching the earth and disappearing isn't the right way to go about things.'

'You're just focusing on the wrong things,' Mum replies. 'Your grand-dad's barn has made a lot of people very happy. You don't need it. And you're worried about seeing how things go because of what people might think. You don't need to.'

'In reality, I don't think people begrudge others a bit of happiness where they can find it,' Heidi adds, taking things seriously for a moment. 'You deserve to be happy, Liv, and so does Hugo.'

Oh, god, I really am being ridiculous.

Why am I so quick to write Hugo off as another rich idiot who thinks he can do whatever he wants? Obviously I'm still reeling from figuring out what kind of man Teddy really is, and that's all the more reason to stop and think before getting involved with anyone else, but I shouldn't have just shoved Hugo away like I did, I should have talked to him.

'What do I do?' I ask no one in particular.

'Go to him,' Heidi says in a sort of jokey way. 'But seriously, go find him.'

'Just be honest with him,' Mum adds. 'And he'll be honest with you.'

'But probably go and put some clothes on first,' Heidi adds. 'As fetching as that shorts-and-vest combo is, turning up in your nightwear might make him think you're knocking on his door for something else.'

'Well, while you're up there,' Mum jokes quietly to Heidi.

'Mother!' I say, shocked. 'Okay, I'll go put some clothes on, and I'll go talk to him.'

'Just don't worry about it and go and see what happens,' Mum says.

I puff air from my cheeks.

'Okay... okay.'

I head to my bedroom, unsure what I'm supposed to wear to such an occasion, but I'm sure Heidi is right, anything but pyjamas.

I don't know what the right thing to do is, but I know that whatever I do should be the right thing for me, and not for anyone else. So I'm going to get dressed, head up to the cottage, and hope that I know what I want when I get there.

And that Hugo is still willing to talk to me, of course.

36

I hover nervously at the cottage's front door. I can tell, by the lights glowing in multiple rooms, that Hugo must still be awake. If I had come up here and found the place in the darkness, I probably would've been too scared to knock. I would have run away. I suppose I still could...

Who am I kidding, there's no turning back now, although I am still scared to knock.

Hugo opens the door, which makes me jump, not only because I wasn't expecting him, but because I'm not ready. I don't know what I'm going to say.

'Hello?' he says, making it sound like a question. I'm not surprised he's wondering what I'm doing here. 'Were you going to knock?'

'Erm, yes,' I reply. 'How did you know I was here?'

Hugo points to a small camera above him.

'It only points towards the doorstep, to keep an eye on the place while I'm out,' he explains. 'I don't use it to spy on the hot tub or anything like that. Is that why you're here? Do you need it turning on?'

Hugo is wearing grey tracksuit bottoms and a white T-shirt. He looks tired, despite leaving the wedding early.

'No, actually, I was looking for you,' I say after only a second or two of awkward silence. 'Can we talk?'

'Erm, yeah,' he says. 'Do you want to come in or...?'

'Can we go to your mum's bench?' I ask. 'It feels like a good spot to talk, away from everything.'

'Let me grab my trainers,' he says. 'Back in a second.'

I wait anxiously, still wondering what I'm going to say, how I'm going to say it, what I even want...

'Okay, let's go,' he says.

I follow Hugo along the path, down to his secret space, where we both sit and look out to sea.

'What time are you heading home tomorrow?' he asks me.

'What time is checkout?' I ask through a laugh. 'I know you own the hotel.'

'Ah,' he replies. 'Well, it's not exactly a secret, but I did start to wonder if you knew. I wasn't sure if you had got the wrong end of the stick, or if you preferred not to think about it, because the last thing you would want is another person with money seeming completely out of touch with reality.'

'I suppose I got the wrong end of the stick,' I tell him. 'I was quick to think the worst of you because I found out something else you hadn't told me. You're the one who isn't going to be hosting weddings any more, and you're the one knocking down the wedding barn my granddad built.'

'Liv, I'm so sorry,' he tells me. 'All that, it's just business, I'm just doing what I need to, to keep the hotel going.'

'With all the fancy weddings and stuff, surely it's a gold mine?' I reply.

'Things aren't always as they seem,' he says. 'I know how much you wanted to get married here – and I promise you, I was doing everything I could to make sure you had the perfect wedding. But hosting weddings here just isn't possible, at least for a while. Can I explain?'

'Sure,' I reply. 'That's why I'm here.'

'When Mum and I stayed here, we got to know a lot of the locals,' he starts. 'And one thing they all thought about this place was just how much it had gone downhill. All the footballers' weddings and the influencers coming here just because it was trendy – people wanted the place back to its glory days, when it was a place for the local community to have their parties and events, where families could come on holiday.'

I appreciate that. That's what the place was like when we used to come here.

'Before I bought the hotel, I put together a committee of locals, to find out what they wanted, and everyone agreed that taking the place back to basics was for the best,' he continues. 'Weddings might be off the table, for now, but only until we have somewhere new to host them.'

'Right, but you are demolishing the barn,' I remind him. 'The barn my granddad built. It's practically iconic and you're just going to tear it down.'

'I didn't know that but, Liv, I'm lucky it hasn't been condemned already,' he admits. 'I don't want to knock the barn down, it needs knocking down. I'm going to do everything I can to rebuild it, with as much original material as possible, but it's taken a real beating over the years.'

'Oh,' is about all I can say.

'I'm sorry, if I'd known that was the part that was sentimental to you, I would have explained.'

'So, that's the plan?' I reply. 'Rebuild the barn and then start doing weddings again in the future?'

'Yeah, I guess,' he replies. 'When the place isn't cool any more. Locals don't look twice at the place these days. It's such a shame no one from here wants to get married here, but everyone I spoke to said that no one felt like they could, like they were priced out, that high-profile people always seemed to get priority. You would be surprised how often we get people throwing big chunks of money at us, or at other people, to have their wedding here, no matter what the cost. We had one couple get married here after buying someone else's booking from them.'

'I know more about that than you think,' I remind him.

'Well, there you go,' he says. 'Although it isn't usually relatives of people who helped to make the place what it is who are trying to tie the knot here. I just want it to mean something again.'

I smile.

'I've never met anyone who wanted to decrease business,' I point out. 'To make less money.'

'Well, what can I say, I'm special,' he jokes. 'But there are plenty of ways to make a living here and most of them don't involve billing people thousands of pounds to get married in a barn that could fall down on them if the wind picks up.'

I'm sure he's exaggerating, but I take his point.

'Well, it makes sense why you live in the cottage now, and have a bench for your mum in the garden,' I say. 'You're not going anywhere, are you?'

'I am moving,' he tells me. 'But only into the house, and not just yet, as soon as I possibly can, though.'

'That's a big house for just one person,' I point out.

'Big house, small living,' he says, repeating my words back to me. 'It sounds nice.'

'I'm sorry for being so mean to you earlier,' I tell him. 'I thought you were just another rich arsehole, putting his work first, keeping things from me that he didn't think I needed to know, or could possibly understand.'

'That's not me,' Hugo insists.

'I know, but I've met similar before,' I point out.

'Well, I should have just told you about everything,' he replies. 'If I had told you about the barn, when you told me you wanted to get married here, I could have explained.'

'You don't need to apologise,' I tell him. 'But I'm happy to call it a draw.'

Hugo laughs.

'So, is that why you pushed me away earlier? Just because of the hotel stuff?' he asks, and I nod.

Hugo reaches his hand out towards me and intertwines his fingers with mine.

'I really like you, Liv,' he tells me.

'I really like you too,' I reply. 'But I think being so fresh out of a relationship is making me a bit... odd. I think I'm taking all the problems I had with Teddy and projecting them on to you. It's like I'm waiting for you to lie to me, to put business or money first. I just don't know how to let my guard back down again.'

'That makes sense,' he replies. 'But it's a shame because, I don't know if I've mentioned this, I really like you. From the moment we met, I just knew there was something special about you. But I was never out to get you. I did everything I could to help with your wedding. It was only after you called it off that my feelings snuck ahead of me, they were there before I could stop them.'

'The first week, when we were hanging out, I was realising more and more every day that I didn't want to marry Teddy,' I admit. 'But then, once I was past that, when it was off my plate, I got to focus on the real you, and who wouldn't fall for a guy like that? You're wonderful.'

'I appreciate that the timing is terrible,' he replies. 'I wish we had met sooner – or much later.'

'So do I,' I reply. 'And as much as I'm feeling everything I could possibly wish for, for you... I know that it would be a mistake to rush into anything. At least not while I'm judging all men by my ex's standards.'

In hindsight, I do feel like I overreacted to finding out Hugo owned the hotel, and I do have feelings for him that grow stronger each time I see him, but I know that I'm right, it's far too soon for me to be thinking about striking up anything with anyone new just yet. I need to go back to London, back to my flat, back to my day-to-day life and figure out what I want. I need to put everything that has happened to bed before I jump into a new one with someone else. There's no way that can work.

I came to Cornwall expecting to get married, not to fall in love – or in like, or whatever. But whatever has happened while I've been here, it's irrelevant. I'm leaving here single. That's just the way it has to be.

'Well, I know you're going home tomorrow, but I'm just going to throw it out there,' Hugo starts. 'I'm going to start rebuilding the barn as soon as I possibly can. Maybe you can let me know what colour your granddad's eyes were, I can see about getting a streak of resin put into the door, and maybe you can come and see us, for the grand opening.'

Now, that I can work with.

'Well, that sounds nice,' I say with a smile. 'I'd really like that.'

The timing might not be right for me and Hugo right now but – I know, we only live once – I think I can take a minute to step back, move on from my past, and look forward to my future. And for the first time, it does feel like I could have a future that looks like the one I have in my head. But we'll just have to wait and see.

37

Today is the first day of the rest of my life – or maybe it's the last day of my previous life. Either way, when I woke up today, I knew it was both a beginning and an end.

The holiday is over. Heidi has gone, Eden's parents have left too. Dougie and Eden are about to set off to the airport, to catch their flight to Maui for their honeymoon – a surprise wedding gift from Dougie to Eden. And then all that will be left is me, my mum and my dad. Obviously given that they drove me here, and there's no one else around to drive me, they're going to have to take me home too, only this time we hopefully won't lose Mum over the other side of the motorway.

Saying goodbye to Hugo last night was hard. I feel so awful saying it, but I genuinely found it easier saying goodbye to Teddy. I suppose that's because I knew I was doing the right thing. Leaving Hugo, when it really feels like there could be something amazing between us, doesn't feel right. I am really putting it all in fate's hands, leaving him behind, with no idea what's in store for me in the future, but if it's meant to be, we'll find a way to come back together again when the time is right.

So I pulled myself out of bed, packed up my things, and now I'm sitting outside the beach house front door, perched on the wall, swinging my legs as I wait for everyone else to join me. I'm going to miss this place – I feel like I never really got to make the most of it, I always had something else on my mind. It's such a shame.

'Oh, good morning,' Hugo says.

'Er, hi,' I say kind of awkwardly.

I don't think either of us was expecting to see each other again – well, not before I left, anyway.

'How are...'

'I was just...'

We talk over one another. I place my hand over my mouth, to let Hugo know that he can go first.

'I'm just heading into the town, I've got some work errands to run,' he says. 'I'm in a bit of a hurry but... it's good to see you again. I wasn't sure I would, before you left.'

'It's good to see you too,' I reply. 'Perhaps we can say a more normal goodbye. Just, like, a regular see you later. Not one off the back of a deep and meaningful conversation.'

He laughs.

'Yeah, a normal goodbye sounds good,' he said.

God, any goodbye goes against my gut, but I'm doing what is best – or what seems best, at least.

'Hugo!' Eden squeaks excitedly. 'Aw, come here, let me say goodbye. We owe you a big thank you.'

'We really do,' Dougie says, waiting his turn to give Hugo a hug. 'Hopefully we can see you again soon.'

'Yeah, you guys are always welcome back,' Hugo replies. 'Anyway, I was just telling Liv that I'm heading into town. But safe travels, all of you.'

'Thanks,' I reply. 'Have a good day.'

'You too,' he says as he hugs me.

I hold him perhaps a little too tightly, for a little too long. I let him go eventually. I need to let him go.

Hugo heads towards the hotel. Eden looks as though she's waiting to say something the second he is out of earshot, but Mum and Dad join us before she has the chance.

'What are you two still doing here?' Mum asks in disbelief. 'You've a flight to make.'

'Excuse me for wanting to say goodbye to my parents before I jet off on holiday,' Dougie jokes.

'Oh, go on then,' Mum sings. 'Oh, I'm so proud of you both. It was such a wonderful wedding. I wish you a lifetime of happiness – but before that, have a wonderful holiday!'

'We will,' Eden says excitedly. 'I honestly can't wait. Watch my Instagram because I have never been to Hawaii before and I am going to absolutely spam you all.'

'Spam didn't mean anything good in my day,' Dad jokes. 'Or the day after my day, come to think of it. Have a great time, though. If it's good, I'll have to take your mum for our big anniversary this year.'

'*After* our anniversary,' Mum corrects him. 'We celebrate these things as a family.'

Eden hugs me.

'Thanks again for everything,' she says.

'You're welcome,' I tell her. 'Have an amazing time. You too, Doug.'

Dougie hugs me next and kisses me on the cheek.

'Thanks, Liv,' he adds. 'Honestly, you've made this wedding for us.'

I bat my hand casually but this really is a lovely, lovely moment.

'Oh, Liv, can you nip in and pay the bill for us?' Mum asks.

I go cold.

'What?'

'Oh, not the bill-bill,' she says quickly, highly amused at how bad things seemed for a second. 'Your dad and I had a meal in the restaurant, which we charged to the house, but it never got added to the bill. There was an invoice through the door this morning. I'll give you the cash.'

I laugh with relief.

'Of course,' I reply.

I say my goodbyes to Dougie and Eden again and then head inside to settle the bill.

I reach the front desk of the hotel and press the bell. Eventually, Hugo appears.

'Erm...'

'Hello again,' he says with a smile. 'Our receptionist is running late. I'm just covering. She should be here any second.'

'I did wonder what you were doing there,' I reply. 'I just have a bill to settle from when Mum and Dad ate in the restaurant.'

'Oh, don't even worry about it,' he says. 'Tell them it's on me.'

'Are you sure?' I reply.

'Yeah, anything for those guys,' he insists.

Why do people always look so good when you're saying goodbye? His eyes look kinder than they ever have, his dimples so deep I feel like I could dive into them. And that smile... I'm really going to miss that smile.

'Sorry I'm late,' a frazzled-looking woman says as she hurries past me. 'Thanks for covering for me, boss.'

'No worries,' he reassures her before turning to me. 'Anyway, goodbye... again.'

I laugh.

'Goodbye again.'

Hugo heads outside. I don't follow him, I nip into the toilets, to try to compose myself. I really could've done without a third goodbye. They're getting harder each time. Not to mention how it feels more and more like a mistake, with every chance fate gives me to make a different call.

Back outside, I can't say I'm surprised to see Hugo chatting with my parents. I can tell my mum and dad really like him because they have the biggest smiles. I feel like they've both really bonded with him. You can just see it in the way they're hugging him.

I hang back for a moment, keen to avoid yet another goodbye. Eventually, he says a final farewell, gets in his car and drives away.

With the coast clear, I head back to my parents.

'Right, are we all good to go?' Mum asks.

'Yep,' I say with a bit of a sigh.

'No,' Dad says at the same time. 'I don't have my phone charger. I've just remembered that I've forgotten, I couldn't find it.'

I can't help but laugh at his confusing choice of words.

'Well, I emptied the room,' Mum tells him.

'Well, it's in there somewhere,' he claps back.

'Right, okay, fine, do you want to be loading up the car, Liv?' Mum suggests. 'I'll go help your dad find his charger – and try not to wrap it around his neck.'

She says this last bit under her breath, just to me. I really hope that, in the future, I find this kind of happiness with someone I still love so much, who I can be so happy with, even if I do want to murder them.

I do as I'm told, loading up the car, hovering next to it until Mum and Dad emerge from the house again – Dad bright red and Mum with a face like thunder.

'In his pocket,' she says simply through gritted teeth. 'Come on, let's go.'

I can't help but stare back at the hotel as we drive away. I'm going to miss so much about this place. So, so much.

Am I making a mistake? Should I not be going or, even if I do go, should I not be making plans with Hugo to see him again? Am I being ridiculous, walking away from something amazing, just because the timing doesn't seem quite right? I just wish I knew what to do, I just need some kind of sign.

'Hugo,' Dad shouts.

Then I realise he's gesturing at traffic and what he actually said was 'you go' – ha! As if it was ever going to be that easy, as if a sign would be something so unsubtle.

But then, of course, as we turn a corner into town, I am confronted with a giant photo of Hugo. Me and Hugo, to be more specific. A massive billboard with our photo on it, under big letters that say: 'Congratulations to Cornwall's Cutest Couple'.

I decide not to point it out to Mum and Dad, I'd never hear the end of it, but now, more than ever, seeing how happy we both look in the photo, it's almost as though I'm being given a glimpse at how wonderful life could be if the two of us were to get together.

The car slams to a halt, snapping me from my thoughts.

'Be careful what you're doing,' Mum ticks him off.

'I am,' Dad replies. 'I think we've got a puncture.'

Seriously? Are you joking? It's almost as though Porthian Sands is refusing to let me leave.

'I've got a spare in the boot,' he says. 'We're in the town – why don't you two pop into the shops while I change it?'

'Can you change a tyre?' I can't help but ask.

'Of course I can,' he replies, almost annoyed.

'Alone?' Mum adds. 'Come on, let's take a look.'

The three of us crowd around the flat tyre, all looking down at it, no real idea what we're supposed to do.

'Need a hand?' a voice that is music to my ears asks.

When I turn around and see Hugo standing there, I grab him and kiss him. He drops whatever he's holding but I don't care. You've got me, fate, I'm reading you loud and clear.

'I meant with the car,' he jokes when I finally let him go.

Mum and Dad politely ignore my dramatic display of affection.

'If you don't mind,' Dad says with relief. 'I'll grab the spare.'

'And I'll pop into the shop and get some sweeties for the road,' Mum adds. 'Lord knows I'll need something stronger, though.'

A moment alone, just me and Hugo, I compose myself and pick up the papers I knocked out of his hand.

'Oh, you're selling the cottage,' I blurt, looking at the estate agent documents.

'Renting it out,' he corrects me. 'I'm going to stop taking bookings and move in to the house as soon as possible, you inspired me.'

'You're welcome,' I say playfully. 'This cottage you're renting – reckon it's in my price range? It seems like the perfect place to write romance novels.'

'I'm sure we could arrange something,' he replies with a smile. 'We have to stop meeting like this – best we do it on purpose instead.'

'If the last hour has taught me anything, it's that we're probably going to see each other again, whether I like it or not,' I reply.

'Oh, no, you definitely will,' he informs me. 'Just before I set off, your mum invited me to her and your dad's wedding anniversary party next month.'

I smile. Whether fate is trying to get me and Hugo together or not, my mum definitely is, and she's an even stronger force to be reckoned with.

It just goes to show that, even if it feels like you've met the right person at the wrong time, sometimes you have to meet the wrong person first, so that you can find yourself in the right place, at the right time, to meet the right person.

Today is most definitely the start of something. The start of something new with Hugo. It's early days, but I know that I'm exactly where I'm supposed to be, and I can't wait to see what the future has in store for us.

ACKNOWLEDGMENTS

Thanks so much to my wonderful editor, Nia, and to everyone else at Boldwood HQ for all of their brilliant work with my books. It's so fantastic, to be publishing *another* one.

Massive thanks, as always, to everyone who takes the time to read and review my books. Your support and kind words mean so much to me.

Thank you to my family for all of their love and encouragement – and for being my biggest cheerleaders. Thanks to Kim, Aud, James and Joey – I'd be lost without you guys. And thanks to Darcy, for always being by my side.

Finally, thanks to my husband, Joe. I really am so much better off for marrying you.

MORE FROM PORTIA MACINTOSH

We hope you enjoyed reading *Better Off Wed*. If you did, please leave a review.

If you'd like to gift a copy, this book is also available as an ebook, paperback, large print, digital audio download and audiobook CD.

Sign up to Portia MacIntosh's mailing list for news, competitions and updates on future books.

http://bit.ly/PortiaMacIntoshNewsletter

Discover more laugh-out-loud romantic comedies from Portia Macintosh:

ALSO BY PORTIA MACINTOSH

One Way or Another

If We Ever Meet Again

Bad Bridesmaid

Drive Me Crazy

Truth or Date

It's Not You, It's Them

The Accidental Honeymoon

You Can't Hurry Love

Summer Secrets at the Apple Blossom Deli

Love & Lies at the Village Christmas Shop

The Time of Our Lives

Honeymoon For One

My Great Ex-Scape

Make or Break at the Lighthouse B&B

The Plus One Pact

Stuck On You

Faking It

Life's a Beach

Will They, Won't They?

No Ex Before Marriage

The Meet Cute Method

Single All the Way

Just Date and See

Your Place or Mine?

ABOUT THE AUTHOR

Portia MacIntosh is a bestselling romantic comedy author of over 15 novels, including *My Great Ex-Scape* and *Honeymoon For One*. Previously a music journalist, Portia writes hilarious stories, drawing on her real life experiences.

Visit Portia's website: https://portiamacintosh.com/

Follow Portia MacIntosh on social media here:

facebook.com/portia.macintosh.3
twitter.com/PortiaMacIntosh
instagram.com/portiamacintoshauthor
bookbub.com/authors/portia-macintosh

Boldwd

Boldwood Books is an award-winning fiction publishing company seeking out the best stories from around the world.

Find out more at www.boldwoodbooks.com

Join our reader community for brilliant books, competitions and offers!

Follow us
@BoldwoodBooks
@BookandTonic

Sign up to our weekly deals newsletter

https://bit.ly/BoldwoodBNewsletter